Another death in Venice

The eminent barrister and amateur sleuth Sir Patrick Scott and his novelist wife Virginia return by the Orient Express to the scene of their honeymoon, Venice, the most visited city in the world.

Their host is an old Etonian Italian American, Bernadetto di Montebello, whose family *palazzo* on the Grand Canal is the fashionable venue for the cultural and social élite of the ancient city.

Effortless hospitality, delicious meals and carousing of such sophistication as only the very rich achieve – these delights are rudely curtailed when an Australian they have just met on the Orient Express is found floating in a canal.

And the death soon overshadows the dinner parties at the home of Peggy Aschenheim, New York heiress and art-collector, and the quaffing of champagne at the fabulous Hotel Danieli, where Peggy tries to persuade Philip Bouncer, a Texan worth about half a billion dollars, to donate his art collection to the Metropolitan Museum in her native city.

The Scotts are joined by a Chilean painter, whom Peggy has collected along with his work, and the dowager Lady Hawksworth, a famous beauty, whose husband has left an even larger fortune than Philip Bouncer's; and they come across a full complement of Venetians, from the magistrate investigating the murder – the charming and cosmopolitan Signor Montenari – to some of the seedier characters hanging about in the Piazza San Marco.

The theft of legal papers from Sir Patrick's bedroom at the *palazzo* and the sudden fatal collapse of Philip Bouncer pitch Sir Patrick into his habitual role of 'professional amateur' private eye and into a final dramatic confrontation with a line-up of sinister but distinguished suspects.

Anthony Appiah, the author of two previous Sir Patrick Scott investigations, matches his Venetian scene with the elegance of his subtle storytelling in this exceptional novel of murder and retribution among the international *haut monde*.

Also by Anthony Appiah

Avenging angel (1990)
Nobody likes Letitia (1994)

ANOTHER DEATH IN VENICE

Anthony Appiah

Constable · London

First published in Great Britain 1995
by Constable & Company Ltd
3 The Lanchesters, 162 Fulham Palace Road
London W6 9ER
Copyright © 1995 by Anthony Appiah
The right of Anthony Appiah to be
identified as the author of this work
has been asserted by him in accordance
with the Copyright, Designs and Patents Act 1988
ISBN 0 09 474430 0
Set in Palatino 10pt by
Pure Tech Corporation, Pondicherry
Printed and bound in Great Britain
by Hartnolls Ltd, Bodmin

A CIP catalogue record for this book
is available from the British Library

1

A word of advice to those of you with fond memories of Venice in your youth: you have forgotten the steps. There are scores of them up and down over the Ponte dell'Accademia and the Rialto, to be sure, that you may not have forgotten. But every little bridge over every little rio takes you up and then down in exactly the sort of motion that my dear son, Sebastian (who is medically qualified to volunteer such information), apprises me is just the thing to strengthen the heart. Alas, what strengthens the heart also takes away the breath – at least, if you are, as I am, a gentleman in your early seventies, used to treating a modest half-hour's saunter pubwards into Chewton Ampney and back (with a stop in the middle for refreshment) as a serious outing. So that even in the early summer, when the temperature is high in the sixties and a cool breeze blows up the Grand Canal (passing, as it goes, between the *vaporetto* stop in the Piazza San Marco and Santa Maria della Salute), one finds oneself constantly pausing, half-way up this flight of stairs or that, affecting breathlessly to glance at some detail, however implausibly humdrum, of the brickwork and plaster of the Serenissima.

I offer this warning from the painful depths of experience. For, not long ago, in the grip of the romantic notion that Virginia, my wife, and I should return to the scene of our honeymoon, in what was then the fortieth – it seems impossible, but there you are, fortieth – year of our connubium, we set off to revisit the most visited city in the world.

Those of you who recall the year of Our Lord nineteen hundred and fifty will perhaps also remember that Sir Stafford Cripps had decided that what Britain needed in the years after the war was a continuing dose of the spirit of the blitz. The result, of course, was that rationing was still in place, and travel abroad, which had been easy enough to arrange in the early forties if one was willing to don a uniform, required the most elaborate of arrangements. Churchill had once observed of Cripps, 'There, but for the grace of God, goes God,' but one assumed that even without the full panoply of divine omniscience the fellow knew what he was doing. Still, these difficulties with travel had not made him popular with my father and his friends. And so Papa, who sat on the opposition benches in the Commons in those days, oscillating between fits of apoplexy at another socialist cataclysm and quiet snoozing, took a certain grim pleasure in arranging for Virginia and me to have the most ferociously luxurious time in Italy, while conforming to the letter of the Bank of England's restrictions on the transfer of sterling.

It was a painful business for him. For if there was one thing my father disliked more than an English socialist it was a foreigner. He himself had rarely travelled out of England – it amused him, despite our name, to refer to his shooting holidays in Argyll as 'going abroad' – but a cousin of ours, by the name of Jamie Leith, had made friends at Eton with a chap called Bernadetto di Montebello, whose family had a *palazzo* on the Grand Canal. Papa, recalling this fact not long after I had told him that Virginia and I were intending to be married, had decided to telephone Jamie and arrange for the three of them to have lunch at the Athenaeum.

My father was perfectly capable of presuming on acquaintance, 'auld' or not, but, in this case, he knew that his overtures would be welcome. Jamie and Bernadetto had stayed with us from time to time at Chewton Ampney, the ancestral pile in Gloucestershire, during the war. Bernadetto was only a few years younger than I was; but at the tender age of eighteen, a fellow in his mid-twenties can seem awfully impressively grown-up. My father once asked me if I thought that Bernadetto's affection for me was 'healthy', and I confess that this rather astounded me at the time: I had thought my father quite unnoticing of ordinary human relations. But it appears that even Papa had observed that Bernadetto looked up to me (largely, I suspect, because Jamie had told him that my war work was so top secret that enquiries about it could not even be whispered).

Papa had time neither for Americans nor for Italians: he was aware that the former had joined us, rather belatedly, in battling the Hun, while the latter had drifted, more out of muddle than malice, into the grubby embrace of the Führer, and he regarded them as equally unreliable as a result. But Bernadetto – Papa alone referred to him as Bernard – was the model of a charming young

Englishman, and his mother's family had lived in our part of the world for several centuries longer than ours had, so his father's American citizenship and Italian antecedents were things Papa could put out of his mind.

Bernadetto's looks were a greater difficulty, not least because they were, of course, present whenever he was. Papa had always been suspicious of handsome men – he once told me I should be grateful I had inherited his looks and not my mother's; but Bernadetto, unlike me, had come into rather stunning looks from his father's side of the family. His fine features – the aquiline nose, the thin, sensitive lips and his almost feminine eyelashes – caught the eye of many a girl – and, no doubt, the occasional boy – when he was at school. Papa overcame his natural resistance to this unmanly beauty because Bernadetto overcame *him* with an easy masculine charm.

Knowing that Virginia had an unaccountable taste for Italian art and having discovered from Mother that Venice was crammed with the stuff, he decided that we should have a honeymoon-full of it. A taste in art, Papa felt, was quite suitable in a wife. (He was also clear that honeymoons were for the pleasure of the bride: any son of his, it went without saying, would rather have a week or two fishing in Scotland.)

The Montebelli (as they were known to the Scotts; Bernadetto referred to us, in consequence, as 'I Scotti') were a rather peculiar lot. To begin with, despite the Italian name and the Venetian connections, Bernadetto's father was, as I say, an American. His English education was the decision of his mother, who, being English herself, and having visited a whole host of American schools, whose names – Phillips-Exeter, Andover Academy, Deerfield – Bernadetto never tired of reciting, decided that her husband's country, while a fine enough place in which to live and make money, was no place to get an education. Mr di Montebello's notion that a collection of large buildings a stone's throw from Windsor Castle might not be the ideal spot to hide from the Luftwaffe produced in Margaret di Montebello only scorn. 'I am not going to have that horrid little German deciding where B. goes to school,' she was reported to have said.

I assume that Jamie prepared Bernadetto for the conversation with Papa, for, by all accounts, it went swimmingly. Bernadetto listened politely to my father's announcement of my plans to be married and opined, a little while later, before Papa could quite get round to the subject, that the *palazzo* would be a perfect place for a honeymoon and that he would ask his parents – if Papa would permit it – to make it available for the purpose. Jamie told me that Bernadetto had persuaded Papa that we would be doing the Montebelli a favour, since 'the servants get frightfully bored because we're never there'. Nowadays, of course, this elegant fiction would seem, at best, to be the half-truth of a generous host, but Papa's knowledge of the mental life of servants did not extend very far and his grasp of the psychology of foreigners was a complete blank; and so he was not one to question the claims of someone who was plainly better qualified than he was, about the psychology of the Italian servant class. A few days later, having bought us a pair of first-class railway tickets to Venice, he summoned me to dinner at his club.

'Patrick,' he announced over the sherry, unable to hold in the secret a moment longer, 'I have arranged for you to honeymoon in Venice.' He paused, his watery eyes darting about mischievously. 'Bernard's parents have put their house at your disposal, and I have purchased a pair of railway tickets on the Orient Express.'

'I say, Father, that's awfully good of you.'

'Think nothing of it, dear boy.' He ran his hand carefully through his distinguished white locks, scanning the room before he turned to look me straight in the eye. 'I know that Virginia is keen on that sort of thing and you must start off married life on the right foot. Women' – he leaned forward confidentially – 'are very appreciative of such attentions.'

And that, give or take the odd detail, is how Virginia and I had ended up waking a few mornings after we exchanged our vows to the sound of water slapping below our balcony, and the hearty singing of a Venetian gondolier.

Four decades later I wrote to Bernadetto, who now lived mostly in Venice (accompanied, I gathered, much of the time, by Jamie) to ask where we should stay in his adopted city. We had met often over the years – Bernadetto had acquired a pretty little country house at West Maulding, a few miles from us, where he spent a few weeks a year, and we had often stayed, at his invitation, at his place in Spain (where, for some reason, Virginia was able to write her Bella Sharpe novels at astonishing speed). Because I wanted to surprise Virginia, I did not mention to her that I had written to Bernadetto, and I was rather taken aback, as a result, to find myself reproached for it by my good lady, early one morning in April, a few weeks after posting my letter.

'It's very naughty of you to invite yourself to stay with Bernadetto di Montebello, Patrick.' The tone was stern: those unfamiliar with my good wife might have thought her ladyship was not amused.

'I did no such thing.'

I should have learned after nearly four decades not to contradict Jinny's account of the facts.

'Then, why has he written to say that, of course, we must stay with him?'

'Might I be allowed to read the letter?'

'Did you not invite yourself?' Diversions don't work either.

'Certainly not. I simply wrote to the only person I knew in Venice to ask if he could suggest a place for us to stay.'

'Really, Patrick, that's as good as instructing him to invite us. Why on earth didn't you ask Sheila at Thomas Cook's in Banbury?'

'Because I was hoping to surprise you, my dear, and Sheila is about as discreet as the *Daily Mail*.'

'It appears that Bernadetto is no better at keeping secrets.'

'If you don't want to spend our fortieth anniversary in the *palazzo* where we spent our honeymoon, just give me the word. I can always go fishing with Jamie Fitzgibbon.'

'Don't sulk, Patrick, my pet. It was a perfectly nice idea, and we shall just have to tell Bernadetto that we meant to stay in an hotel.'

'Why can't we just take him up on his offer?'

Jinny gave me one of her looks. I used to think I was imagining them, that they were what that old Austrian fraud Sigmund would have called a 'projection'. But Sebastian has confirmed that they are an objective phenomenon. The English language is extremely rich – richer, I dare say, than any other – but it does not contain the words to describe the withering scorn that Lady Scott can infuse into a glance. It was such a look that inspired the myth of Medusa: but my wife's glance was intended to have the opposite effect of the Gorgon's, turning one to a quaking jelly. I glanced away nervously and waited in humble silence while she finished reading the letter through her lorgnettes. As she placed the letter on the table within my reach she issued a sort of hurrumphing sound that suggested something other than pleasure.

I picked it up. It was written in Bernadetto's elegant hand on heavy cream-coloured paper.

Venezia
Palazzo Longhi,
3rd April 1990

My dear Scotti:
One must begin all letters here with a discussion of the Italian post, much deteriorated in quality since it was taken out of the hands of the Thurn und Taxis family. Despite which, I hope you will get this before you make other arrangements – and I shall telephone if I do not hear from you in a week or two.

But, of course, you must come and stay with us. Jamie will be here and we would both be thrilled to see you on the anniversary of your honeymoon: can it really be thirty years already?

I shall put you in the room you had then, though, alas, we cannot promise the same level of staffing!

Jamie and I have just returned here from a few weeks at the villa in Gorée: Senegal is pleasant in the winter, and Venice, though always serene, is nicer when it is warmer. We were delighted that we were here to get Patrick's letter.

No time for more news: we shall, after all, be seeing you soon, and talking to you sooner.

With all my love,

B.

PS Patrick. Ignore Virginia's protestations that you cannot take up my offer. I shall be very cross if you don't come: and I might even punish you by denying you a visit in the autumn to Sevilla.

PPS Jamie says it is not thirty but forty years. Ridiculous!

'He's become rather Italian, hasn't he, over the years?' I remarked, thinking it best not to gloat over the decisive refutation of Jinny's arguments in the first PS. 'But he's still the same generous fellow he always was.'

'What do you mean, "rather Italian"?'

'Well, I mean, "with all my love" . . . it's a bit, you know, . . .'

'I think it's charming.' (Virginia in this mood is as contrary as Mary, Mary in the rhyme.) 'He *is* one of our oldest friends.'

'Indeed. It's just more . . . effusive' – I was delighted at having fallen on the right word – 'than one is used to in England.' I tried a new tack. 'It's rather extraordinary his putting up with Jamie all these years. I mean, Jamie's a very nice chap, and all that, but really he does rather sponge off Bernadetto.'

'Patrick, sometimes, just sometimes, you can be enormously dense.' Virginia chuckled.

'What on earth do you mean?'

Another glance, this time over the lorgnettes. I was reminded of Nanny warning me to be careful, because 'the wind might change', freezing an unpleasant look on my face for ever. And I would have said something similar in a nannyish voice, had it not been abundantly clear that Virginia was not in the mood to be cheered up by teasing. Whatever I had said, I judged it best not to pursue the topic further.

Two days later, as I anticipated, Jinny reopened the matter at breakfast in a friendlier spirit. 'Sheila says the Orient Express has opened up again. We could go by train.'

I was just about to ask whether it might not be more comfortable to fly, when I saw the slightest suspicion of firmness in the set of Jinny's jaw. Forty years teaches you something. 'Wonderful!' The exclamation mark probably overstates the extent to which I succeeded in producing a convincingly enthusiastic tone: but Jinny was in a mood to ignore this failing.

'Good, it's settled then. I shall write to Bernadetto. We shall stay with him for two or three days and then go up to Lake Como.'

'Of course. That will be perfect, darling.' I got up from my side of the kitchen table and went round and leaned down to kiss Virginia on the head.

My good wife evaded this friendly gesture, ducking out of the path of my descending face. 'Don't be soppy, Paddy. You've got marmalade on your lip.'

Somehow, I felt, the omens for this trip were not all one might have hoped.

2

It was not, in any case, the most convenient of times to be away. I was in the middle of trying to disentangle some legal matters that had come up a few months earlier, after the sudden death of Milo Hawksworth, a client whose family I had advised off and on over my career at the Chancery bar. I had agreed to be a trustee for Milo's son twenty years earlier, when he reached the age of eighteen: while Milo was alive, this had been a fairly routine business, and while I had kept a dutiful eye on the paperwork that crossed my desk and thought, from time to time, about taxes, Milo had made all the decisions. Among the properties in trust was the house at Hawksworth, which Milo had opened to the public. He and his son, Alexander, each had a small flat in the west wing, and between them they spent a good deal of the summer there together.

When Milo and Alexander were not in the country, they lived in good style in a house in Mayfair or in a small château in the South of France, a few kilometres to the east of St Paul de Vences. Milo was separated from his wife, Melissa, but they seemed to be on good terms and she was often to be found at Hawksworth, staying with her son. Alexander was not over-endowed in the intellect department – he had never managed to pass more than one O-level at Fettes – so there was not much hope of finding a career for him. He was a robust lad, though, and rode and shot like a champion. Marriage posed some difficulties: the girls Milo and Melissa thought were good enough for him were not interested in this friendly dullard, and the ones that *were* interested in him were plainly after his title and his money. Milo protected Alexander from these gold-diggers by taking the girls aside when they came to stay and telling them politely what he would have done to them if they did not leave his son alone. At six foot two inches and a good seventeen and a half stone, he could put on a pretty menacing performance.

I always assumed these threats were all bluff. Milo Hawksworth wielded his great bulk with enormous grace: and though he was ruthless in business, he was, so everyone agreed, a gentle, amiable, amusing fellow in private life. When we were young he had cut a great figure at dances, his vastness gracefully enfolding some slip of a girl as he wafted her around the floor. Milo was not only prodigiously proportioned: his activities, too, were all rather larger than life. He had inherited a good deal of money and land from his father, but his frequent appearances on the business pages suggested that he was busy making a good deal more.

His appearances on the society pages were rather rarer. Years ago, when Alexander left school, he and Melissa had separated, without any apparent rancour. They occasionally accompanied each other to charity dances; but, by and large, Melissa's social life was conducted on her own. She spent much of her time in Italy – 'I do so love the sun, Patrick,' I recall her saying to me once, in rather the tones that Jinny would adopt in reporting her love of Giorgione or Trollope. Milo clearly gave her a generous allowance. Not only was she able to disappear off to sunnier climes whenever she felt like it, she was always out and about in London in dresses that Jinny assured me must have cost an arm and a leg. She was chaperoned by a variety of men, most of them confirmed bachelors, and there was never even the hint of a suggestion that her relations with them were less than proper.

This must have required a good deal of restraint on the part of these various companions, since Melissa is, simply put, a stunner. Even now, in her late fifties, she is one of London's great beauties. She has the most gorgeous pale blue eyes and her golden hair has turned to purest white: and each of her features is exquisitely sculptured. Over the years she has been painted by a dozen artists, some of them great ones. None of them has ever quite captured the mixture of strength and frailness that makes her so endearing.

One summer, ages ago, when Milo and Melissa were still living together, our friend Patrick Windermere had us down for the weekend. On Saturday, he arranged a scavenger hunt – an activity that in my experience does not display the upper classes in the best light – that took us all about the estate and through the nearby towns and villages. The list of things we had to collect was particularly extensive and it included 'a cap off the head of a local villager'. For years, Jinny and I would recall Melissa's extraordinarily reckless behaviour that weekend. It was Melissa who leaned out of the window of their Austin-Healey, as it shot at seventy miles an hour through Much Madding, and grabbed the cap of an astonished burgher. (This was a much more direct approach than the one I had adopted, which was to enter into negotiations with what must have been the oldest inhabitant of Lower Madding, at the end of which he was a hefty guinea the richer.) It was Melissa, too, who was seen climbing the roof of the stables to collect an empty bird's nest. And, despite her denials, everyone knew she had deliberately tripped up Michael Montagu-Borden as he was running through the kitchen garden towards the greenhouses. This little act of sabotage allowed Milo to acquire the only green tomato within easy reach of the house. (Jinny and I spent an hour in the company of one of the gardeners begging for an unripe tomato at the cottages of various estate workers.) One thing was clear: Melissa may have looked frail, but she could be resolute in pursuit of victory.

Then, as I say, after Alex left school, Melissa and Milo separated quietly. If she had ever wanted to marry again, perhaps Milo would have accepted divorce: but I suspected he took as much pride in having this beautiful wife as he took in the splendours of Hawksworth and his inheritance. Still, neither of them ever seemed to have found anyone else, and so they had drifted on for the two decades in a loose and friendly alliance, until Milo's unexpectedly early death.

The Barony of Hawksworth was an Elizabethan one, and Hawksworth is a fine house built around a stately Elizabethan heart. The great beamed hall accommodates some fine seventeenth-century paintings of Milo's ancestors – including the first Baron, whose martial bearing was, in fact, the cover for an intelligent and rather unmilitary courtier and poet. It is one of the essential stops on any serious tour of the great houses of England. In the last few years, Milo had summoned me there occasionally to talk about his affairs. Sometimes Jinny and I would spend the weekend, shooting or fishing, or walking the splendid woods of the estate. We were not invited for Milo's occasional large house-parties, because, I gathered, these were for his business 'associates'. 'It's so nice to be able to have a quiet time here with civilized people,' he once said to me, in a sudden and surprising access of intimacy. 'Sometimes, you know, I have to have thirty people for the weekend – we close the house to the public. Frightful. The things one does for money!' It was offered as a small gibe at his own expense: but someone of Milo Hawksworth's ambition could not have meant it.

Then, in the year or so before he died, Milo started expressing anxiety about the transfer of the title to his son, Alexander. He seemed, at first, to think the fact that his wedding to Alexander's mother had taken place in Australia placed the boy's legitimacy in doubt. Milo had spent the period after the war down under, enjoying the rugged life of a farm in the outback. Melissa travelled out to Australia the year after she was presented at court and they had met in Sydney and married after one of those whirlwind romances that delight the press. They had returned when Milo's father died suddenly a few months later.

When he first put his worries to me, I dutifully reassured him that there was really no question but that Alex was the heir to the title. Milo was so insistent that I found myself explaining on one occasion that even if Alex were not his son – 'And', I said parenthetically, 'I don't for a moment wish to impugn Melissa's virtue' – the law would *presume* that he was. 'A child born to a married woman is presumptively her husband's son.'

Finally, I had even taken the trouble of persuading my kinsman,

Charlie Ivor, who has sat in the Lords for a good many years, to explain the process of establishing succession to Milo (who had only been in the chamber of the House once, when he first inherited the title, though he had taken various of his business partners there for lunch over the years. 'An invitation to the House of Lords dining-room', he remarked to me matter-of-factly one day, 'is worth a very great deal if you're trying to get an American to sign on the dotted line. With a Japanese, it's worth even more.').

'Mad as a hatter, your chum Hawksworth,' Charlie said to me on the telephone after the meeting. 'Can't seem to get it into his head that an Australian marriage licence is practically as good as an English one. In the end I reminded him that the Queen was monarch of Australia, as well, and that seemed to reassure him a bit. But I don't understand how someone who's such a successful business man can be quite so harebrained.'

'Well, I'm very grateful to you for trying to reassure him,' I said.

The next day Milo had telephoned me and asked if I would mind arranging for someone to get a copy of his son's birth certificate. I obliged. Then he wanted a copy of his Australian marriage licence. We got that, too. Then we had to engage an Australian detective to see if he could dig up affidavits from the few people who were at the wedding. (The bill for this chap's services was positively enormous: I made a mental note to avoid Australian private detectives in future!) Then he had Melissa write up an affidavit swearing that she had been married to Milo, had conceived a son by him, and that son was, indeed, Alexander John Hawksworth.

'Isn't this all a bit bonkers?' Melissa said to me, when we met at her house in Kensington to sign the papers.

'He's got a bee in his bonnet. I've tried explaining to him that this is all unnecessary. But it seems easier just to humour him.'

'Poor, dear Milo. I think he hates the idea of something important to him that he won't be able to control. He'd just love to be able to reach back from the grave and hand Alex the title.'

I mumbled something non-committal – best, I find, not to get between a man and his wife's opinion of him, even if they've not lived together for years – and went my merry way, with an accumulating pile of unnecessary documents in my Gladstone bag.

And then, suddenly, a few months before he died, Milo stopped mentioning the succession. When I once raised the question, somewhat gingerly, to make sure that his mind was at ease on the subject, he laughed outright. 'You must have thought I was absolutely barking mad,' he said. 'I'm sorry. Just one of my odd notions. No, I'm not worrying about it any more. Alex is my son and heir and even the Lords won't be able to tamper with his rights.' The whole episode was entirely out of character: I would never have thought of Milo as having 'odd notions'. But I was reassured that his anxieties were over and I put the matter out of my mind.

When Milo died suddenly in January 1990, however, I discovered that, while his worries about Alexander's inheritance had, indeed, been groundless – Alex was to be installed as the seventeenth Baron Hawksworth of Hawksworth, without fuss, six months after Milo's demise – there were some murky details to the finances which had made possible their lavish style of life. I had rather assumed that the enormous sums of money in stocks and various other investments held by the trust, along with the shares he held in the many companies of which he was a director, constituted the bulk of Milo's holdings. It came as a great surprise, as a result, when I discovered that there were companies in Monaco with holdings in Panama of stocks in companies in Brazil. Obviously, Milo kept his family finances and his businesses quite separate: as his personal lawyer, I had not been involved in these matters, and that, I suppose, was why he had not asked me to draw up his will. The will required the various executors to spend two years establishing control of these properties in various jurisdictions so they could be managed through a trust – of which Melissa and I were to be trustees – for the benefit of his eldest son. Milo also instructed the executors to provide me with a great body of documents to read, documents I presumed were somehow connected with my duties as trustee.

The trust itself seemed straightforward enough. There were provisions for distribution of the trust after the boy's death: and, for the first five years, he was to have a huge income but no access to the capital.

'I assume', David Mellor – one of the executors, who was a financial expert of some sort – said to me as we were reviewing the will, 'that this language was from before Milo knew that he wasn't going to have any more children.'

Over the next four months, the sums accumulated: I mentioned to Alexander, at one point, that his father's will seemed to have left his eldest son – or, to be more precise, his trustees – in control of several hundred million pounds' worth of international assets, in places and through devices that would keep it far from the clutches of Her Majesty's Inspectors of Revenue.

Alexander, who was standing at the time, looking out of the window of our flat, staggered back a few feet, collapsed into a chair and wondered if he might have a glass of malt.

'Several hundred *million*?' he squawked in a strained falsetto, when he had recovered enough to speak. 'Several hundred million *pounds*?'

I nodded slowly, so as to leave the young Lord Hawksworth in no doubt as to the enormous size of the sum in question. Alexander, as I say, is not terribly bright and one has, sometimes, to put on this sort of show to get things into his head. 'I'm so sorry, I should have prepared you better for this,' I said. 'It's not the sort of thing you can calculate precisely, they tell me, and the accountants are still busy trying to work it all out as best they can. But, yes, something of that order.'

'No wonder he was always disappearing to South America,' Milo's son said. 'Odd that he never mentioned this to me . . . or to you.'

'Indeed. But your father always played his cards close to his chest.' I winked at him, man to man.

Alexander laughed his good-humoured laugh and then paused thoughtfully, as if he had suddenly understood what I had said. 'I never saw him play cards, actually.'

'Not one for metaphor, eh?' I mumbled. I soon regretted my words: it took me several minutes to explain to him what I meant.

In the weeks prior to our trip to Venice, I found myself reading the endless documents that Milo had directed I should review. Milo's instructions were simply that I should read the papers he had had copied for me. The originals were in a safe-deposit box, whose key I was instructed to keep secure. The note, in Milo's hand, that accompanied the files managed to be at once curiously melodramatic and quite uninformative.

> My dear Patrick:
> I am sorry to have to impose on you a final burden. My executors are fine money men but do not have your experience and discretion. They need not know about these matters. And as you will see, there are things here I cannot leave to Melissa.

Please keep from Alexander, too, if you can, anything that will hurt him.

I must ask you to review these documents, once I am dead. That is all I ask. If it becomes necessary for you to act, you will find the information essential. If it does not, you will only have had to carry the burden of some of my secrets.

There are some who would go to great lengths to steal these documents, if they knew you had them. I have told no one, save Ellis, who will send them to you. Even he does not know what is in them, however.

You have been a loyal friend all these years, Patrick.

I thank you.

Milo Hawksworth

I asked John Ellis, Milo's personal secretary, if he had any idea what I was supposed to do about the papers and he told me he knew only that I had been asked to read them.

Puzzled, I set about the task.

The first thing that became clear was that Milo was worried for Alexander's physical safety. There were copies of papers explaining arrangements that had been made for him to be accompanied by bodyguards. Milo had written a note on one of these documents, asking me to make sure, through Ellis, that all these instructions were carried out, and to impress on Alex himself his father's insistence that he stick with them. 'As soon as anyone knows how rich he is, he'll be a target for kidnapping for ransom. I've explained it to him myself. But it wouldn't do any harm to reinforce the point.' I did as I was bid.

In the first lot of files I reviewed there was also more evidence of Milo's earlier bizarre obsession with Alexander's succession: there were, for example, medical documents demonstrating that samples of tissue that Milo had provided had 'no nucleic acids that were inconsistent with the subject's being the biological offspring of Lord Hawksworth'. The probability that the person from whom the tissue came was a son of Milo's was 'of the order of 0.999 . . .'. (Frankly I don't remember the exact number of 9s; but that – as my gambling great-uncle Freddy would have said – is close enough to a sure thing.)

'Very peculiar the way these scientists put things. Here's a chap who was born to his mother while she was living with his father and they tell me that the evidence is "not inconsistent" with his being his father's son,' I said to Virginia. Since my dear wife had already made it plain that she was more bored than piqued by Milo's eccentricities, I was somewhat surprised when she stretched out a hand from her armchair by the fireplace. I handed her the report and, the *Times* crossword apparently forgotten, she set about reviewing it.

'The evidence they're talking about is evidence from comparing Alexander's DNA with Milo's. And they seem to think the chances that their nucleic acids would match so closely if they weren't father and son are one in several hundred million. That's about as conclusive a piece of evidence as you'll get.' (I have long ago ceased puzzling as to how Jinny knows everything, but it is sometimes the result of research for her writings. So I wasn't a bit surprised when something about this sort of genetic hanky-panky turned up in the next of her Bella Sharpe detective novels.)

'Good. Well, it obviously satisfied Milo. You remember I told you he stopped talking about it a few months before he died? This form is dated 11th October 1989. If you count back from January, when he died, that's about the right time.'

'What are these papers about, darling? Why did Milo want you to read them?'

'I don't know yet, my sweet. They're about all sorts of different things, none of which seems very important. But one thing's clear. Milo wants me to be prepared if anybody challenges the trusts he's established for Alex.'

'Why would he want to do that?'

'Oh, I don't know. Melissa once said she thought that Milo couldn't bear to think he wouldn't be able to control Alex's fate from beyond the grave.' I pantomimed a pair of hands reaching up from beneath the earth.

Virginia laughed. 'Will you be finished before we go to Venice?'

'I don't suppose so.'

'Then you'd better bring those papers with you.' It may seem a small matter to those of you who have been married for less time than I have, but this sort of thoughtfulness – anticipating that I might have wondered whether she would mind my bringing the papers and granting the waiver before it was applied for – is the kind of thing that makes me offer up regular prayers to the Almighty in thanks for his gracious loving-kindness ... even in seasons when I seem not to be in Jinny's best graces.

3

We arrived in Venice in a state of nervous exhaustion. (On our latest trip, I mean, not on the honeymoon.) In the ordinary course of things I am, I think I can honestly claim, an enthusiast for the railway. I always liked the old steam engines. I remember the thrill of setting off alone on one for the first time on the way to school. This was such a memorable moment that I was overwhelmed by a great rush of nostalgia when I waved Sebastian off on the steam train to Ampleforth for the first time, thirty-odd years later. My initial doubts about the wisdom of taking Jinny on an exhausting train journey across the Continent were overcome by her insistence. Even though the modern locomotive rather lacks the distinction of the old steam engine, as the day approached I found myself anticipating our jaunt through the European countryside. It was, I felt, a most romantic notion.

Our journey to Venice for the honeymoon had also been extraordinarily enjoyable. Mother had somehow tipped the steward off that we were newly married, and we were treated with enormous kindness and generosity from the moment we left Victoria Station. The only slight inconvenience was the hangover with which we staggered to breakfast in the dining-car in the morning, due to the preposterous amounts of champagne we drank the night before.

For a whole host of reasons this second trip never had quite the same feel to it. To begin with, my dear mother was not, alas, on hand to inform the staff that we were making a fortieth-year pilgrimage on the route of our first married journey. Not, I suspect, that Jones, our steward, was the sentimental type. He loaded us very efficiently into the carriage and explained all the modcons. But he smiled at none of my little jokes and seemed generally not disposed to *bonhomie*.

As we walked past each cabin, we read the names of its incumbents, written in a beautifully calligraphed hand (which Jinny informed me was almost certainly done by a computer). In our carriage, all of the cabins were occupied by couples. It was clear, from the heads that popped out to call cheerfully down the corridor to each other, that they were a party of young people, many of them not much older than I had been when I had set out on this journey for the first time. The men were dressed in the sort of clothes I associate, from Sunday colour magazine articles, with excesses in the City in the eighties. The ties just a little louder and wider than one favours oneself; the pin-stripes somehow slightly off; the collars too large and I should have said rather under-starched; the cuff-links perhaps heavier than I would expect to be comfortable. And despite their smooth young faces, I detected a certain coldness about them, as if they were taking this junket only to show each other that they could afford it.

Jinny observed that, the presence of lady companions with Gucci shoes and silk scarves bought in Sloane Street notwithstanding, there were no wedding rings in sight. (There were, however, a great number of signet rings of a size rather larger than I am used to.) They were clearly all set to have a whale of a time, and I did not begrudge them their noisy enthusiasms.

Five minutes out of Victoria Station, Jones entered, his face lugubrious as it had been throughout our first encounter, and begged our pardons. 'You have the only cabin in this carriage that doesn't belong to the party of young people going to Istanbul.'

We nodded, all ears, and I wondered whether Jones was planning to wander in from time to time with general intelligence of this nature. 'Thank you for telling us,' Virginia said brightly.

'No, I mean, I was wondering if you would mind if I moved you into the next carriage. There's one couple in the group that was booked in there by mistake.'

Virginia looked at me. 'I don't see why we shouldn't, Patrick. It'll no doubt be quieter.'

'Very well,' I told Jones. 'If you'd give us a minute to do some repacking, we'll be ready for the exchange.'

'The young gentleman has arranged for a bottle of champagne for you, in the other cabin. I'll move the luggage.'

When we met the 'young gentleman' in question, he turned out to be a chap in his late thirties with an Australian accent. He was extravagantly grateful. 'I say, it's really great of you to let us have your cabin.'

'Think nothing of it. Enjoy the trip.'

'No, really, I mean it. If there's anything I can do for you...' Naturally, this was all rather embarrassing and we hurried away as fast as we could, resolved to keep ourselves as much as possible henceforward to ourselves.

This resolve did not communicate itself very efficiently to our young companions. As we made our way to the dining-car for dinner, we came across a crowd of them in the bar.

We had stopped only in order to establish a way through them, when we were addressed by the tall, good-looking young man who had taken our cabin, his tie now slightly loosened at the neck. 'We're very griteful, Marilyn and mai.' I confess these Australian vowels have always grated mildly on my ear.

I mumbled an acknowledgement and attempted to move ahead with Jinny. But he was insistent on continuing the conversation. 'Been on this train before, 'ave you?' The enquiry was entirely friendly. I noticed at the same moment, via the nostrils, that this young man was unusually fragrant, positively doused in something a good deal more complicated than Trumper's Extract of Lime, and, via the old eyes, that he had on his arm an extremely attractive dark-haired girl who smiled constantly, as if, like the Mona Lisa, she was keeping a most delicious secret. (Virginia referred to her throughout our journey, when we were alone in our cabin, as 'the cat that swallowed the cream'.)

'Been on this train before, 'ave you?' We were so preoccupied that the first time he had spoken we had neither of us taken in that he was talking to us. But the second time he addressed himself directly to Jinny, and I should have left her to field the question. Unfortunately, I replied to him with rather greater particularity than is probably wise with a complete stranger. 'Indeed, we have, though not for forty years.'

Gary Mitchell – for that, as we were to discover in a few moments, was his name – pantomimed complete amazement at this intelligence. His mandible dropped towards his sternum (you learn this sort of lingo if you loiter about the coroners' courts) and his eyes opened enormously. He looked for a moment or two at each of us, attending, as any red-blooded Englishman would, a good deal more to my good wife than to me, and then turned to his mute and smiling companion. 'D'yerhearthat Marilyn?' It really did sound like one word. 'They've not been on the Orient Express for forty bloody years... oops, I beg your pardon, madam.' I formed the impression that Gary had probably spent some of his time at Victoria Station in the bar: certainly he was in good *metaphorical* spirits. 'Well, well, well... hold on,' he said. 'I must tell the others.'

For the next ten minutes, Gary introduced us to his dozen or so travelling companions, among them Marilyn Rimmer (the cat that swallowed the cream), Gerald Miller and his lovely companion Rita Spender, and a host of others whose names did not long reside in the ageing grey matter. They were all Australians, it seemed, making a European grand tour.

'It's Gary's birthday,' Gerald said. 'You must have a drink.'

'Yeah, go on,' Marilyn said. 'He's an old man of thirty-seven, now.' She laughed. In the circumstances, it would have been churlish to refuse.

One after another, they insisted on buying us drinks, and I had to avoid Jinny's eye in order to get in my order for a third large gin and tonic before she forbade it.

Gary and Marilyn and Gerald ('Call me Gerry, everyone else does') were not only amazed that anyone had done anything forty years ago, they went through a whole series of new expressions of astonishment when we introduced ourselves as Sir Patrick and Lady Scott. (I have almost always found titles a great source of muddle, and not only when one is dealing with foreigners. Most of Sebastian's contemporaries at Clare were really frightfully vague about how they work: one of his chums once sent us a thank-you letter addressed to 'Sir Scott and Lady Virginia'.)

'Golly,' Rita said, 'did you inherit your title?' Australians have an engaging directness, do they not? Her pretty blue eyes looked up almost reverentially from below her blonde fringe into mine. I was mildly distracted by the mascara on her eyelashes and the bluish make-up on her eyelids: if ever there was a case, I thought, of painting the lily, in the Bard's fine phrase, this was it.

'Partly,' I said, after a slightly embarrassing pause, while I resurfaced from my reflections on her adornment. (Perhaps I should have said more, but I've never really known how to deal with this sort of question.)

'How'd you get it then?' Marilyn took up the inquisition.

'I'm a QC.' Virginia later described my tone here as brusque: I should have said I was firm. Jinny also did not see the vague smile I gave Miss Rimmer, to indicate gently that this was as far as I was keen to go with the subject.

Marilyn looked blank for a moment and then smiled as if she had worked something out. Jinny, who did not wish to leave her in her state of confusion, explained to her over the next few minutes that one might be knighted if one was a successful enough lawyer, but that I had also inherited a baronetcy, which was why I had said 'Partly.' Rather than helping, however, this seemed to confuse matters further, and Jinny, exhausted by our exertions in getting to the station – we'd had a frightful time getting a taxi, but that is another story – took her off to a plush corner and settled in for the long haul.

'Sorry about Marilyn's curiosity,' Gerry said to me. 'Titles aren't so common in Australia . . . except for politicians and some business magnates. And most of them aren't inherited.' In the course of the conversation, it transpired that Gary, Marilyn, Gerry and Rita were stopping off in Venice, while the rest of the party went on through the Balkans to Istanbul. 'Got a little investigating to do in Venice,' Gerry told me mysteriously.

'Ah, investigating, eh?'

'Yup. I'm looking for a beautiful and mysterious woman who holds the key to my destiny.' I glanced involuntarily towards Rita and he laughed. 'It's not that sort of destiny I have in mind.'

I may have coloured slightly. 'Well, at all events,' I said, 'I wish you the very best of luck.'

It took nearly three-quarters of an hour to disentangle ourselves from the enthusiastic affability of this crowd of young people. I was very grateful that I had not mentioned the *occasion* of our earlier journey on the train, since that would no doubt have produced more exclamations of astonishment and pourings of gins and tonics.

After this exhausting encounter, dinner was rather later than we had expected, and Virginia forbade me wine with the meal, on the grounds that my ethanol ration had been exhausted by my two or three gins in the bar. Despite this, the food was excellent. We began with an elegant sort of mushroom dish, whose name I don't recall, but whose combination of tastes and textures has stayed with me. As I savoured it in silence – Jinny being unaccountably unresponsive to my occasional cheerful nods and winks – I imagined how it might have complemented the Muscadet that was being quaffed in prodigious quantities at the table across the aisle from us. When the plates from our hors-d'oeuvres were being taken away I winked at Jinny again to see if she was cheered up by her salmon.

'Are you developing a twitch, darling?'

I contemplated going along with this notion; but, after a moment's thought, I issued, rather gingerly, a mild challenge: 'Actually, I was hoping to cheer you up.'

'I don't need cheering up. Gary and his friends have done enough cheering up to last me a good few weeks. What I need now is a good night's sleep.' While the tone was even, and the voice was not raised, there was no mistaking the mood. I inferred that it would be best to spend the rest of the meal in silence.

As we progressed by way of sorbet and salad to the excellent *entrecôte*, accompanied by lightly sautéed string beans and parsnips, cooked – as they almost never are – exactly right, I imagined a whole series of wines, rising, by way of a Gevrey-Chambertin I remembered from a recent dinner at Lincoln's Inn, to a rich Sauterne, fragrant and smooth, that would have done well with the *tarte aux pommes*. By this stage I was obliged to imagine both the wine and the dish, since Jinny announced that I had also passed my calorie quota somewhere half-way through the sorbet. Decaffeinated coffee being unavailable, and tea after dinner being, in my view, an abomination, Virginia and I were up and away from the table a mere forty minutes later, and installed in our bunks not long after that.

Virginia has almost never been known to go to sleep without a wee spot of reading. She withdrew from her overnight bag a slim volume, which turned out to be a mystery novel by Dame Agatha of blessed memory. It was called *The Mystery of the Blue Train*. Virginia's reading when she is in the midst of composing one of her Bella Sharpes invariably has some connection with the subject matter of her current book. It occurred to me that we might be taking the train to Venice less out of sentiment than out of Jinny's desire to establish the 'atmosphere' of Miss Sharpe's latest adventure. Not an hypothesis, I felt, to raise with my good wife even in jest. I dropped off eventually in a mood soured by my unexpressed suspicions.

Virginia had said that all she wanted was a good night's sleep. This, at the beginning of a railway journey, even on a train designed with the comforts of the new Orient Express, was not something to be relied on. I will pass over in silence the loud knocking on our door at three in the morning when Gary, even more immersed in his cups than when we had seen him before dinner, attempted to persuade us to get up and look at the moon. Jones, our steward, revealed himself to be something of a master at dealing with such situations, however; and Gary apologized with a sheepish fulsomeness at breakfast, urged on by a now unsmiling Marilyn. 'I see the cream's gone sour,' Jinny observed *sotto voce*.

For the rest of the ride, my wife sat wordless, her Parker poised over one of the large pads of lined paper on which she constructs her Bella Sharpe novels, the nib occasionally swooping down to write the next perfect phrase.

I do not interrupt the Muse. And so I set about deciphering more of the Hawksworth papers, resisting the temptation to read aloud even the juiciest titbits. Jinny did not hear, therefore, of the Bolivian ranch, where Milo kept not only several hundred horses but an Indian woman, now in her fifties, whose children appeared to be as clearly descended from William, first Baron Hawksworth of Hawksworth, as was Alexander. These two daughters had had large settlements made on them, on condition that they never came to England. They had been notified of Milo's death: knowing that when it happened, they were to move to the home in La Paz that Milo had bought for them. I pondered what it would be like to move from the idyll of a ranch on the shores of Lake Titicaca to even the most gracious flat in what cannot be the most charming city in the world. Unless their elder brother died within five years, they would get nothing more. If he did die within that time, they'd get everything. I wondered if they knew *that*.

I also wondered what on earth Milo had expected me to do with all this information. Somewhere, I hoped, I would find the answer. Milo had written: 'If it becomes necessary for you to act, you will find the information essential.' So far, I had read nothing that seemed likely to be useful for any obvious purpose: perhaps, I thought, I would just have to wait for the grand event that would make it necessary for me to act. I only hoped I would notice it when it happened.

Jones kindly brought us lunch in our cabin, so that we could avoid facing the by-now most unwelcome attentions of Gary and Marilyn, Gerald and Rita and the rest of the Australians. 'You were lucky you moved yesterday. Somebody broke into Mr Mitchell's cabin while he was at breakfast. He lost his briefcase. Fortunately, he had his passport and his traveller's cheques on him.'

'How awful,' Jinny said. 'Does that sort of thing happen often on the train?'

'Good lord, no,' Jones replied, shocked by the suggestion of a slander against his train. 'Nothing like that has ever happened while I've been on the Express. It's very unusual.'

'Glad to hear it. I gather that pickpockets and villains of all kinds flourish in Italy, however.'

'That may well be, Sir Patrick. But we can usually keep 'em off our train.'

The weather was sunny and the cabin became hot and stuffy, even with the window open: finally, as we passed through Brescia, I summoned Jones and asked him if there was anything he could do.

'You haven't got the air-conditioning on,' he said matter-of-factly. I felt supremely silly. Ten minutes later we were shivering. Try as I might, I couldn't seem to get the temperature anywhere near comfortable. I attempted to make these arrangements discreetly, knowing that Bella Sharpe's world is not to be interrupted, but Jinny peered at me over her glasses from time to time, with the sort of enquiring look to which the best response is not an explanation but an apology.

'Sorry, darling. Just trying to cool us down,' I would say, only to have to respond to the next querying glance with a 'Sorry, darling. Just trying to warm us up.' By the time we arrived at the Ferrovia station in Venice the next afternoon, neither of us was as fresh or as cheerful as we would have liked.

Jinny ordered a taxi boat in her efficient Italian (or so I assumed, my own Italian being somewhat primitive). I heard her announce, as the bags were settled in the baggage area, that we were going to the Palazzo Longhi. The captain – if that is the right word for the operator of a motor-boat – looked mildly askance at her (in rather the sort of way you might look at a nun who asked to be driven to a bordello) but nodded and mentioned what sounded to me like an outrageous fee. I was, by now, in no mood to question any of Jinny's judgements, and I was certainly not going to express scepticism about her bargaining capacity. When I settled back on the plastic seat, my eyes closed and my face raised to the warmth of the afternoon sun, I prayed fervently to St Simeon the Lesser, whose domed church faced us as we set off, that the worst of the trip was over.

On the whole, the days that followed did not reinforce my faith in the celestial influence of the good Simeon.

4

Bernadetto's remark about the level of staffing had led me to expect something other than the welcome that greeted us. (I gathered later that, since we had insisted that we could find our own way, he had placed a servant to witness our arrival in the Ferrovia, whose task had been to telephone ahead of us. Very Bernadetto, this: to arrange to be waiting for us, as if by some psychic means, when we arrived.) The result was that as we struggled out of the boat and approached the grand portal of the Palazzo Longhi, the door was opened by a handsome young man in white livery with gold epaulettes, who came out to greet us followed by three others, similarly attired. They bowed slightly and greeted us. 'Welcome, Sir Patrick; welcome, Lady Scott,' each of them said in a remarkably light accent. And then they peered down into the taxi, obviously expecting enough baggage to occupy them all mightily. Once they realized how lightly encumbered we were, the leader of this band of four liveried stalwarts then directed two of the others each to take one of our suitcases, while he pointed to our overnight bags and directed them into the hands of the fourth. Finally, he waved grandly towards the open door and invited us to precede him into the vast hall of the *palazzo*.

And there, smiling at the base of the stairs, dressed stylishly in a white suit with a large and very American-looking bow-tie, was Bernadetto. He bowed low in welcome and said genially, 'Darlings, *mi casa e su casa*,' repeating the greeting he always offered us when we arrived at his Spanish house. Behind him, I saw my cousin Jamie (dressed, I was glad to see, in more conventional English summer clothing, with a blue blazer that would have delighted the Royal Yacht Club during Cowes Week) descending the sweep of the grand staircase. Bernadetto strode towards us and gathered Virginia, who had suddenly become unaccountably cheerful, into his arms, kissing her enthusiastically a good deal more than once on both cheeks. Once this was done, he approached me with what looked threateningly like the same intention, and so I thrust out my hand, as I always find myself doing with him, hoping that he would take up the offer of this more manly form of welcome.

One thing you can say for an English education: manners. Bernadetto obliged. Indeed, he combined a firm handshake with a most reassuringly conventional welcome: 'How do you do, Patrick? Marvellous that you could come.'

Jamie's welcome, though courteous, was more subdued. 'Hallo, Patrick, old man. Virginia, my dear.' This was followed by a reliably English kiss an inch or two to the left of Virginia's cheek.

Throughout this process the four young men in livery stood in a row with the baggage, waiting, as it turned out, for Bernadetto's command.

'Let me take you up to your room,' he said. '*Avanti*, Giorgio,' he went on, addressing the leader; and we proceeded up the stairs and round to the room at the front of the *palazzo*, overlooking the canal, where we had not been for four decades. The servants set about unpacking our cases and hanging up our clothes.

'Changed much?' Bernadetto asked.

We looked around. One thing was immediately clear. The bedroom as it had been, with the peeling plaster on the ceiling and the fading wallpaper, coming off in strips, was no more. Everything was in perfect order. The canopy over the bed, a vast but slightly tattered nineteenth-century affair when we had been here last, had been replaced by a modern fabric – 'What a lovely brocade,' Jinny said quietly – and the painted Venetian furniture that I remembered had been carefully restored. On each side of the bed on the marble floor was a vast rug – one of those great French things made by Aubusson. The result of all these changes was to make me feel as if I was visiting the *palazzo* now at a time long *before* my last visit, in the century when its furnishings were newly purchased by the Venetian Count whose chattels Bernadetto's father, old di Montebello, had bought lock, stock and barrel when he acquired the *palazzo*.

'I'd say it has,' Virginia said, as she scanned the room. 'Changed, I mean.' At this moment, Giorgio flung open the casement on to the canal, and we saw, for the first time, the one thing that had not changed: the extraordinary, timeless view of the Grand Canal.

'But the view, I think, will not have changed much,' Jamie said, echoing our thoughts in the sort of pompous tone that suggested it might have been almost entirely his doing. 'We'll leave you to settle in: *apperitivi* at six on the *terrazzo*. Then we're taking you out to dinner.' It did not occur to me at the time that it was strange to adopt so proprietary a tone in someone else's house: Jamie and Bernadetto had been keeping each other company for so long they seemed more like brothers than friends.

As they left, Virginia and I were staring out in silence over the canal. When I turned to kiss her modestly on the cheek, there was, I thought, a touch of moistness about her eyes. She smiled at me, one of her radiant smiles. It is the east, and Jinny is the sun, I thought. Funny how there's always a phrase from the Bard to match the moment.

In the previous few days I had been competing with Bella Sharpe for Jinny's attentions. Now, she must have solved some problem in the writing of the novel: her mood had lifted and she seemed suddenly to be completely enthusiastic about our adventure. 'Paddy, darling, we're here. I'm going to try and be nicer to you, if you'll be nicer to me.'

Eager to celebrate this escape from several days under the dark clouds of her disapproval, I uttered the magic formula: 'Kiss and make up.'

And we did; and we did.

*

Drinks on the terrace, overlooking the canal, were served by Giorgio, who was obviously the major-domo. Aiming to get into the Italian spirit, I had a Campari, with a slice of orange, and a single lump of ice; Jinny displayed her newly recovered good spirits by having a Martini; and Bernadetto and Jamie abstemiously sipped champagne. Since we were going out to dinner, we had dressed, though Jinny had persuaded me not to put on the old dinner-jacket. This turned out, of course, to have been good advice, since our host was dressed with a stylish informality: his trousers were pearl grey, with black Italian moccasins peeking out from below the cuffs; on top he wore what looked like a white silk dinner jacket, and a cream silk shirt, open at the collar, with a bright silk scarf. It was, as Virginia put it later, 'a smart and rather dashing look', especially for a man in his sixties. Jamie, as before, was more conventionally dressed in a pale grey suit (though his tie was of a colour that Jinny tells me is nowadays called aubergine).

'We're going to dinner with some friends, a little bit down the canal. She's an American called Peggy Aschenheim: she collects paintings, and she's got a Chilean painter by the name of Claudio Occampo staying with her. And there'll no doubt be others.' Bernadetto smiled a beatific smile. 'It'll be fun and we don't have to stay too late.'

'You'll like Peggy,' Jamie said. 'She's very, very bright. And she's a fan of Bella Sharpe's.' He laughed. 'She'd never have forgiven us if we had kept you to ourselves.'

Bernadetto muttered something to Giorgio, who vanished downstairs, reappearing a few minutes later at the helm of a little motor-boat, which appeared out of a rio that runs between the Palazzo Longhi and its neighbour. I noticed that he was sporting a rather splendid nautical cap, in the same white and gold braid pattern as his jacket.

'How handsome Giorgio looks,' Jinny said.

'Doesn't he just.' Jamie's remark had a slightly unattractive leering tone. I wondered if he really thought it appropriate to interpret Virginia's innocent appreciation in this vulgar way, or whether this was just his idea of grown-up humour.

Bernadetto evidently thought the latter, because he gave Jamie a stern look, before turning to offer Jinny his arm: 'Shall we?' He was smiling cheerfully again. We walked downstairs to the boat.

Peggy Aschenheim was a striking woman. She had masses of

curly hair, of a colour I believe is called platinum, and the sort of creased skin that comes from years in the sun. Her eyes were lively and intelligent; she gazed about her as if nothing escaped her notice and she understood everything. Her pleasant and interesting looks were impaired, however, by one notable flaw: in the centre of her face sat a tiny well-formed, retroussé nose that looked utterly out of place. As we approached the door of her *palazzo*, Jamie whispered to us: 'Don't stare at her nose, she's very sensitive about it. The surgeon has never been forgiven.' This sort of instruction is very hard to obey, and so I found myself shiftily glancing in every direction as we were introduced. As a result, Mrs Aschenheim treated me throughout the evening as if I were slightly unbalanced, smiling unnaturally and coaxing me with the occasional 'Yeees . . .' said on a rising tone, as one would urge on a slow child. I cursed Jamie inwardly on several occasions.

Mrs Aschenheim greeted us in the hall of her *palazzo* – the Palazzo Aschenheim, it said on the brass plate outside the front door – and led us down a candle-lit corridor to an enormous sitting-room. On the wall above the fireplace was a very large modern painting in bright colours, composed, so far as I could see, by hurling paint randomly at the canvas. I knew, at once, from Jinny's reverential glance, that it was an 'important' work. 'Jackson Pollock,' Jinny murmured in my ear.

'I see.' Of course, I did not.

There was nobody in the sitting-room, because the guests were all out on the *terrazzo*, which was lit with hundreds of candles: their reflection in the water must have delighted those who passed by in *vaporetti* and gondolas as the day drifted into the night. And there, beautiful as always, in a pale blue evening-dress and a single string of pearls, was Melissa Hawksworth.

I had spent so much of the last few days thinking about her husband and his affairs that it took me a moment or two to realize how strange a coincidence it was that she was here.

'You know Melissa, Lady Hawksworth, don't you?'

'Indeed, we do, what a lovely surprise,' Jinny said. I was unable to think of anything to say, and so I smiled blankly and followed Bernadetto's example in kissing her hand.

'Goodness, Patrick, a day in Italy and you've gone native,' she said, her laughter tinkling across the canal.

I blushed, naturally. And as I recovered my sang-froid, it occurred to me that in all the years of our acquaintance I had never asked Melissa *where* in Italy she went to, and she had never told me.

'And this', our hostess continued, indicating the man to whom

Melissa had been talking, 'is Claudio Occampo, *the* Chilean painter.' The stress suggested that there was no other Chilean painter of note. On the whole, this did not surprise me. 'He is the author of the masterpiece over the fireplace.'

'A wonderful painting,' I said to the dark-skinned man in the white linen suit, 'rather reminiscent of Jackson Pollock.'

Jinny, for some reason, kicked my shin and took over the conversation. 'And yet it extends his ideas in an entirely new direction. A deeply original painting. I liked it immediately.'

'You don't need to worry that you've upset Claudio. He doesn't speak a word of English,' Mrs Aschenheim said to me in a slow and serious voice. 'It simply thrills people in New York to know that they are paying hundreds of thousands of dollars for paintings by someone who just won't learn the language.' She laughed pleasantly. 'Unfortunately, my Spanish is quite useless, so we've been chatting in French.' Then she flashed Señor Occampo a smile and went on: '*Sir Patrick est un grand amateur de vos oeuvres. Il m'a dit qu'il préfère la peinture au-dessus de la cheminée à toutes les oeuvres de Jackson Pollock.*' Even with *my* French, I could tell that this was not, shall we say, a wholly accurate account of my views. I resolved to believe none of Mrs Aschenheim's translations in future. As she turned away to move on to the introductions of her other guests, she winked at me.

Mr Occampo inclined his head towards me solemnly. '*C'est un très grand honneur de faire votre connaissance, monsieur.*'

'*Moi aussi* . . .' I stopped and smiled vaguely, not wishing to risk my grasp of the French language any further, and followed Virginia and Mrs Aschenheim towards the final person on the terrace, a middle-aged woman, seated on her own looking gloomily out over the water.

'Honey, this is Sir Patrick and Lady Scott. My daughter, Georgie, Georgie Aschenheim Bishop.'

Mrs Bishop looked up at us blankly for a moment and then offered a bejewelled hand. 'Delighted, I'm sure.'

We shook hands.

'So, Lady Scott, how long are you going to be with us in *la bella Venezia?*'

'Just a couple of days. And then on to Como.'

'Hardly enough time to pick up our atmosphere . . . a pity. I'd love to see Bella Sharpe deal with the Italian police.'

'So would I, Mrs Aschenheim, but I must accept my limitations: and one thing I know is that I can only write about places I know extremely well. I tried to send Bella to New York once –'

'*Poisoned Apple*,' Georgie Bishop chimed in. 'I read it.'
'Well, I'm not sure it worked.'
'Worked for me.'
'Thank you.'
'So,' Mrs Aschenheim continued, 'maybe if you spent a week or two here and took some notes we could entice Bella here.'

I saw the slight tension that was beginning to build in Virginia's jaw. She does not like talking about Bella Sharpe novels that are as yet unwritten. And, I suspected, she was especially cross about being asked to discuss the possibility of bringing Bella to Venice, when she had already decided to do so. The note-taking on the train had been followed, I noticed, by a more than usually scrupulous attention to various details of our trips to and from the Palazzo Longhi. And I had heard her suggesting to Jamie, on the ride over to the Palazzo Aschenheim, that she would like to be taken on a tour of some of the less familiar parts of the city the next day. So I knew that it was time to divert the Aschenheims, *mère et fille*, from their pincer attack on my favourite novelist.

'I fear, Mrs Aschenheim, that my wife finds it difficult to talk about Bella Sharpe's unwritten future.'

'Oh, of course, I'm dreadfully sorry. It's terribly bad luck, I know, to talk about what you're working on. Albert, my late husband, used to say that it stifled the creative juices. Please forgive us . . . we're just such fans.'

'There's really no need to apologize,' Virginia said. 'Patrick always exaggerates my sensitivity about Bella Sharpe.' Sometimes, I regret to say, my wife does not exactly hew to the truth.

Señor Occampo's French was certainly plentiful. I had never heard a Chilean speaking the language, but the impression I formed was that a Chilean French accent was much like an American one. Certainly, I would have been hard put to it to tell his accent apart from Mrs Aschenheim's. I gathered from our conversation that the painting above the fireplace was a new turn for the painter, and that until recently his work had been '*hyper-réaliste*' (a word I translated freely to myself as 'hyper-realist,' while still remaining pretty much in the dark). Mrs Aschenheim told me, with a smile and a wink towards the painter, that '*l'année dernière Claudio a fait un mouton, qui était plus mouton qu'un mouton.*' I smiled complaisantly, while trying to work out what this might mean, and decided that it was probable that Claudio had done a painting of a sheep that was photographically exact. Pleased that I had grasped *something* of our conversation, my smile broadened. But then it occurred to me to wonder why, in an age of fine cameras, anyone would bother to do such a thing: and this thought, I'm afraid, renewed my perplexity. I don't suppose my smile lasted long.

'He's not at all how I expected him to be,' Peggy Aschenheim confided. 'He's famous for being kind of reclusive, so I thought maybe he'd be shy. We are so lucky, don't you think, to be able to just spend time with a real artist? Isn't it a thrill to finally meet someone whose work you've been collecting for years?' Mrs Aschenheim continued. (The split infinitive, I have noticed, is a defining feature of the American idiom.)

'I'm sure it must be,' I said, more out of politeness than anything else: not having met anyone whose works I had collected 'for years' (except, of course, Sebastian, my boy, whose every daub since prep school has been framed and hung somewhere at Chewton Ampney) I was not really in a position to comment honestly. As for this business of spending time with a real artist, it didn't seem to me that Occampo ranked with, say, John Betjeman as a dinner companion: though, of course, you'd expect a literary genius to be more amusing than a painter.

At this moment, my hostess chose to leave me alone with Mr Occampo. We bowed and smiled at each other for a moment, and, when it became clear that the next move was up to me, I ventured out on the ice with a good deal less enthusiasm than I affected. '*Votre oeuvre . . . magnifique.*'

Occampo took this compliment in good part and began what seemed to be a long account, starting '*il y'a vingt ans,*' of the whole development of his style. I tried to divert him towards discussion of Bolivia – a country I knew to be in the same general vicinity as Chile – hoping to learn something of relevance to interpreting Hawksworth's strange bequest. '*Avez-vous fait des peintures de Titicaca, le lac bolivien?*'

He seemed rather more discomfited by this question than one might have expected, positively bellowing: '*Non, je n'ai jamais voyagé en Bolivie.*' I wondered if, perhaps, confusing Bolivia and Chile was as much of a solecism as muddling up, say, us with the French. This was obviously not the right person with whom to pursue the question of Hawksworth's Bolivian possessions. I made an attempt to patch things up: '*En Chile . . . aiment-ils vos oeuvres?*'

'*Pour moi, le Chile n'existe pas.*'

We returned to an exhaustive review of the challenges of painting in the Occampan manner.

I was in the middle of this difficult discussion with Señor Occampo, which had, so far as I could gather, arrived at a phase involving something called '*l'expressionnisme abstrait*', when the final guests arrived. I welcomed their presence with the enthusiasm that must have met the troops relieving Khartoum.

Everybody but Jamie, Jinny and I seemed to know them already. They were an American couple by the name of Bouncer – Philip and Jo-Ann Bouncer, to be exact – and they were old friends of Peggy and Albert Aschenheim's, who had been brought over by a little motor-boat skippered by a chap in the livery of an hotel. Mrs Bouncer was wearing dark glasses, despite the fact that the sun had set, a fact that gave her a certain glamour.

They were staying not too far away at the Hotel Danieli, which Mr Bouncer described as 'f—ing terrific, f—ing expensive.'

I confess I winced slightly at this free use of the old Anglo-Saxon: in my day I don't think even an American would have used language of that sort with ladies. But I was so grateful to be back in a conversation in my native tongue (even if Mr Bouncer spoke a less than exalted dialect of it) that I forgave him pretty immediately; especially since Jo-Ann – an attractive woman in her mid-fifties, with a great many more diamonds about her person than I would have thought safe, even in the boat of the Hotel Danieli – whispered something to Philip that produced a mild blushing followed by an apology for his language. The apology proved sincere: Philip Bouncer's manners fell away with each of the glasses of brandy he insisted on drinking before dinner and positively vanished when he started on the wine at dinner, but he did not use a single further swear-word the whole evening.

When we were introduced, Mr Bouncer pricked up his ears when he heard Jinny was a writer. 'You're not a journalist are you?' he all but snarled. 'I hate journalists.'

'Actually, I write fiction.'

'So do most journalists, if you ask me.'

'I'm sorry, Virginia.' Jo-Ann patted her husband firmly on the forearm and made a quiet shushing noise. 'You must excuse Phil: he's just kinda sensitive about journalists right now, being as how some guy calls himself an investigative journalist is out to get him. I told him that Peggy had promised us a famous British novelist for dinner, but he doesn't always remember what I tell him.'

'Now, honey, that ain't fair. I *never* forget a word you say. But my wife's right, Lady Scott, I'm sorry. Just kinda touchy right now about journalists.'

'I quite understand. I've never had much time for the press myself.'

Once Mr Bouncer had had a chance to calm his nerves by knocking back a few glasses (which took, on average, two minutes per fairly-healthy snifter), Peggy Aschenheim rang a bell and, after a brief discussion with the liveried servant that this produced, announced that dinner would be served in a couple of minutes.

'We're eating on the roof . . . I think you'll enjoy the views . . . so we can start making our way up in the elevator . . . it only takes three or four people comfortably. Bernadetto, my dear, will you take up Patrick and Jinny . . . and maybe Melissa – you are all so slender.' This last adjective was offered in a spirit of accuracy in relation to the others: it took a very generous spirit to apply it to me.

We rose in stately style together, Melissa and Bernadetto standing stiffly side by side, facing me, with Jinny on my arm, chatting briefly about the Bouncers.

'Too amazing,' Melissa said, giggling slightly. 'Peggy does know the most extraordinary people. I met them with her last time I was here and they stayed with me in London a few weeks ago. I can't understand how someone so dull could have made so much money.'

'They own an area of Texas that's larger than the Home Counties, endless oil wells, and hundreds of thousands of cattle.' Bernadetto leaned towards us and went on *sotto voce*: 'And, according to Peggy, Philip Bouncer has the best collection of nineteenth-century American painting outside the National Gallery in Washington. He *was* planning to build a museum for them in San Antonio.'

'A patriot, I gather.' I gathered from Bernadetto's dismissive tone that older American art could not be collected for its quality, so to speak, *as* painting. (Actually, we have always bought a couple of new British watercolours from Christie's every year or so on rather the same principle ourselves.)

'Keeping nineteenth-century American painting off the market is not just an act of patriotism, it's a service to mankind.' Melissa laughed. Jinny cast me a surprised glance, and I knew at once what she was thinking: I, too, had always thought of Melissa as more of a huntin'-shootin' sort than a greenery-yallery Grosvenor Gallery gal. As we waited for the lift's door to open, so we could step out into the warm night, on the roof garden of the *palazzo*, I was impressed.

5

But I was even more impressed by the sight that greeted us when the doors opened. There, on the roof of the *palazzo*, in the middle of Venice, overlooking the Grand Canal, Peggy Aschenheim had planted a fabulous garden. I say 'fabulous', because that was what it was: like a landscape out of the Arabian Nights or some other Oriental fable. There were orange trees, in tubs, fruiting with tiny bright oranges, azaleas, massed and colourful, which seemed to be planted in deep stone troughs; and everywhere, on little candle-lit tables, there were miniature roses, in pots. Behind the domed gazebo, which housed the lift, was a vast unlit forest of rosemary bushes, which filled the air with their resinous smell.

Jinny and I looked at each other amazed and wandered about this flowered landscape, breathing in the perfumed air, and admiring the large, extremely modern, glass table, which was richly laid for the ten of us. Five of Mrs Aschenheim's gentlemen in livery stood silently in front of another table, set a few yards away, which was laden with wines and plates and various other appurtenances of the dinner-table. They looked like a set of Indian quintuplets – I, at least, found them less than easy to tell apart, with their dark brown skin, curly hair, and bright, toothy smiles. Mrs Aschenheim must have searched long and hard for a matched set of Indians this handsome.

Bernadetto waved cheerily at them and they smiled, equally jollily, back. '*Buona sera.*'

And a quiet chorus of '*Buona sera, signore e signori*' came back in reply.

In a minute or two, Mrs Aschenheim arrived with the Bouncers; and Jamie came up last with Mrs Bishop.

'It's marvellous up here, Mrs Aschenheim. How clever of you to invent such a glorious secret garden.'

'Why, thank you, Lady Scott, I'm happy to take the credit; but the fact is the whole thing was Jamie's idea.'

Another surprise. In all the years I had known him – and our acquaintance began when he was about four – Jamie had never manifested the slightest interest in gardening. 'What a gift you have, Mr Leith,' Mrs Bouncer gushed. (It was a natural enough error, since Jamie insists on being introduced always as 'Jamie Leith'. This is exactly the sort of muddle one gets into with titles. And it would have so thrilled Mrs Bouncer to know that she was talking to a real English Lord.) 'You must come and give us your help in Texas. We have this penthouse in Dallas that really needs a roof garden. Don't we Philip, honey?'

'That's right. We do. If Jo-Ann says we need a roof garden, then we need a roof garden.' The blush on his cheeks this time was the result of the spirits he had imbibed.

Mrs Bouncer was predictably delighted by this pronouncement, and Jamie bowed modestly, treating the invitation as a piece of friendly flattery. This turned out to be a misunderstanding. For, throughout dinner, whenever I overheard Jamie's conversation with Mrs Bouncer, who was seated next to him, she was busy explaining to him how easy it would be to fly into Dallas; the exact configuration of the roof in question; or the needs of a dozen of her friends whose taste for roof gardens, or gardens of all other sorts, was similarly intense and immediate. It seemed that Mrs Bouncer had misidentified my dear cousin as a glorified gardener. If he resented it, he was too courteous to let it show. And Mrs B. was not one to be put off.

Mrs Aschenheim had placed Bernadetto at the opposite end of the table from herself. To her left sat Occampo; I was at her right, surrounded entirely by Aschenheims, since Mrs Bishop was to my right. And Mrs Bouncer, unencumbered with even the minutest knowledge of French, smiled in a friendly way to Occampo, on her right, from time to time, in the rare pauses in her disquisition on the demand for roof gardens in urban Texas.

Peggy Aschenheim's cook was a gem. From the first course – a marvellous summer cold soup involving a veritable cornucopia of vegetables – by way of the elegantly Dovered sole to the succulent slices of duck's breast served with a fennel and potato purée and finely julienned carrots in a sauce of orange and ginger – passing by a salad of endives and radicchio and a blackberry sorbet whose memory still brings delight – we reached a charlotte russe that I will remember for the few years remaining to me (and may remember longer if such corporeal thoughts are permitted in the hereafter). The wines, too, were heavenly: many of the reds were Italian wines I did not know, rich with fruit, heavy on the palate, subtle and resonant. The Bollinger with which we cleansed our palates before the duck (with the sorbet) and after the pudding (by itself) was wonderfully refreshing: the Sauterne with the charlotte russe was even better than the one I had imagined on the train. (Existence, the monks taught us, being a perfection, is superior to non-existence; and sipping a great wine confirms their teaching, since, I am happy to record, a real taste is always better than an imaginary one.) The effect of the meal, at least on me, was to cause a gratifying warmth to spread over one's body and one's mood. Virginia tells me that Dante was not a Venetian. But if he had been, he would have found an evening of feasting on the roof of the Palazzo Aschenheim a most suitable inspiration for the *Paradiso* . . . as well, I fear, as an occasion of the sin of gluttony, that might be rewarded in the *Inferno*.

'How did you start collecting Mr Occampo's work?' I asked Peggy as the soup course was cleared.

'Saw something in a gallery. Fell in love with it. I think it was one of those sheep that Phil liked, too.' Mrs Aschenheim beamed down the table at Philip Bouncer: 'So, Phil, are you gonna buy some of Claudio's pictures?'

'You bet. I called the dealer in New York on Friday.' He waved heartily and returned to his conversation with Melissa.

Mrs Aschenheim lowered her voice confidentially and turned her attention once more to me: 'Yeah, I showed Phil a photograph of one of the paintings from the hyper-realist period and it just blew him away. So he said he was going to call Claudio's agent and have him send slides over here.' Peggy smiled. 'He never was one to wait, Phil.' She paused, glancing reflectively at Occampo, who was in earnest conversation with Jamie, across the bows, so to speak, of an obviously uncomprehending Mrs Bouncer. Then our hostess assumed an even more confidential tone. 'You know, Patrick, it's kinda strange. I've been collecting for forty years now. This is the first time an artist has just invited himself to stay with me.'

'He must have taken to you. Did you meet at one of those New York openings?'

'No.' Peggy was still whispering. 'He just knew I liked his stuff. I mean, I talk about it all the time.' She looked across the table towards Claudio. 'Course, he doesn't understand English, does he, so I guess I don't have to whisper.' She waved across at him. '*Ça va?*' Señor Occampo nodded meekly.

*

I gathered from a conversation between Jo-Ann and Virginia that Philip Bouncer and Al Aschenheim had started out in business together. 'You've known Mr Bouncer for quite some time,' I said to our hostess as the sole arrived.

'Yup,' Mrs Aschenheim said cheerfully. 'Guess Phil and Al made their first few million together.' I gathered, too, that Phil and Jo-Ann were having a disagreement about how safe it was to wander about Venice without the bodyguards that apparently accompanied them everywhere in America; and this reminded me that I had been meaning to have a word with Melissa about getting her to make sure Alex understood how important it was to respect the security precautions his father had designed for him.

But I confess that, on the whole, with such a feast before me, I paid less attention than I no doubt should have to the brilliant conversation going on in French and in English about me. I was rather caught off my guard, as a result, when Mrs Aschenheim sweetly raised her glass to toast our anniversary. 'Bernadetto tells me that you two have been married for forty years. I think that deserves a little recognition here. So let's all raise our glasses and drink a toast to Virginia and Patrick Scott. To many more happy years together.' Jinny reported to me later that my blush was clearly visible to all.

Bernadetto's occasional Italian remarks to the Indians – 'Tamils,' Mrs Bishop whispered to me at one point, 'from Sri Lanka, not Indians at all' – were the only linguistic concession to the Serenissima and her language. 'Do stop talking to them in Italian,' Peggy Aschenheim roared at Bernadetto after he had addressed his fourth aside to them in the language of Dante. 'You know perfectly well that they much prefer English. Don't you, Sujit?' This last remark was addressed to the servant who seemed to be in charge. He nodded and smiled merrily. 'Yes, indeed, madam; English much, much better.'

This was exactly my own sentiment and I was relieved to have it expressed. While Mrs Aschenheim translated for a puzzled-looking Occampo – '*Il disait que l'anglais est beaucoup mieux*' – I murmured a couple of 'here, here's of endorsement and waved at Sujit and his cohorts. Unfortunately, in returning my arm to the table, I knocked over a glass in front of me, and the seepage of champagne in my lap through the cloth of my trousers brought home to me, in a very direct way, an urgent call of the physical man.

'I wonder, Mrs Aschenheim...'

'Peggy...'

'Indeed, Peggy, whether there is a...' (I paused, the proper American euphemism escaping me for a moment) '...a bathroom, in the vicinity.'

'Oh yes, of course there is. Sujit, take Sir Patrick to Mr Aschenheim's bathroom.'

I realized, as I stood up, that the cumulative effect of a great many wines was going to make a dignified exit something of a challenge. But Sujit had anticipated this problem and supported me discreetly at the elbow as we approached the lift. 'Not far, sir, not far at all,' he murmured encouragingly as we went down a single floor. When the door opened, we were in a vast room, with a great wall of windows looking out across the canal, over the roof of the facing *palazzo*, and down towards the Giudecca island. There were two large easels with unfinished paintings on them; and the inner wall of the room, facing the windows, was hung densely with paintings of Venice, all in the same style. Even a fellow as aesthetically off-beam as myself could tell at once that these were not the works of a great talent. I am aware that in modern art, paintings do not necessarily have to look like the things that they are paintings of, if you follow me: but these paintings were off in an unintended sort of a way. They were also in colours – purples, greens and browns – that suggested the artist might perhaps not have been endowed with normal colour vision.

I stared, for a moment, at this wall of horrors, until Sujit nudged me gently: 'Toilet, sir; toilet is important.'

Once more, I felt, he had said something with which it was hard not to agree. 'Nail on the head, old man,' I said, beaming at him. Sujit looked at me blankly. He did not seem to be familiar with the expression.

I followed my Indian friend across this room to a little bathroom. Three minutes later I had wiped off the champagne and satisfied the urgings of nature and I re-entered this room, which was, of course, the studio of the late Mr Albert Aschenheim, with my vigour renewed. On the desk by the bathroom door, which was covered with crayons, pens and pencils and various pieces of paper, as if it had all lain undisturbed from the moment Mr Aschenheim had left for the last time, was a faded wedding photograph. The woman in it was easily identified as a younger Peggy Aschenheim. Her pleasant face had, in those days, a kind of proportion, even a sort of beauty: for her large pleasant features were complemented by a large pleasant nose. The man in the picture was older than she was. He was large in every direction: towering over her, his vast girth cinctured with a cummerbund. Mr Aschenheim looked like a man who took his pleasures seriously. And the leer he directed at his young wife left very little to the imagination.

Sujit was waiting patiently by the lift, standing to attention, as if awaiting the Colonel Sahib's inspection. In my moderately intoxicated state I fear I raised a hand to my forehead and gave him a lazy salute: and I was rather astonished when he responded with a very smart and soldierly salutes, combined with a shout of 'All present and correct, sir.'

My wide-eyed stare of amazement caused Sujit to collapse in a fit of giggles. 'Upstairs, sir,' he gasped, between fits of laughter. 'Time to go back to party.' You couldn't help but like the fellow.

Mrs Aschenheim insisted, upon my return, that I express my view of the paintings I had seen. A subtle indication of her own view came in the way she phrased the question: 'Don't you think my husband was a genius? Such a masterful hand.'

'Ah yes, the paintings,' I began, looking for inspiration towards Jinny. 'They are certainly very . . . Venetian.'

'Ah . . . so you, too, feel that he has captured the place.'

As I succumbed to the temptation to nod my head in a manner that was bound to be interpreted as agreement with this preposterous claim, I made a mental note to ask Bernadetto to tell me where I could find an English-speaking confessor. (I wondered whether the approach taken by my confessor, Monsignor Galsworthy, on this sort of white lie would be endorsed by an Italian priest. Galsworthy has always held to a very firm line, being himself a man of great honesty. I once heard him tell a mother at a christening that he could not say that he thought her bawling infant beautiful, but that he did think the child was healthy. Jinny, I fear, who has rather given up on the Church recently, thinks Galsworthy a prig.)

'Patrick's not a great judge of painting,' my beloved wife chimed in helpfully at this point, hoping, I assume, to get me off the hook.

'Oh no, I think he has excellent taste, excellent,' Mrs Aschenheim pronounced, beaming at me. 'And a good eye, too: he immediately saw the affinities between Claudio's recent work and Jackson Pollock.'

Claudio grinned broadly at the mention of his name in conjunction, once more, with this fellow Pollock. As we rose from the table to stroll through the flowers to the elevator, everyone seemed to be in very good spirits.

The Bouncers had arrived, as we had, that afternoon (though they had wisely chosen the less sentimental approach to the city of flying in first class on Alitalia). Peggy Aschenheim was right when she boomed: 'You must all be very exhausted after your travels.' She had her people bring out her motor-boat, so that the Bouncers could be carried off back to the Hotel Danieli. Mr Bouncer grasped the opportunity provided by the few minutes it took to summon the craft to accept and down a hefty slug of Delamain. When I displayed just the slightest hesitation in declining our hostess's offer of a snifter, and looked, for the briefest moment, longingly at the brandy bottle, Virginia coughed discreetly and communicated a clear message that this was not an idea that met with her approval. Mrs Aschenheim had wisely provided on the drinks tray the option of fizzy mineral water, to begin the process of undoing the damage to the system wrought by the feast we had just consumed, and all of us in the party from the Palazzo Longhi took up her offer.

We began our farewells.

'A brilliant dinner, as usual, Peggy,' Bernadetto announced, kissing her theatrically on both cheeks. 'We are forever in your debt.'

'It really was quite terrific,' Virginia said. 'It was very kind of you to invite us.'

'I wouldn't have missed the chance to meet Virginia Scott. My daughter and I', she told the Bouncers, 'are just the greatest fans of her Bella Sharpe novels.'

Mr Bouncer nodded exaggeratedly. 'Aha, novels.' The word was no more slurred than anything he had said over the last couple of hours. 'Novels. Aha.' Mr Bouncer's conversation and tone were those of Eeyore in a reflective mood.

His good lady cast a bright apologetic smile at me and took him firmly by the arm, just at the moment Sujit arrived back from commissioning the boat. 'Boat, madam.'

'Thank you, Sujit. It's been great seeing you, Jo-Ann, Phil. We're meeting for lunch tomorrow at about one, right?'

'Uh huh. Would you care to join us, Sir Patrick?' Jo-Ann gushed. 'We've hardly had a chance to talk.'

'We are in the hands of our generous host.' I thought it best to leave planning to Bernadetto: he had said nothing to us, since we arrived, about what we might do on our stay.

'I'm afraid we have a little day-trip lined up for our guests tomorrow,' Bernadetto said. 'But why don't we all gather at my place for dinner tomorrow night? Nothing as fancy as Peggy's table: but we'll rustle something up.'

'Super. That *will* be fun,' Melissa said with a toss of her elegant coiffure. 'One always has such fun staying with you, Peggy darling.' As Jo-Ann Bouncer walked past Melissa to their boat, it struck me how similar they were physically, despite the fact that their lives and characters couldn't have been more different. Both of them were slender; they were of the same medium height. Both had fair hair (though Melissa's, of course, was now white). And each of them had, as the French say, *beaucoup sur le balcon*. In their evening shoes, with their high heels, each of them walked with the style of a fashion model. Mrs Bouncer was a good fifteen years younger than Melissa: and the gay vulgarity of her make-up and clothes – she was wearing what looked like a blue-velveteen suit – contrasted sharply with Melissa's muted elegance. I couldn't imagine Mrs B. trading in her vast collection of diamonds for the pretty string of pearls at Melissa's neck; I couldn't, on the other hand, picture Melissa wearing sun-glasses to dinner. Jinny tugged my elbow to withdraw me from these ruminations and murmured, 'You're staring.'

'I'm sorry. I was just thinking how similar Mrs B. and Melissa are,' I whispered.

'Really, Patrick.'

It didn't seem worth explaining what I meant.

Bernadetto kissed Mrs Bouncer's hand and shook the enormous fist of her husband as we gathered in front of the *palazzo* to see them off. Once they were gone, we said good-night to Mrs Aschenheim and her house-party. The Chilean painter leaned elegantly against the wall of the *palazzo*, watching. As we were chatting and making plans for our meeting the next night, I noticed, out of the corner of my eye, that he was inspecting his palms. He had placed them against the wall and they had picked up some dirt. I watched as the realization that he was leaning in his white suit against a dirty wall spread in a crimson rage across his face. And I could have sowrn that I heard this fellow who allegedly knew not a word of English muttering a series of American swear-words that might have brought a blush to the ruddy visage of Philip Bouncer. I cast a glance at Jinny to see if she had heard what I had. She raised a hand to her mouth and touched her lips pensively with a graceful finger.

Bernadetto hugged Peggy, kissed the hands of Melissa and Mrs Bishop and waved at a rather cross Mr Occampo, and we set off home.

6

'There's something going on between Bernadetto and Melissa,' Jinny announced once we were settled in the semi-darkness under the canopy in our enormous bed. After we had arrived back at the *palazzo*, we had prepared ourselves swiftly for sleep and Jinny had read five minutes of *Mr Norris Changes Trains* before turning off the light. (Also on the bedside table was a large volume entitled *Railways, Then and Now* by the aptly named Edwin Course. As I say, Virginia's reading when she's writing her books always has some strange logic to it.)

A bedroom over the Grand Canal, with the windows thrown wide open to catch the breeze, is not the quietest place even at one in the morning and, despite the exhaustion of our long journey and the dinner party, we were both having difficulty getting to sleep. Still, on the whole I thought chatting wasn't likely to help, and so I merely hurrumphed in response to Jinny's remark. This turned out to be insufficiently discouraging.

'There's definitely something going on. They were sitting next to each other at dinner, and they ignored each other quite to excess. Bernadetto has exquisite manners – and so, for that matter, does Melissa. It's quite out of character for both of them. There's definitely something going on.'

'Well, Bernadetto's always been a bit of a dark horse on the sexual side,' I mumbled. 'I thought you thought he was . . . you know.'

Virginia took no notice of this contribution. She was pursuing her own thoughts. 'You know what it reminded me of? Do you remember when Celia Carter-Bledsoe and Dicky Nelson were having that affair? One used to see them all the time at parties: and whenever they were sitting together they each behaved as if the other wasn't there. Made what was going on obvious to anyone with half a brain.'

'I don't recall Tony Carter-Bledsoe ever noticing until it was too late and so far as I know he had both halves of the cerebrum he was born with.' Clearly, I was going to have to attend to the conversation. I sat up and propped a pillow behind my back.

'The eyes of love', my wife said opaquely, 'are blind.'

I said nothing. I had never thought much about the fact that Bernadetto hadn't married, despite being, for half a century, among the most eligible bachelors in Europe. Virginia had rather shocked me the other day by implying that there was something not quite above-board about his relationship with Jamie. Jamie, after all, had quite definitely been married for a dozen or so years: his son, Anthony, who is a doctor, is rather a chum of my son, Sebastian. When Lucinda, his wife, died, Anthony had been in his teens, and we had gone out of our way to keep an eye out for him because Jamie wasn't exactly cut out to be a single parent. Once the boy had gone up to Oxford, Jamie breathed a metaphorical sigh of relief, and set off gallivanting about the world with his old chum Bernadetto.

Insofar as Jamie had ever had a profession – and, frankly, he had always had enough money for this to be far from necessary – he was a Lloyd's name. He put up everything he owned – including the rather grand seventeenth-century family house near Castle Cary – as security for an insurance syndicate to which he belonged; and each year, in return for this less than onerous obligation, they sent him a large cheque.

In the early eighties, I gather, this cash cow turned out to be rather less of a good thing. But by then Anthony had finished his medical education, and so Jamie disentangled himself from Lloyd's, rented the house to a small order of Catholic nuns, who appreciated the family's long history of loyalty to the faith, and moved into a small flat in Mayfair, from which he continued to make forays to various parts of the world in search of amusement, staying often, as I say, with Bernadetto. For some reason, however, he'd never been in Spain when we were staying with Bernadetto, so, though I knew they were constantly together, I had actually rarely seen them *à deux*. (I had once asked Jamie, years ago, why he never came to Seville. I think the exact words of his response were: 'Filthy country, Spain.' I did not pursue the matter further.)

The appeal of this life to Jamie, who had always been something of a nomad, was obvious. But what Bernadetto got out of it I had never thought about very much: he had, after all, been a generous host to us and to many others over the years, and all we had to offer as guests was Jinny's inexhaustible charm and my appreciation of good cooking. And Jamie *was* his oldest friend.

Ruminations of this general character were carrying me off to the land of Nod; but Jinny had other ideas. Just as I was settling in for a much-desired sleep, she addressed me loudly: 'Well, what do you think?'

'What do I think about what, my love?'

'Why on earth would Bernadetto want to keep from us the fact that he was having an affair with Melissa?'

'Well, Milo's not been dead all that long. Maybe they think it's too early to be decent.'

'I don't think they've just started. It's probably been going on for years. After all, Milo wasn't much of a husband.'

'They were separated, darling.'

'There you are.' She paused. 'And Jamie must know, too. In fact, Mrs Aschenwhatsit is probably in on the whole business: Melissa was probably staying here until we arrived.'

Virginia's capacity for invention is well known and widely admired: and the novel is a fine place for exercising it. But at one in the morning, when you're completely exhausted and trying to sleep, fantasies about conspiracies among one's friends – conspiracies whose whole purpose is to fool one – are probably best ignored.

'I'll ask Sujit, Mrs A.'s chief Indian, in the morning. I think we've rather made friends,' I said, going along as if this conversation was perfectly normal. Unfortunately, I was too tired to get the tone quite right.

'You think I'm completely off my head, don't you?'

'No, darling, I don't. But you must admit that it's a bit far-fetched to suppose that Bernadetto, at the age of – what is he? Sixty-four or five? – would be worried about what we thought of his living in sin with a widow.'

'I didn't say he was worried about that. Though he has always kept that side of his life very far from view. We've never, in all the years we've known him, been introduced to a girlfriend . . . or a boyfriend for that matter.'

'Or even a cat . . .' I said, knowing as I said it that this was not going to be appreciated, but too tired, as I say, to restrain myself.

'You are an utter beast, Patrick. Give me a kiss and go to sleep. I can see I should keep my thoughts to myself.'

Obediently I gave Lady Scott a chaste good-night buss, and an apologetic hug, and retreated to a very interesting dream about trout-fishing in Kintyre.

I awoke at ten – which is a couple of hours later than I have managed to sleep for years – to find a pair of the gentlemen in livery standing at the end of the bed with two trays of orange juice, coffee and croissants and a scrawled message from Bernadetto suggesting we get up slowly and meet on the *terrazzo* at about midday. 'If you want anything else for breakfast, just tell the servants. We've most things in the kitchen.'

I inferred that Jinny had invited the servants in before I surfaced. They had opened the curtains to the balcony so that the sunlight streamed in, along with the bustling sounds of a summer Saturday morning in the City of the Doges. Our *Buon giornos* accomplished, we settled down dutifully to consume this light repast.

Virginia installed her glasses, picked up the Italian newspaper and began to read.

One of the servants left, but the other hovered about by the door to the bathroom for a minute or two before summoning either the courage or the English to enquire whether 'the lady and gentleman is want to bath?'.

Jinny looked up at him for a moment and then nodded at him. I followed her lead.

'Ladies and gentlemen, 'ot, medium, or cold?'

'On the hottish side of medium for my lady wife, wouldn't you say, dear?'

'I would, darling, but I don't suppose he has the foggiest notion as to what that means.' And then she reeled off some Italian, which produced enthusiastic discussion from her young Venetian interlocutor, in the course of which I thought I heard Jinny say that she wanted her water *'caldo'*.

'*Caldo*, eh,' I offered, with just a modicum of scepticism.

'Yes, Paddy, it means hot.'

'Bit confusing that, isn't it?'

'One gets used to it. He's volunteered to run you a bath of the same temperature in the bathroom across the hall.'

'Very nice of him. Could you ask him to come back when he's set the thing in motion and lead me there? I shall be finished with my croissant in a *momento*.'

Jinny addressed our *valet-de-chambre* briskly and then went back to her reading.

I returned refreshed from a long soak in a vast old claw-footed bath, of the sort I associate with visits to my grandmother's house in my youth, to find Jinny stylishly dressed and raring to go. 'I slept marvellously. I've had a lovely bath, and now I'm going to have coffee on the terrace of a *palazzo* on the Grand Canal with two of my favourite people.'

'Actually, there'll be three of us, darling.'

'Jamie is not one of my favourite people, sweetest. After all, I spent all those years looking after Anthony. But Bernadetto comes quite high up the list . . . and even after a few decades, you, my sweet, are still a long way above the rest.'

I kissed my bride of forty years. 'Do you realize that it was almost forty years ago to the day that we got up on our first morning in Venice and went to Mass at Santa Maria della Salute?'

'It took hours to find a confessor . . . we had to go to the second Mass.'

My wife's face fell into the beautiful – almost saintly – composure that she adopts when she is about to say something serious. 'We've had a lovely life together, Paddy, my love.'

'The best is yet to be,' I mumbled, thinking of Browning's rabbi.

I was rewarded with another little kiss. 'All right, darling, now we've been soppy for a bit, let's go and have some more fun.'

After a light lunch we set out on the day-trip Bernadetto had promised. We began by taking the motor-boat over towards the railway station. We were accompanied by Giorgio, who carried a fine old wickerwork hamper. Once we reached the Piazzale Roma, we walked for two minutes to the spot where Bernadetto's Rolls-Royce was waiting, in the square on the other side of the canal from the station, where all the buses arrive in the city. The driver was amusingly dressed in the sort of outfit that one doesn't see much nowadays: a dark jacket, buttoned up to its high collar, trousers plunging into black boots, and a cap. The poor chap was sweating profusely in the hot sun, as he held open the door for us. Bernadetto said something to him in Italian and the fellow smiled sheepishly. When I looked enquiringly at our host he said: 'I told him to shut up the car and turn on the air-conditioning so that we could freeze and he could enjoy the warmth of his uniform. I've instructed him over and over again to wear something lighter in the summer, but he thinks he looks ever-so-stylish in his outfit.' Bernadetto paused. Then he smiled and added: 'Italians!'

Soon we were flying west on the *autostrada* towards Milan. Neither Bernadetto nor Jamie was willing to tell us where we were going. We purred along at the ridiculous speeds that the Italians favour on their motorways, past signposts to Padua and Verona and a whole host of smaller places with equally magical names.

There seemed to be a slight coldness between Bernadetto and Jamie, but they were both too polite for it to show very much. Each of them was rather inclined to withdraw from our bantering chit-chat when the other took it up, as if they could neither of them quite bear to be in the same conversation. When Jamie was engaged in amusing us, Bernadetto stared out over the landscape; when Bernadetto was being charming, Jamie appeared preoccupied, as one might when engaged in composing *in pectore* a difficult letter.

After an hour or so, at about half-past two, we left one motorway and turned on to another, up towards the green hills to the north. Not long after we left the main road altogether and drove down towards the broad southern end of Lake Garda. The view was gorgeous. But when I commented on it, Bernadetto said: 'This is nothing. You wait.'

And so we did. As we drove north along the eastern shore of the lake, it narrowed, and the mountains rose to towering cliffs on both sides. We stopped in a small village on the lake, called Pai, and stood at the water's edge gazing across towards the other side. 'Now, this, this is spectacular.'

We drove back down to the Punta di San Vigilio, a headland just north of Garda, and wandered into the cypress groves by the tiny church. And there we sat on a rug and sipped champagne and ate tiny cucumber sandwiches. Bernadetto seemed utterly caught up in the view, gazing out over the lake in rapt silence.

Meanwhile, Jamie watched out of the corner of his eye in awed astonishment as Jinny peeled the skin off each cucumber slice and remade the sandwiches. Naturally, he said nothing. I've grown accustomed to this one tiny eccentricity, which stems from a conviction implanted in Jinny's mother by an Indian guru that the skin of the cucumber is bad for the digestion. Stafford Cripps had the same guru and I once chatted to an old India hand – chap by the name of Giles Stourton – who confided that he had watched Austerity Cripps do the same trick at a hill station in Simla in between bouts with Mr Nehru and bouts with Mr Jinnah. Giles probably adopted the same awed look.

'How wonderfully English,' Jinny said, as she nibbled her sandwich insouciantly, blissfully unaware of the effect she had had on my cousin.

'The view, the champagne, the cypresses?' Jamie said teasing.

'No, the sandwiches, silly.'

'I thought you would like them. You know,' Bernadetto went on, 'this is one of my favourite places. So peaceful. Unlike Venice.

After the man-made splendours of Venice, it is good to remember the sublimity of nature.' I had never fancied Bernadetto to be much of a philosopher, and he did not stay long in this sententious mood. In fact, a moment later he laughed. 'Maybe I should build myself a tomb here, like one of those crazy Italian archbishops and princes.'

For half an hour, in the shade of the cypresses, we looked out over the lake, as the ferries plied their way up into the romantic fastnesses of the northern end of Lake Garda. The water was a wonderful blue. There cannot be many more beautiful places on earth.

The clock on the front of the railway station said it was a little after six. As we walked back across the Piazzale Roma to the motorboat, I thought I saw Mrs Bouncer climbing the steps of the Ponte degli Scalzi, by the church of St Simeon the Lesser. 'Isn't that Jo-Ann Bouncer?'

'Where?' Jinny asked.

I pointed. 'In that enormous white hat.'

'Darling, in those enormous sun-glasses and that perfectly ridiculous hat, it could be anybody.'

'She's got her figure . . . and that funny bouncy way of walking. What an enormous handbag.'

Jinny was not convinced.

We were back in the Palazzo Longhi by half-past six. We travelled down the Grand Canal in the bright evening sun, a Saturday evening bustle on each of its banks. The sunlight on the warm stone of the *palazzo* was a rich, almost orange, colour; the sky was a clear Venetian blue; the T-shirts and dresses of the tourists all had a sharpened colour in the intense light: it was a scene of almost dream-like clarity. Giorgio had been summoned by car phone to collect us, and he was as spruce as always, in the uniform of the *palazzo*. As we entered the house one of the other servants delivered Bernadetto a handwritten note on a silver salver.

Bernadetto definitely blanched, Jinny and I agreed later, as he read it.

'What's the matter?' Jinny asked.

'Oh, nothing serious. Melissa won't be joining us for dinner: she's sprained an ankle and Peggy's daughter is going to keep her company. But Peggy and the Bouncers will be here . . . and so will Mr Occampo; so we shall still be able to make a party of it.'

'Well, Bernie, should we pop over and try and cheer Melissa up?' Jamie asked. (It was the first time I had heard Bernadetto called 'Bernie' since he was a teenager: it seemed utterly wrong to me.)

'I'll go,' Bernadetto said quickly. 'No need for anyone else. Dinner will be at about nine – this *is* Venice – but they'll all arrive at about half-past eight.'

'You go off,' Jamie said. 'I'll organize things here.' He turned to us. 'I'm sure you'll want to bathe and dress for dinner: we'll have drinks on the terrace from half-past seven.'

'Do give Melissa our love and tell her we wish her a speedy recovery,' Jinny said, as Bernadetto set off with Giorgio to look after Melissa's health. Bernadetto nodded distractedly.

And so we went upstairs to our room to gird up our loins for the evening.

'There you are. What did I say? Did you see how he reacted when he heard that Melissa was hurt?' Jinny had barely waited until the door of the bedroom was shut. 'There's no doubt about it. They're having an affair. Too thrilling.'

'Perhaps. But it could just be that he's an anxious friend.'

Jinny smiled her pleased-with-herself smile (making a face rather like Marilyn Rimmer, the cat that swallowed the cream). 'We shall see.'

We settled on half an hour's rest as the preliminary to the evening, and I fear that I fell asleep as soon as my head hit the pillow. Jinny roused me gently at twenty past seven. She was bathed and dressed, in a very pretty pink Moroccan caftan, with gold braid about the neck, which Bernadetto had given her for Christmas a year or two ago. Her hair was up, spiked through with an elegant pin. She looked like one of Cleopatra's hand-maidens. (If she had been wearing more jewellery, she might have looked like Cleopatra.) I know a chap isn't supposed to boast about his wife, but she really was breath-taking.

'I suppose you know that you look absolutely ravishing,' I said, as I woke to this heavenly vision.

'I've put out your clothes and run your bath.' She kissed me primly. 'I shall see you on the *terrazzo*.' And she was off downstairs.

7

We dined in a vast old dining-room on the second floor, overlooking the canal. The high ceilings and huge windows of the *palazzo* kept the place remarkably cool, considering how sweltering a day it had been. We gathered again with the same company, diminished by the absence of Mrs Aschenheim's daughter and Melissa. Bernadetto was rather less than his usual self, though he did his level best to play the gracious host. The Bouncers had apparently spent a very relaxed day. They had arisen, even later than we had, more or less in time for lunch with Peggy Aschenheim, a magnificent meal at the Danieli. Then they had, of course, taken a siesta. At about half-past four they had settled in at Florian's in the Piazza San Marco. And, no doubt, throughout it all, Mrs Bouncer had worn her dark glasses.

'Tea', Mrs Bouncer pronounced, 'is just the best thing for refreshment on a hot day.' I nodded in hearty agreement, but was rather puzzled to hear her continue: 'But do you know what they brought when I asked for tea? They brought a pot that was steaming hot.' Mrs Bouncer laughed.

I'm afraid I must have looked blank, because Mrs Aschenheim explained to me, in the same pleasantly condescending tone she had adopted the night before, that the Bouncers had, of course, expected iced tea, since no sane person would want to drink hot stuff in this climate. I was gearing up to explain that the habit of drinking tea in mid-afternoon was practised by the English all around the globe, in climates as boiling hot as Simla in summer and as icy as a winter in Northumberland. But I reflected on how modest my success had been over the years in explaining our ways to our transatlantic cousins and thought better of it. Bernadetto explained how to ask for iced tea in Italian, and Jo-Ann Bouncer opened her reticule, took out a small diary and a pencil, and wrote down carefully his instructions. 'It is so good having someone to help you who really knows the local customs.'

After 'tea' – which I was convinced must have involved at least a couple of stiff drinks for Mr B. – they had walked over and into St Mark's cathedral. 'All that gold, everywhere, and those mosaics. It's kind of like one of those mosques we saw in Cairo, wasn't it, hon?'

'Yup,' her hon replied. 'But at least it doesn't take too long to get through: we were back in the hotel by five in time for a little drink and a rest.' He beamed. 'What a day!'

'So it wasn't you, Mrs Bouncer, that I saw up by the railway station, when we arrived back at the Piazzale Roma this afternoon?'

'Me? Lord, no. I've never been anywhere near the railway station.' As she answered my question Jo-Ann Bouncer was suffused with a subtle and, to me, somewhat gratifying flush of embarrassment. 'Is there anything worth looking up over there?'

'There's the ghetto,' Peggy Aschenheim said.

'They have ghettos here?' Mrs Bouncer seemed genuinely astonished. 'I didn't know there were any blacks in Italy.'

'Actually,' Bernadetto explained, 'it's the original ghetto.' Jo-Ann Bouncer smiled blankly at him. 'I mean, it's where the word comes from. Originally, it was where Venetian metal-working went on: *getto* means to cast metal. But the Jewish community of Venice has lived there since the sixteenth century. You'll find a couple of synagogues and a rather interesting art museum.'

'My, my,' Philip Bouncer declared. 'Your people do get around, Peggy.'

Jo-Ann Bouncer blushed again – displaying, I thought, a sensitivity that must make life with her husband rather nerve-racking. 'You do know such interesting stuff, Mr Montebello.' I had the impression from the toss of the head and the pout that accompanied this remark that Jo-Ann was flirting with Bernadetto.

There was a lull in the conversation into which I launched a few compliments on the food in Bernadetto's direction.

'I must say this is all absolutely delicious. This lamb is just wonderfully –'

Jinny interrupted. 'I'm afraid, Bernadetto, that if we let Patrick start enthusing about the food – which is, by the way, perfectly exquisite – we shall be talking about it all night.'

It was an old point of contention. Jinny's nanny was under the impression that it was bad manners to discuss the qualities of the food one was eating and had fixed in her the notion that the only fair comment was a compliment to the hostess (or, as in this case, I suppose, the host). I, on the other hand, have always felt that a good meal is worth discussing; that it is enhanced by a contemporaneous verbal appreciation of its finer points. (It also helps fix the best meals in memory, where they can be a source of solace in the long gustatory troughs between the rare peaks of *haute cuisine*. I suspect that I would be better able to establish proper memorials for great meals, if I knew more about how they were made. Indeed, I have often thought about taking up cooking now that I am a little less busy: but Virginia says that Cordon Bleu looks askance at male septuagenarians and I have never had the courage to set out to prove her wrong.) At all events, Jinny had made her point. I avoided the subject of food for the rest of the evening.

I had not had a chance to return to reading the remaining Hawksworth papers since we got off the train and I was feeling mildly guilty that I still did not know what I was supposed to learn from them. And so, since I was seated across from Señor Occampo, I set about trying once more to elicit from him some information about his native continent.

I suppose I should have known better. A person who has announced – if only in French, a language which, in my limited experience, tends to encourage hyperbole – that his homeland no longer exists for him, is likely to be reticent about it. Probing questions being out of the question, in view of my rather loose grip on the whole French business, I was at a double disadvantage. Still, I did my best. '*Avez-vous visité le fameux pampas de Chile?*'

'*Non, jamais. Je déteste la campagne.*' This is, in itself, in my humble opinion, a sign of weakness of character. I don't think I have ever met a truly honourable person who had no time for the country. Dr Johnson is supposed to have said that anyone who was tired of London was tired of life. Though I have lived in that fair city for many a long year, I cannot entirely agree with him. My cousin Mary Tilworth, for example, left London at the end of the season she came out, having met and married a frightfully charming Welsh solicitor, and has never been seen in the great metropolis since. And Mary – who has, after all, given birth to nine red-blooded (and red-haired) Welsh children – has as much zest for life as anyone I know. So I am confident that it's possible simply to lose one's taste for London. But taking against the country, as Mr Occampo claimed to have done, strikes me as another order of thing altogether. I'm suspicious of someone who claims so unwholesome an antipathy.

Nevertheless, having started on this line of conversation, I felt obliged to continue. Perhaps, if the Chilean countryside was so unappealing to him, he had some residual affection for the towns and cities of his motherland. '*Eh bien: vous connaissez certainement donc . . .*' I paused, realizing that I had forgotten for the moment (this sort of thing happens increasingly often, I fear) the name of the Chilean capital. '*Vous connaissez, j'en suis sûr, les villes principales?*'

'*Oui. D'accord. Mais il n'y a pas une seule ville en Chile qui est aussi intéressante que . . . Brescia.*' Mr Occampo made it clear that he had picked at random from the air the name of an exceedingly uninteresting Italian town. We were patently not on the same wavelength. I distinctly recalled, even after many decades, the appeal of Brescia, with the old fortress sitting high up above the town. Anyone who could give up on the country and on Brescia was not worth talking to on the subject of places. I gave up and returned to the subject of painting.

Had Señor Occampo seen the work of Mr Aschenheim? I asked. Apparently, he had. For he nodded at me and then, looking to his left to make sure that Mrs Aschenheim was otherwise engaged, he took the thumb and first finger of his right hand and placed them on his nostrils. His meaning was plain: and I am bound to say that this was rather my sentiment, even if *I* might have found a way to avoid indicating quite so directly my distaste for the work of the late spouse of my widowed hostess. I was not really inclined to encourage this un-guestlike disloyalty (especially in a fellow whose views were generally so unreliable) and so I nodded sternly at the Chilean painter and returned to the delicious lemon pudding that Bernadetto had had made because he knew how much I liked it.

Jinny's ban on the discussion of food was proving rather demanding: but orders is orders. I simply beamed at Bernadetto when I next caught his eye, gestured with my spoon at the bowl, and mouthed the words: 'Thank you, old man.' I reflected once again what a kind and charming chap Bernadetto was, and how lucky we were to have known him all these years.

Peggy Aschenheim naturally wanted to go home and see how Melissa was doing, and the Bouncers were obviously exhausted by the strain of a whole day of eating, drinking and resting. Señor Occampo had started yawning ostentatiously not long after I had brought our conversation to an end. As a result, we were all perfectly happy when the party broke up almost immediately after we left the table. Bernadetto suggested to Mrs Aschenheim that he might accompany her home.

'My dear Bernadetto, how sweet of you. But I think Claudio will be able to chaperone me quite satisfactorily.' Bernadetto looked mildly crestfallen, if such a thing is possible, and I think Peggy Aschenheim realized belatedly that he might have wanted to see Melissa, because she went on: 'Don't worry, I shall give Melissa your best wishes for a speedy recovery. And I gather she's expecting to see you in the late morning.'

Jinny's suspicions were now thoroughly supported by the evidence. As we mounted the stairs, I prepared myself to be reproached for having doubted her.

But my good lady was in a most forgiving mood. 'You see, we were right, darling.' I enjoyed the 'we'. 'They *are* having an affair. I bet you anything that he's on the telephone to her at this very moment.'

'I'm sure you're right, my love. What I can't understand is why the whole thing is so hush-hush.'

'I think I'll have a little chat with Mrs Aschenheim tomorrow.' Jinny yawned. 'What a life they all lead here. Drinks and meals, interspersed with visits to some of the world's sublimest painting, and architecture... and landscape. Makes me feel like a real country bumpkin.'

'We'd pretty soon get bored with it,' I said. 'But it's a lovely place for a nice peaceful holiday.'

Looking back, I should say that uttering this sentiment was probably tempting fate. And fate, as you know, can resist everything except temptation.

We woke, much rested from a good night's sleep. I was in the middle of wrapping myself in my dressing-gown and wandering over towards the door to find my bath, when Jinny shouted excitedly.

'Patrick. Come here. Look at this.'

Virginia's tone was excited and troubled enough that I fairly dashed to her side. And there, on the front page of the Venetian paper that had been delivered to us at breakfast, was a photograph of Gary Mitchell, our friend from the train. Gone, however, was the perpetual grin, the genial expression. Gone, in fact, was the whole lively spirit. For Gary Mitchell had been fished out of a canal the previous evening, not far from the Ghetto Vecchio. And he was floating, not swimming, when they found him.

8

There was not much more to the story that Jinny translated from the paper. Gary Mitchell's body had been found in the Rio della

Misericordia, up by the old Jewish ghetto, in the middle of the evening. The police were of the opinion that he was probably dead before he was tossed into the canal: there was a deep knife wound in his chest that had almost certainly reached his heart. ('Subtle reasoning,' Jinny said.) An autopsy was to be performed overnight.

'Poor chap.' It seemed somehow particularly awful that this jolly, friendly, young man should have been murdered and dumped so unceremoniously in a back canal of the Most Serene City. 'What awful luck. First time out of Australia ... and they were having such fun.'

'That poor girl. The cat that swallowed the cream. What was her name?'

'Rimmer, Marilyn Rimmer.' It's astonishing what the old grey matter sometimes retains. 'And they were travelling with Gerald Miller and Rita Spender. I wonder why they're not mentioned in the article.'

'Perhaps the police haven't found them yet. After all, they don't seem to know his name. They say that anyone who knows who he is should come forward.'

'Is there a phone number?'

'Yes. But I think we should talk to Bernadetto before we contact the police.'

'Absolutely.'

We dressed hurriedly and in silence. Neither of us was able to finish our breakfast. We positively hurtled downstairs, looking for Bernadetto and Jamie, but nobody seemed to be about. In the drawing-room, I rang the bell and Giorgio appeared a minute or two later.

'*Buon giorno*,' he said, smiling pleasantly. Once he took in our grim faces, however, he adopted a severer countenance.

'Good morning, Giorgio. Where is Mr di Montebello?'

''E is at de Palazzo Aschenheim, sir.'

'And Lord Leith?'

''E is asleep, sir.'

I looked at Jinny for guidance. 'I think we should telephone Bernadetto, darling, at once.'

'I will bring. I phone for you.'

Giorgio returned in a moment with a portable telephone and handed it to me. 'Is ring.'

I raised the telephone to my ear and said: 'Hallo.' And then I heard it was still ringing. 'Still ringing,' I said to Jinny. A moment later, a voice on the line said: '*Pronto*. Palazzo Aschenheim.'

'Ah. I wonder if I could speak to Mr di Montebello.'

'It is Sir Scott, yes?' Sujit's voice said.

I allowed as how it was and wished him a good morning.

'Good morning, sahib. I will fetch Signor Bernadetto.'

When Bernadetto came on the line, I explained that we felt we should make a report to the police. We knew the dead man's name, at least, and we knew how he had come to Venice. We also knew the names of some of his travelling companions. They might or might not have seen the newspaper – they did not, so far as I could tell, speak much Italian, so there was no reason why they should buy an Italian newspaper.

Bernadetto seemed rather doubtful. 'Don't you think that his friends are likely to contact the police?'

'Well, they might . . . unless *they* were somehow involved in his death. Though I can't say that I think that's very likely. Of course, their bodies may turn up later as well. I do think it would help the police to know who he is as early as possible.'

'The trouble with the Italian police is that they're always getting the wrong end of the stick. If you turn up they're as likely to charge you with murder as to thank you. And they'll certainly want you to hang around for a day or two.'

'Well, I realize that that might inconvenience you somewhat, old man. But we could easily –'

'My dear Patrick. Don't be silly. That wasn't what I was thinking of at all. But you're supposed to be having a second honeymoon. Aren't you due in Bellagio in a day or two?'

'Our hotel reservations are for Tuesday. But we've enough time to cancel or change the dates without inconveniencing the hotel.'

'Well, you were always very public-spirited, Patrick. So, if you feel you must, you must. I'll call the police station – I know one of the officers there – and ask him to send someone over to take a statement. You'd better tell me the dead fellow's name, so I can pass that on at once.'

'Gary Mitchell.'

For a moment I thought I detected a sort of gasp from Bernadetto. Then there was an uncanny silence. And then, a moment later, he sneezed. I started. And Jinny looked at me interrogatively. I shook my head to indicate all was well as Bernadetto replied, 'Frightfully sorry, Patrick. Must be allergic to some of Peggy's flowers. Mitchell, did you say? Gary Mitchell? And his friends?'

I was frightfully pleased with myself for being able to rattle off the names of the three who had not gone on to Istanbul.

'All right.' Bernadetto repeated the names back to me. I assumed he was jotting them down. 'Good. I'll pass all that on. And if they want to talk to you further, they'll send someone round. I'll be back by the time they get there. Their English may be a bit rudimentary: and their questioning is not always . . . how shall I put it . . . refined.'

'Thank you, Bernadetto. I'm sure we're doing the right thing.'

As I was about to put down the phone, Jinny, who had been listening to my end of the conversation, took the receiver from my hand. 'Bernadetto?' She paused. 'It's Virginia. I don't know if Patrick made this clear to you: Rita Spender is Gerald Miller's wife.'

While she was saying her goodbyes to Bernadetto I was wondering how I could have been expected to make clear something that I didn't know. 'How do you know they were married? You yourself pointed out that they none of them had wedding rings.'

'I've no idea about the rings, though she did say they didn't really believe in marriage. They "got hitched", she said, six years ago to please Gerald's mother.'

'Well, why on earth didn't he at least introduce her as his wife?'

'It's not done these days. Women keep their names. Men don't introduce them as "my wife". And, Paddy darling, it isn't only happening in Australia.'

An hour later, at about half-past ten, Bernadetto arrived back from *chez* Aschenheim. He was accompanied by Melissa, her ankle wrapped in bandages. She was carried from the motor-boat into the drawing-room by two of the Sri Lankans, who placed her gently on a sofa. One of them dragged over an ottoman and she rested her leg on it. Her face was a little pale, I thought, but she looked well enough otherwise.

'How *are* you, Melissa dear?' Jinny smiled sympathetically as she perched herself next to Melissa's foot on the ottoman.

'It's too silly. I slipped on one of those endless Venetian flights of stairs and twisted my ankle. Luckily Peggy was with me. Too silly. We came back from lunch with the Bouncers at the Danieli, and we were just walking back to the *palazzo*, when I slipped and fell. I hobbled home on Peggy's arm and she summoned a delicious Italian doctor, who was so comforting. Sat with me for an hour. And then Peggy made him stay to tea. But there's no permanent damage. I must just rest a little. Peggy has been spoiling me something rotten. Actually, to tell you the truth, it's been rather heavenly.' She paused for a brief moment to catch her breath and then rattled on. 'But how awful this murder business must be for you two. You actually knew the man?'

'Not really. We exchanged cabins on the train, because he wanted to be near his friends, and then he insisted on thanking us by filling us with gin.' (I realized that I was speaking rather faster than usual, caught up in the whirlwind of Melissa's speech.)

'He may have filled you with gin, Paddy, my sweet. *I* had a vermouth.' Jinny is always one for precision.

'But what was he like, Patrick?' Melissa was thrilled with the whole business; and she was not doing much to conceal the fact.

'Tall, Australian, frightfully jolly. His friend, Mr Miller, said they were here looking for a beautiful, mysterious woman who held the key to his destiny.' Melissa grimaced and then adjusted her leg on the ottoman. Bernadetto moved to her side solicitously, but she waved him away.

'You didn't tell me that,' Jinny said to me sharply during this little interlude.

'I didn't think it was all that important at the time.' I did not point out that *she* had not thought it important to tell me that Gerald Miller and Rita were married until a mere hour or so earlier.

'What on earth do you suppose he meant by that?' Bernadetto asked. 'Did he explain?'

'No. Though he did say that it had nothing to do with romance.'

'It's rather Australian, isn't it, to be looking for a beautiful, mysterious Venetian woman while avoiding romance?' Melissa said. 'You know Milo and I met and married in Australia. I always had rather a soft spot for the Aussies. They're so frantically unpretentious. So good for one.'

'I suppose he might have been done in by his friend,' Bernadetto wondered aloud.

'It's possible. Did the police tell you whether anyone else had come forward and identified the dead man?'

'Couldn't get a peep out of them. They just took down the names you gave me and told me to ask you to wait here until they could send a man over to talk to you.'

Bernadetto summoned Giorgio and ordered tea for everybody and it arrived not long afterwards, along with some delicious Venetian biscuits. They were thin and flavoured with almonds and they managed both to be crisp and to melt in one's mouth. Jinny tapped me on the wrist when I reached for my sixth.

Jamie surfaced a little while later and we caught him up on the latest events while we waited for the police.

The two *carabinieri* who finally arrived to take our statements were a splendidly odd couple. One was tall, fair-haired, young, extremely tidily attired – his uniform crisp enough to please a sergeant-major – and tremendously genial and polite. The other was a good deal shorter than any of us, older, roughly round, grubby and as rude as one can be in a language one does not quite understand. It turned out that they had both been selected for their claimed knowledge of English. How much they really understood of what we said was not entirely clear.

'We met him on the train from London,' I began.

'You 'ad appointment?' Shorty interpreted.

'No. We happened to be on the same train and we met because they wanted to move cabins.'

Shorty looked extremely sceptical. 'It is chance you meet 'im.'

'Absolutely.'

'Hah.'

At this point the tall fellow intervened. 'We 'ave only to make sure we understand.'

'Absolutely.'

'So: you are on the train.'

'Exactly.'

'You meet for the first time this Mr Mitchell.'

'You've got it.'

'And . . . ?'

It took them rather a while to grasp that we had met Gary Mitchell on the train and exchanged cabins at his request. Bernadetto and Melissa sat quietly and listened, Bernadetto intervening occasionally to correct, in Italian, misapprehensions due to the language barrier. When they had asked all their questions, I asked, in turn, if Mr Miller and his wife and the other lady had shown up yet.

At first, they pretended not to understand what I was asking. And then, when Bernadetto asked for us again, in Italian, they apologized and said that the investigation required absolute secrecy.

Bernadetto asked them rather naughtily at that point what we should say to the press if we were contacted by them. He was smiling politely as he asked. It would have been very hard to prove it was blackmail. Naturally, the *carabinieri* both expressed horror at the suggestion that this might happen. How would the press know that we had given statements? Surely, Bernadetto did not think that the Venetian police would reveal such compromising information? At all events, it would be better to say nothing to the press, would it not? Signor di Montebello was an old friend of the city. Murders of this sort were bad for the tourist business and the city of Venice would be grateful to the Signori and the Signora if we did not aid in spreading hysterical rumours.

'I can't say that I think that anything we know could lead to hysteria,' I said, after Bernadetto had translated for me the gist of this conversation. 'But I'm all for avoiding the press when one can.' Once they had had this explained to them, they looked immensely relieved.

The younger officer was extremely apologetic as he asked for our passports. 'Is a formality.'

Shorty, naturally, would have none of this namby-pamby courtesy. We should have registered when we arrived, he said to us sternly. It was the law. But Bernadetto pointed out that the Office for Foreigners had not been open since we had arrived and that we were going to register on Monday. 'Today is Sunday. They arrived on Friday evening.'

'Then is okay,' the younger officer said, relieved to be able to follow his natural inclination and be nice to us. And, smiling, he followed his sour-faced colleague out of the *palazzo*, winking at the general company as he went, as if excusing his boorish comrade.

'I see what you mean about the Venetian police,' I said to Bernadetto as Giorgio closed the door behind them.

'The tall chap must have been new on the job. They'll have him as unpleasant as the rest in a wee while.' Bernadetto sighed loudly. 'Lunch now. But first an enormous drink for everybody. Jinny, Melissa, what'll it be?'

It was during our siesta as we lay under the canopy not quite snoozing that Jinny showed the first signs of what was to be a persistent brooding on the death of Gary Mitchell. It began innocently enough.

'I wonder, darling, if we shouldn't have mentioned the theft of his briefcase?'

'Won't they find out about it from the railway people, now they know which train he came on?'

'But will they realize it might be significant?'

'I'm sure they know their job.'

'Not if Laurel and Hardy were anything to go by.' I had been calling the short, round *carabiniere* 'Shorty' to myself, but this was, of course, much better. I laughed. 'Mr Hardy was not the pleasantest policeman I have ever met. Mr Laurel, on the other hand, was quite charming.'

'But not, I should have said, totally confidence-inspiring in the competence department.'

We returned to our snoozing. I was just about to doze off completely, when a warm gust of afternoon wind carried the sounds of sloshing water up from the canal, and we heard the voice of an American tourist. All I could make out, I fear, was the single word 'quaint'. 'Americans *are* funny.' I could hear that Jinny was smiling. I could also hear that she was wide awake.

'I expect they think we're rather amusing, too.' Jinny says I am inclined to sententiousness when I am half awake. Knowing that this was my condition she ignored both the slightly reproving tone and the content of my remark. (Jinny is used to my defending the Yanks. I have always had a soft spot for our transatlantic cousins; one just has to know their limitations ... as in the matter of not understanding why iced tea is an abomination.)

'What do you suppose the secret of his destiny was ... the secret he was looking for from the beautiful, mysterious Venetian?'

This was one of those questions to which the answer is clearly: 'I don't know. What do *you* think?' I obliged.

'Well, darling. An Australian, in Venice, looking for his destiny, is probably looking for an Australian.'

'Possibly.'

'So maybe the police should be looking for an Australian woman. Probably someone older. Perhaps the ageing sister of his grandfather who emigrated to Australia?'

'Possibly,' I continued, hoping that if I was non-committal enough, Jinny would eventually allow me to return to a peaceful siesta.

'Or perhaps a dying aunt visiting the city for the last time.'

'Possibly.'

'Or perhaps an Australian poodle.'

I wasn't going to be caught out like that, even in my semi-comatose condition. 'Darling, I *am* listening. I just haven't got anything to contribute at the moment.'

The 'Hah' that my wife produced in response to this excuse suggested to me that I was going to have to play along. As I fell asleep, I promised myself to collect together all we knew of Gary Mitchell and his chums, and see if there was any clue in it as to what might have happened to him.

It was hot. I was in a desert and I knew, somehow, that it was in Australia. Gary Mitchell and Gerald Miller were standing in front of an enormous cactus talking to a tall woman, shrouded in a black lace mantilla, wearing black lace stockings and high-heeled shoes. She looked like a flamenco dancer in mourning, though she bore an uncanny resemblance to Miss Malster, the matron at my first prep school. In the background kangaroos were leaping across the landscape. The mysterious Spanish lady was pointing across the sands to a figure far away, walking over the dunes towards us. As he approached, I recognized him as Milo Hawksworth. He was trailing a series of three pack donkeys on the first of which was an ageing Amerindian woman, who was followed by two very beautiful, brown-skinned girls. Milo arrived and spoke to the group gathered in front of the cactus.

'I say, does any of you know the way to Lake Titicaca?'

From out of the blue, the voice of Claudio Occampo, speaking, unaccountably, in perfect English, said: 'It's too boring. Why don't you go to Brescia?'

And then I woke up.

'Most extraordinary dream,' I said to Jinny. 'All about Milo's illegitimate children and a Spanish dancer talking to Gary Mitchell.'

'What illegitimate children?'

'The ones in Bolivia.'

'You've never mentioned them before.'

'I only read about them in the train on Friday.' I paused, concerned to go carefully here. 'You will recall, I am sure, that the Muse was on you. I didn't want to disturb you.'

'That was more than two days ago.'

'I'm sorry. It slipped my mind.'

'Well. Out with it, then.'

I gathered that I was to be forgiven and so I set about passing on what I had picked up from the papers.

'Maybe you should read the rest of them in a hurry. There may be something else of interest.'

'I can't really tell Melissa about these children, can I?'

'Good lord, no. If Milo had wanted her to know he would have left her a letter himself. What happened in your dream?'

When I recounted it, it seemed awfully silly. But Jinny was amused. 'I'm glad your aunt Helen isn't here. She'd be telling you it was a message from the beyond, a clue to the murder.'

Aunt Helen was an active member of the Society for Psychical Research. (She once opined that she might be the reincarnation of one of its Founders.) And while her earliest involvement was the result of a desire to re-establish contact with Uncle Peter, who died in the Great War, by the time she began discussing these things with me, during the Second World War, she had moved on from mediums to telepathy. I was extremely fond of Aunt Helen, not least because she was the sort of free spirit who cared little for what others thought of her. In her mid-fifties, just after the war, she took to wearing large baggy trousers of a sort I associated with harems, and large shapeless jumpers that she knitted herself. And while this was something of an embarrassment if you were a smart young nephew being entertained to tea at Fortnum's, I rather admired the *élan* with which she carried it off. But I cannot say that her opinions on telepathy (or, for that matter, on almost any other issues) struck me as particularly plausible.

'Perhaps it was a message *from* Aunt Helen,' I said.

'She was probably trying to wake you up so that we could go downstairs for tea.'

'I have always obeyed Aunt Helen's every wish or whim. Let us descend.'

We tidied ourselves up a bit and walked in stately fashion, Virginia on my arm, down to the *terrazzo* for tea.

9

'I'm sorry you weren't able to come with us yesterday to the Punta di San Vigilio, Melissa. It was really quite wonderful.' Jinny and Melissa were chatting side-by-side on one of the sofas in the drawing-room, Melissa's foot resting, once more, on an ottoman. Apparently, our invalid friend had not left the house after luncheon, and I felt rather guilty thinking that she would probably be staying in the Palazzo Longhi if we were not here.

'My dear, I was too busy having a lovely time twisting my ankle. And if I hadn't twisted it, I shouldn't be being pampered so deliciously.'

'Besides,' Jamie said, 'you have been there before, haven't you, Melissa?' The look that passed between them was not exactly friendly. I wondered if Jamie was unhappy about the deception involved in keeping Bernadetto's fling with Melissa from us. I resolved to take advantage of our kinship and ask him to tell me frankly what was going on, just as soon as we could have a moment alone.

'Indeed, I have, Jamie, my dear. It is a wonderful place for a picnic.'

An unfriendly silence descended on the room. Bernadetto suggested we all have another cup of tea and summoned Giorgio for the purpose.

'So, I wonder when the police will be back with your passports,' Melissa said brightly. 'I do hope they won't be too tiresome about all this.'

'That reminds me' – this was Bernadetto – 'that we should telephone the Hotel Serbelloni in Bellagio and tell them you will be a couple of days late. It's the beginning of the busy season on the lakes – I'm sure they'll be grateful to have an extra room.'

'When should we tell them we're coming?' I asked.

'I haven't the faintest idea when the police will release you. Why don't I just tell them that you've been held up here and you're not sure when you'll be able to come and you'll give them a call again when you know?'

At this point Giorgio appeared to announce that Peggy Aschenheim's boat had arrived and that the two Tamils were ready to collect Melissa. It was about a quarter past five. 'Well, it's been a fascinating day, but I think I must go home to Peggy's and rest. She's having the Bouncers and a lot of Venetian grandees to dinner *ce soir*. I asked her to send over a boat at five.' She lowered her voice to a conspiratorial whisper. '*Entre nous*, it turns out that she's trying to persuade Philip B. to give his art collection to the Metropolitan Museum in New York, of which she's a trustee.' Melissa's laughter tinkled through the room. 'When she first asked him, do you know what he said?' We all looked suitably interested and ignorant. 'He said: "Give 'em away? Fifty million bucks' worth of paintings? You must be plumb loco." ' I thought Melissa's Texas accent rather convincing. 'But Peggy is not one to take no for an answer.'

'Wish her luck from us,' Jinny said. 'Though I'm not sure I want to have to look at dozens of nineteenth-century American paintings picked by Mr B. when I visit New York. And you take good care of that ankle.' Melissa disappeared out of the room, supported in the seat made by the crossed hands of the two servants, looking for all the world like a wounded Memsahib being carried home for treatment. Bernadetto accompanied her, and so Virginia and I were left alone with Jamie.

'Look here, Jamie.' I adopted the tone appropriate for a frank conversation with a cousin one has known all one's life. 'It's perfectly obvious to Jinny and me that Melissa would rather be staying here because of her . . . because of Bernadetto. I do wish you could tell him that we're not as prudish as he imagines. I mean, damn it all, Milo's dead; and he didn't have much claim on Melissa's affections when he was alive.'

Jamie laughed. He laughed loud and long. 'I told them you'd see through the charade. I've been cross with Bernadetto all along for insisting on dragging Peggy and me into his scheme. But he's frightfully concerned with appearances, you know, is our Bernadetto. Comes from being teased about his father's Mafia connections at school.'

'Mafia?' I was frankly astonished. It had never occurred to me that courtly old di Montebello could have been involved in anything so low.

'How do you think an Italian immigrant made a huge fortune in America – in Chicago, to be exact – in the twenties and thirties?'

'Did his mother know?'

'Never cared to ask, I don't think. She was in England most of the time, or here. And she was old-fashioned, as you know: didn't think it appropriate to worry about where her husband's money came from or how he made his living. And anyway, by the time they met, old Montebello was frightfully respectable. He wouldn't have come within a hundred miles of committing an actual crime himself.'

As Jamie spoke, Bernadetto appeared framed in the vast doorway and he heard Jamie's last few remarks. He didn't notice that I was watching him: Jinny couldn't see him, because Jamie was between them. His jaw was clamped tight; his brow was furrowed; he looked for a few moments more angry than I had ever seen him. I watched with interest as he forced a smile on to his face and entered the room: 'I see Jamie is throwing light on the skeletons in other people's closets again.'

'It's all water under the bridge,' Jamie muttered defensively. And then – in the spirit of the best defence being attack – he went on: 'Patrick and Virginia are puzzled as to why you're keeping your affair with Melissa from them.'

'I am sure you told them what I told you.'

'I told them you probably didn't think it looked very good having an affair with a woman so recently widowed.'

'That's not really what I told you, is it, Jamie, old man? I apologize to you both.' Bernadetto had now quite recovered his equanimity. 'You being English Catholics, I thought it would be in poor taste to carry on an extra-marital affair – to commit a mortal sin – under your very noses.' I don't know if we were really expected to fall for this.

'The winds of the Second Vatican Council had not entirely spent themselves by the time they reached the Channel,' Jinny said, 'and even my dear Patrick, who has a nostalgia for *sub rosa* Tridentine Masses, has mellowed.'

'At all events' – this was all very embarrassing and I was rather hoping I could get us on to a new topic pronto – 'it isn't that it's any of our business. I was merely asking Jamie to pass on the message that we really wouldn't mind if Melissa was to move back here.'

'Move *back*?' Bernadetto seemed genuinely astonished. 'She wasn't staying here before you came. She only arrived a week or so ago, and she was to stay with Peggy for at least another week; until Peggy goes back off to New York.'

'If I'd known that I wouldn't have brought it up . . . it was just the idea of our having displaced her.'

Bernadetto shook his head and smiled ruefully. 'Really, Patrick, you are too comical. I'm grateful for your thoughtfulness. If you're still here when Peggy leaves Venice, I promise that Melissa will join us.'

As we dressed for dinner – we had asked to be allowed to take Bernadetto and Jamie out – we reviewed the various disagreeable happenings of this all-in-all rather disagreeable day.

'Remember you told me that there might be some connection between the robbery on the train and Gary Mitchell's premature demise?' I asked. Jinny was putting up her hair and had hairpins in her mouth. She nodded her assent. 'Well, on reflection, I don't think so.'

Lady Scott finished adjusting her hairpins and looked at me intently. Then she pronounced: 'You think that whoever broke into the cabin must have been looking for *us*.'

Trust Jinny to take the wind out of one's sails. 'Actually, that *is* what I think. Jones never changed the labels on the doors, and nobody else was broken into.'

'I'd had the same thought.'

'So I gather. But then, of course, we have to wonder what anyone would have been looking for in our luggage.'

'They *took* a briefcase.'

Light dawned at about the same time for both of us. 'Milo's papers,' we said in unison. And then, we both looked over towards my battered Gladstone. I strode over and opened it up. So far as I could see, everything was there. But, of course, I didn't really know what 'everything' was, since I hadn't finished reading it all.

'It's not likely that anyone has been at them here. There are servants around the house all day, and you'd be a bit conspicuous climbing up on to a balcony in full view of the Grand Canal.' Jinny paused. 'But who would want to steal Milo's papers?'

'That depends on why he wanted me to have them. I must really finish reading them as soon as possible.' I paused. 'In the meanwhile, my darling, I think we should make a list of the people we told about our jaunt on the Orient Express.' For the next few minutes, as we dressed, Jinny announced names as she thought of them and I wrote them down on my notepad. With the names I came up with, we soon had a fairly substantial listing.

'Gosh. Extraordinary how many people one tells when one isn't trying to keep one's movements secret,' Jinny said, as she peered at the list over my shoulder. 'Now, darling, would you mind doing me up?'

I helped Jinny zip up the rather super evening dress she was planning to wear for our dinner out. We moved together across the room to inspect ourselves in the elaborate mirror over the fireplace. 'You look very dashing in that white dinner-jacket,' she said, addressing my reflection.

'I thought it looked summery and rather Italian. And, if I may say so, you're looking pretty spiffy yourself. We can't let the natives have all the style, now can we?'

I should have known that something at least mildly unpleasant was going to follow the ominous pause that ensued. I tensed in anticipation. 'I wonder,' Jinny began in that uncertain tone which is, in fact, intended to leave no doubt at all, 'I wonder, darling, if those shoes are exactly right.' I was wearing a pair of very comfortable brown walking shoes, of which I am particularly fond. The temptation was strong to rise to their defence.

I resisted. 'You're right, my sweet.'

'I put out a pair of black shoes for you; they're over there by the chair. And there's a lovely tie.'

I was already wearing a tie, naturally: it was a rather dashing thing that Sebastian had given me a couple of Christmases earlier. It had a large Paisley pattern in a whole host of colours: rather like the sort of Liberty's scarf that Jinny seems to favour. 'What's wrong with this one? Sebastian gave it to me.'

'I know he did, darling. He inherited your taste. I don't mind if you want to look like a septuagenarian who last had fun in the sixties, but Bernadetto is rather *careful* about his clothes and I think it wouldn't be fair . . .'

'You needn't go on.' I was determined not to be bad-tempered this evening. 'Your wish is my command.' As I finished tying the shoe laces of the rather tight dress shoes that Jinny had picked for me, I began to undo my tie. 'Do you think Sebastian and Catharine would like Venice?'

'Don't think so. They'd rather go walking in Nepal or bicycling in Swaziland; that sort of thing. Neither of them is a bit interested in art or architecture.'

'Pity. I can imagine them here . . . there really is something very . . .'

This idle chatter was not going to put Jinny off a full review of our day. She interrupted me in my search for a word to capture the essence of the Most Serene City. 'What did you think of that business between Bernadetto and Jamie? And Bernadetto's silly excuse. He knows us both well enough to know that we wouldn't be moralizing about his sins, mortal or not.'

'Very curious,' I nodded. 'Very curious indeed.'

'I thought Jamie's explanation made more sense. I think Bernadetto must just think there's something slightly shifty about descending on Melissa so soon after Milo's death. He must be a little ashamed.'

'Never thought much about Bernadetto and romance, I must admit. I thought he might be one of those chaps who prefers to go without. Like Uncle Charles.'

'I think if you had asked the stable boys at Ampney about Uncle Charles, you might have formed a rather different impression.'

'Uncle Charles?' Virginia really does have a steamy imagination. 'I think not. I hate to bring this up, but you were the one who thought that Jamie and Bernadetto might be . . .'

'I said no such thing.' Virginia doesn't usually rely on technicalities: I deduced that she was embarrassed at having misread the situation.

I pressed my advantage. 'You distinctly insinuated it.'

'It was merely a hypothesis. There must be some other bond between the two of them.'

'I don't see why. They're friends. They've always been friends, ever since school. They used to go on all sorts of adventurous holidays together, climbing mountains, visiting monasteries in Tibet, that kind of thing. And once Lucinda died, they were able to do more of it. That's all there is to it.'

'Do you think Melissa will come between them?'

'Why on earth should she?'

'Well, they live rather a bachelor's existence when they're gadding about to Bernadetto's houses together. Melissa is more settled.'

'I don't know why you say that. After all, she's been disappearing off to Italy ever since we've known them for vast tracts of time. She's a very unusual woman.'

'She is certainly very attractive.'

I know when we are entering dangerous waters. 'Yes, I suppose she is: but I meant more that she's lived an odd life. First, that odd sort of marriage; and she's an odd mother. Of course, she's spent lots of time with Alexander, but she was always able to disappear and leave him with Milo and his nanny for weeks at a time.'

'That's not really all that odd, darling, just old-fashioned.'

By now we were both dressed and ready to make our way downstairs to the *terrazzo* to meet Bernadetto and Jamie, and I acknowledged this observation with a little nod. On the whole, I felt, it was better to move off Melissa, Lady Hawksworth, as a topic of conversation.

We dined outdoors in a restaurant in the Campo di San Stefano. It was one of those charming Italian trattorias with pink tablecloths, and matching linen napkins. 'It's not fancy,' Jamie had told me when he recommended it, 'just very good.' As we arrived, Jinny thought she caught sight of Mrs Bouncer making her way out of the square over the wooden bridge to the other side of the Grand Canal.

'Where?' I asked.

She pointed.

'At this distance, it could be anybody,' I said.

'With your eyesight, perhaps, Paddy, but not with mine.'

I let the matter drop.

Naturally the head waiter recognized Bernadetto at once and found us a lovely spot where we could look up towards the Accademia bridge and the canal. There was a great deal of flapping of napkins and bustling about to produce Pellegrino and bread and butter and *apperitivi*. As we settled down to examine the menus – it was a moment or two before I realized that I, at least, had been thoughtfully provided with one that was in a sort of English – I watched the steady flow of walkers passing back and forth over the bridge, to and from St Mark's Square. On a lovely early summer's evening in Venice, at about nine, there is a great deal of life. Much of it is not Italian: large American women in shorts, accompanied by larger husbands bearing guidebooks; tiny Japanese women, in tidy skirts, accompanied by equally tiny husbands bearing cameras; young Scandinavians and Germans, blond and burdened with knapsacks; and the occasional English couple, often, I regret to say, complaining about the foreign food.

Of course, there is a great deal of bad food outside England. We once stayed with Billy Heath when he was at the embassy in Moscow and eating out there, at least without a Russian guide, is a gustatory experience too ghastly even to summarize. And, of course, for those of us with a taste for the refinements of English cuisine – roast beef, rare, with horseradish; a light crisp Yorkshire pudding; roast chicken with roast potatoes, carrots and brussels sprouts; lemon pudding; you know the sort of thing – it can be painful to be away from it for too long. But how anyone could dismiss the cuisine of France or of Italy absolutely baffles me. And the meal at the Trattoria di San Stefano confirmed me in my opinion that, after England and France, Italy is one of the best places to get a good plain meal finely made of fine ingredients.

It was not a *great* meal, and the details do not stick in my mind: but I *can* recommend the polenta. And while *osso bucco* is, I suppose, really a Roman dish, I should report that it can be quite excellent in Venezia.

Some of the discussion, on the other hand, I recall very well. We began, of course, with idle chit-chat. But conversation soon turned, as I had feared it would, to the death of Gary Mitchell.

'Such bad luck,' Jamie said. 'Venice is actually rather a safe city for tourists . . . of course, people are constantly being robbed by gypsy girls and thuggish, if handsome, Italian boys, but, by and large, there's not much violence.'

'Perhaps he was being robbed and he resisted,' Bernadetto said. 'It's always a good idea to let them take what you've got on you. It can be pretty quiet up there around the ghetto on a Saturday. The Jewish museum is closed on their Sabbath and there's not really much else to see.'

'I don't suppose most Australian men would hand over their wallets without a fight. And you have to remember that he'd already been robbed once on the train.' Jinny addressed herself to all of us.

'Really?' Bernadetto said. He seemed only mildly surprised. 'I'm afraid that theft from tourists is the second biggest industry in Italy: the first, of course, being fleecing them legally.' He paused, smiling, and took a sip of his wine. 'What did he lose?'

'His briefcase. We were all dining at the time. Fortunately, he had his passport and his money on him.'

'Did you mention all this to the police?' Jamie asked.

'Didn't think to. We couldn't see that it would have had anything to do with this murder.'

'I suppose not.' He looked at me, a slight frown of worry on his forehead. 'But the police here can be frightfully nasty if they think you aren't being helpful.'

'Really, Jamie, you mustn't distress Patrick and Jinny like that.' Bernadetto patted me on the back as he spoke, as if to reassure me. 'I can't see how it could have anything to do with a botched robbery in Venice.'

Virginia said: 'We can't be sure it *was* a robbery attempt. I mean, they did say they were here in Venice to meet this mysterious woman. Suppose she had one of her henchmen do him in?'

'We don't know she has any henchmen,' I said. I gave Jinny a look that was intended to urge her to change the subject.

Bernadetto weighed in on my side. 'We don't know she has anything to do with it at all. In fact, we don't even know they weren't just teasing you with all this talk of mysterious ladies.'

A lull descended on our conversation and we turned our attentions to the pastry cart that our waiter had produced. Jinny's gentle patting on my thigh hinted at the direction I should go, and so, when she announced she would have only a decaffeinated cappuccino, and Bernadetto and Jamie followed suit, I looked with longing at the strawberries I had been planning to take as a healthy and non-calorific finale to my evening, but declined.

'How much longer are you going to be in Venice?' I asked Jamie.

'I must go back to England in a week or two. Anthony and I are going fishing in Argyll.'

'What fun. We haven't seen him for months. How is he?'

'Busy, of course. I was rather surprised when he said he had a whole week off. But you know from Sebastian what the life of a young doctor is like.'

At this point the waiter returned with my Barclaycard and we were ready to go. 'Let's walk back,' Jinny said. 'We can go down to where Giorgio is moored and tell him to go home by himself.'

Everybody seemed to think this an excellent idea.

As we were walking away from the table, Bernadetto asked, casually, whether I was having an interesting time disentangling Milo's affairs as Alex's trustee. In the circumstances, I thought this a question in rather poor taste. Milo's widow had every right to ask me about this – she was, after all, the other trustee – but his widow's lover surely would have done better not to bring it up. I muttered something to the effect that carrying out the last wishes of a friend was, unfortunately, one of the inevitable accompaniments of a lawyer's old age. Bernadetto, however, persisted, as we made our way back along the Grand Canal to the *palazzo*.

'Must be fascinating disentangling the life of such a global wheeler-dealer.'

'It's mostly in the hands of accountants.'

'Melissa says you told Alex he would be a very rich young man.'

'Indeed.'

'Do you think he will be able to manage his father's affairs? I mean he's not exactly . . .'

'He will continue to have Melissa and me as trustees.'

Jamie had detected the reluctance in my responses and chose to come to my rescue: 'I wish my father had left me in the hands of some wise trustees. I should have escaped all those Lloyd's losses.'

Virginia had stopped, unnoticed by the rest of us, at the door of a shop selling those Venetian masks (or rather the vulgarized versions of them that are now made for the tourist trade). 'Do look!' she shouted towards us as we drifted away from her. I turned around, asked Bernadetto and Jamie to wait for us, and returned to her. 'Aren't they pretty,' Jinny said to me, smiling. Since they were decidedly not to her taste and I knew it, I gathered something was wrong.

'Indeed,' I said loudly and then added, under my breath, 'What's the matter?'

'We're being followed. It's someone I recognize.'

'Who is it?'

'I don't know. But he was on the train with us. He walked through the dining-car while we were having dinner.'

I knew, of course, what she was thinking. She was thinking: This is the man who stole Gary Mitchell's briefcase. And I was absolutely sure she was right.

10

If we were to have a chance of trapping this man, he mustn't know we had seen him. I told Jinny that if she was sure she could recognize him again, I wasn't even going to take a look at him. 'We absolutely mustn't do anything to raise his suspicions.' We made a show of discussing one of the masks with the proprietor of the stall – or rather, Virginia made a show and I nodded occasionally to indicate that, while not actually able to follow the substance of the discussion, I was a hundred per cent behind my good wife – and then we turned to walk over to the others. 'We'll go home and Bernadetto can call the police for us from there. And let's not mention it to him or to Jamie until we get back to the *palazzo*. They'll probably not be able to resist looking back to see if they can see him.'

A few minutes later we were ringing the bell of the Palazzo Longhi. Giorgio, who had returned earlier at our bidding, appeared at the door and greeted us. He then said something *sotto voce* in Italian about 'Lady 'awkswort'.

Bernadetto gave us a somewhat forced smile. 'Melissa has asked me to telephone her.'

'I do hope her foot is less painful,' Jinny said. 'Give her our love.'

We strolled into the drawing-room, where Giorgio had laid out a good supply of grappa, cognac and various liqueurs, as Bernadetto drifted off to the library to phone Melissa.

We explained to Jamie what had happened on the way home.

'Too extraordinary. Well, we must phone the police just as soon as Bernie has finished talking to Melissa.' I'm afraid that this time he noticed me wincing at his use of the appellation 'Bernie', and he raised his eyebrows in response. 'I've called him that since we were both fourteen. Too late to stop now.'

'Quite,' I said.

'Why on earth do you think somebody's following you?'

'Can't think of any reason,' I answered quickly, hoping to pre-empt Jinny from speculating out loud about the documents in my briefcase. She got the message.

'Darling, I'm rather exhausted. If you could deal with the police, I'll tell them what I saw when they come over. In fact, maybe I should do a little drawing before I go to bed.' Virginia's infinity of talents includes, of course, the skill of capturing, by hand, with a pencil, a most extraordinary likeness on paper. (Sebastian, our son, has always been more impressed by the fact that she could draw elephants with a pencil held in her toes. Until he was nine or ten, when he became self-conscious about his mother's distinctions, he regularly required this trick at birthday parties.) 'Say good-night to Bernie for me,' she added, as she left the room, blowing kisses to all and sundry.

Bernadetto spent only a few minutes in conversation with his inamorata, and returned looking rather less refreshed by the experience than a romantic such as I would have expected. 'Ankle playing up,' he mumbled. 'Hasn't anyone had a drink?'

'Virginia asked to be excused. She's rather exhausted. Actually I am, too, but there's one bit of business I'd like to do before we go to bed.' I explained about the loiterer from the train.

'Good God, why on earth didn't you get me off the phone? He'll have disappeared by now.'

'I think the easiest thing is for them simply to set a man to follow us on our doings tomorrow and see if they can see him. Jinny will draw them a picture. Come to think of it, if he's watching this place, perhaps we should send Giorgio over to the police station with the picture. Then he needn't know we've been in touch with the police.'

'Good thinking. I'll pass on the information to them right away. You'd better wait in case they have any questions I can't answer.' Bernadetto disappeared once more across the hall to the library. A couple of minutes later, he returned. 'They're expecting Giorgio with the picture. They'd like it tonight, if possible.'

'Of course, I'll go up and get it from Jinny now.'

'They also asked whether you had anything in your briefcase that this fellow might have been after. I said I'd ask you.'

'Are they still waiting on the phone?'

'No. I said I'd call back if there was anything.'

'Then perhaps you could tell them in the morning that I have no idea why anyone would have been after my briefcase.'

As I went upstairs, my mind was racing. I hadn't mentioned the possibility that my briefcase was the real target of Gary Mitchell's theft. I hadn't mentioned it to Bernadetto or to the police either.

When I reached our room, Jinny was in bed, with a sketch in her hand. It was nearly done. I looked at it distractedly. The man had long hair and a full face. And Jinny had drawn in his torso, which one could see was well-muscled even through his T-shirt.

'What's the matter, darling?' she asked.

'Bernadetto just spoke to the police. He explained that we were being followed. They've asked us to send over your drawing with Giorgio tonight.'

'That doesn't seem to be anything to worry about.'

'No. That's not the problem. The problem is that Bernadetto told me the police wanted to know what I had in my briefcase. But they didn't know I had a briefcase. And I didn't tell Bernadetto I suspected that this chap might have stolen Gary Mitchell's briefcase. Even if they know about the stolen briefcase now, from the railway people, it's pretty astonishing if it's occurred to them that the thief might have been after my briefcase, just because we swapped cabins. After all, it only occurred to *us* because we knew there were some valuable papers in my Gladstone bag.' I paused. 'There's another thing. If they *did* work it out by themselves, Bernadetto wasn't on the telephone long enough to have the whole business explained to him. So why didn't he ask me why they wanted to know?'

My good wife took my hands and held them gently in her own. Hers felt soft as she touched me. She looked up into my eyes with a sweet, loving look – Penelope to my Ulysses, Isolde to my Tristan – and spoke healing words: 'You're being paranoid, Paddy. It is just conceivable that the Venetian police force, which is probably dedicating scores of able minds, trained in criminal investigation, to this matter, has come up with the possibility that someone might have been after our things because it was, at least originally, our cabin. And it is just possible that Bernadetto thought it was none of his business why they were interested in your briefcase.'

She was, of course, as usual, quite right. I glanced over to the briefcase, which sat, where I had left it, on an armchair, with its back to one of the great windows on to the canal. I kissed Virginia on the nose, and thanked her for her good sense. Then I sat down and took off my dress shoes and slipped on my slippers. I knew that in a minute or two Virginia's sketch would be done. I strolled over and flipped open the clasp of the briefcase and opened it, intending to read.

It was empty. The papers were gone.

*

Now, naturally, I was angry with myself for not having been more efficient about getting through Milo's papers. I offered up a silent prayer of thanks that Milo had not left me the originals. That was a real blessing. Until I got back to London, where the originals were stored, I would have no idea of what significance the papers might have for the theft on the train. When I reported the loss to the police, they would naturally want to know what the documents were about. And I would look a complete ass when I had to tell them I couldn't honestly say.

Jinny pulled on a dressing-gown. 'Never mind, my sweet, we must just deal with it. You *have* got the originals in London. Here, pop this drawing in one of those envelopes and let's take it downstairs. We'd better tell the others about this.'

We went down together to the drawing-room, Jinny reassuring me as we went and holding my hand, which she massaged comfortingly.

Bernadetto had gone to bed. Giorgio stood silently, next to the chair on which Jamie sat waiting for us. They had been chatting quietly when we entered the room, and Jamie looked slightly shifty, I thought, when we arrived. Because we were both in slippers, they had not heard us coming until we were almost through the door. It may have been my imagination, but I thought I had seen Jamie withdraw his hand from Giorgio's, which was now hanging limply against the white trousers of his uniform.

'Bernadetto asked me to hand on the drawing to Giorgio with instructions,' I said.

'I'm afraid that we're going to have to ask him to bring a policeman back with him,' Jinny added.

'I thought we didn't want to stir up suspicions with the chap who's following you,' Jamie said.

'We don't. But there's been a theft from this house. Someone has stolen the contents of my briefcase from our room.' Jamie and Giorgio case sidelong glances at each other in what can only be called a suspicious manner.

'I think we'd better get Bernie up and confer.' Jamie turned to Giorgio and issued instructions. 'I think we should probably consult with the *carabinieri* on the telephone, before we make any decisions. I mean, they might feel it was important enough to catch this other chap that they should just wait until you are out tomorrow to come and look into the burglary here. After all, if he's following you, then he'll not be here if you go off somewhere.' Jamie paused, uncertain as to how to interpret our silence. 'By the way, what *was* in the briefcase?'

'Legal papers. To do with Milo's estate. Not of any intrinsic value. Just copies.' In my tired and enervated condition I found myself degenerating into telegraphese. I roused myself to produce a couple of more coherent sentences. 'I haven't read them all, yet. So I can't say what anyone would learn by reading them.'

When Bernadetto arrived, Virginia and I repeated what we knew about the briefcase. It had been full when we left the room to go out for dinner this evening. The papers were copies, of no intrinsic value, of documents that Milo had left for me to read. I hadn't found anything very startling in them, I said (avoiding the little matter of the Bolivian family, which Bernadetto would be bound to mention to Melissa). Still, Milo's estate was worth a very great deal of money, and he had felt it important for me to have and to read these papers, so perhaps there was some secret lurking in them that was of value to somebody.

'If they come and look tonight,' Jamie made his point again, 'they'll scare off the chap who's following Patrick and Jinny. And since he might be the thief, that would be a pity.'

'We could just not "discover" the theft until the morning,' Bernadetto said speculatively. 'By then, they'll have their men in place. You can go out and they can try and catch him, and *then* they can send someone here for fingerprints while you're away.' He turned to Giorgio. 'Who was in the house while we were out to dinner?' He was conducting the conversation in English, in deference, no doubt, to my linguistic limitations.

'Giovanni . . . Teresa . . .' He counted them off on his fingers slowly. I imagined him scanning the rooms mentally and checking off their inhabitants. 'Piero . . . Enrico . . . Paulo . . .' For a moment he looked somewhat embarrassed, as if wondering whether he should mention someone else, and then he finished: '. . . and Sujit.'

'Sujit?' I asked.

'Yes, Mrs Aschenheim's top Tamil. He and Paulo are very close.' Jamie laid his head back on the sofa at an angle and said archly: 'Practically inseparable. I myself believe that Sujit is trying to convert Paulo to Buddhism.'

'Sujit is Catolic,' Giorgio said seriously.

'Quite.' Bernadetto sounded irritable for the first time. 'It's out of the question that any of them would have taken your papers. My people have been with me for years and Sujit adores Peggy. And besides, they wouldn't have any interest in Milo's affairs.'

'I'm sure you're right about that. But I'm not so happy about keeping this discovery from the police. The quicker a crime is reported, the better the chance they have of solving it. And if we don't report it now, that widens the time interval in which it could have been stolen.'

'I think you could assure them that you would have been woken by anyone coming into the room while you were asleep.' Bernadetto was at his most charming again. Reassuring, commanding, and, above all, oozing charm. Nevertheless, I continued to look sceptical. He smiled again. 'My dear Patrick, trust me. I know these people. I've lived here off and on all my life . . . I even have their blood in my veins. I promise you that we are simply making sure they don't scare your stalker. And that, as I'm sure you'll agree, is the most important thing at the moment.'

We were his guests. It was his house, his country. And he did know the place very well. Whatever my general misgivings about keeping things from the boys in blue, I could hardly insist. Giorgio went off with the picture of our 'stalker', as Bernadetto had dubbed him, having been sworn to silence about the theft. The rest of us retired to our rooms, to get what sleep we could.

As Jinny and I settled in for the night, she snuggled up to me and said: 'Milo's last request may turn out to be a bit more of a nuisance than you bargained for.'

'We shall have to wait and see if it was his papers that have caused all these problems.'

'Never mind, old thing. We can still have a holiday. We must just take as little notice as we can of all these goings-on.'

'Absolutely.'

My dear wife sighed deeply and then sat up and picked up her book. It was another slim novel, *The Train Was on Time*, by a German fellow named Heinrich Böll she rather admires.

I took this as a sign that I was permitted to drift off to Nod. 'Good-night, darling,' I said groggily.

'You know, my sweet . . .' My back was to Jinny but I knew she was peering at me over her book, her spectacles balanced finely on the tip of her exquisite nose. 'I don't see how our stalker could have stolen your papers *and* followed us to the restaurant. He must have an accomplice.'

'Absolutely,' I offered, like one of those complaisant young men in Plato's dialogues, happily going along with whatever is required by Socrates.

'Which means we need to keep our eyes peeled for someone else we saw on the train.'

'Indeed.'

'On the other hand, if he was doing his job, we probably didn't see him at all.' Jinny's mind was plainly abuzz with ideas.

'Hmm,' I offered, Eeyore-like, in hopes that this would both convey sufficient attentiveness and indicate that I was well on my way to sleep. (I don't recall anyone in *The Republic* trying this.)

'Of course, the real question is who sent him ... if it was a him.'

I think I said 'Absolutely' again or, perhaps, 'Indeed.' If I did, it was the last word I uttered before I lost consciousness. Despite all that had happened, I was too exhausted to stay up worrying.

11

The newspapers that arrived with breakfast at nine the next morning were full of more details of Gary Mitchell's death. It was now possible, they said, to confirm that the police believed the victim had been murdered. Suicide had been ruled out. And for the first time they had Gary's name and nationality. They also announced that they were looking for three travelling companions, including his girlfriend, who had still not shown up by the time the newspaper went to bed on Sunday night; and that the Turkish police were trying to find the rest of the Australian party in Istanbul. The three who had stopped off in Venice were all named as well, of course; and there were descriptions, based not only on what we had told the police but also, apparently, on the account of Jones, our steward, who was quoted as saying, among other things, that Mr Mitchell was a very generous and cheerful gentleman.

Gary's wallet had not been found – the police identification of the victim was entirely due to us – and so robbery remained a possible motive. But there were no signs that he had struggled: the police were said to be speculating that the stab wound was delivered from in front by someone he was talking to a moment before, and had come as a complete surprise.

'They mention that he came here on the Orient Express, and they have this little interview with Jones,' Jinny told me, as she scanned the article, 'but they don't say that he was robbed on the train. So obviously the police are keeping mum about that.'

'Well, we know they know about it. That's why they asked about my briefcase last night,' I said.

'Of course they know. Jones would have told them. It would have been reported to the railway security people.'

'Well, they kept their word. They didn't mention us. So Laurel and Hardy are men of honour.'

'Speaking of which, oughtn't we to "discover" the loss of the papers about now and set the whole charade going? If they do find our stalker, we'll be able to see who was the real target of the robbery on the Orient Express.'

We bathed and dressed in comfortable tourist clothes. I was wearing a linen jacket that Jinny gave me some years ago, of which I am particularly fond, and carrying a boater, which Jinny also bought for me, to which I cannot claim to be partial, but which is very good for keeping off the sun. Jinny wore one of those summery cotton dresses that identify one immediately as English (if one is a woman, that is; a chap who wears one is liable to be identified first of all as a wee bit odd). Bernadetto and Jamie were both standing in the hall as we came down the stairs, as if they had been waiting impatiently for us.

'Sleep well?' mine host asked.

'Of course they didn't, Bernie,' Jamie said irritably. 'None of us did.'

'Quite.' Bernadetto paused for a moment. 'You two are a credit to your class and country,' he went on. 'Nobody could mistake you for anything but an English gentleman and gentlewoman on holiday in Italy.'

'Let's hope that the police don't mistake us for the murderers of Gary Mitchell . . . which they may well do, if we don't pass on the news of the theft fairly soon.' I really was looking forward to sharing our little secret with the local constabulary.

'Ah yes. By the bye, Giorgio said that the police were very grateful for your sketch. They've had it copied and circulated. And they'll have a tail on you when you leave this morning. They suggested it would be easiest if we agreed you would go to the Accademia. I hope that's all right?'

'Of course it is, Bernadetto, my sweet,' Virginia said. 'After you, it's my favourite thing in all of Venice.'

'So let's tell them about the briefcase and then you can set off for a morning's art.' As he reached the doorway, he turned with a great beaming smile and added: 'After all, we mustn't let all these disagreeable goings-on stop you having your holiday.'

Bernadetto went off and telephoned the *carabinieri* and got them to agree to our plan. In the meanwhile, I tried desperately to remember which of the paintings in the Accademia were particularly special and which ones I had better not praise. The one lesson I recalled firmly from my honeymoon was that one did not like Tintoretto and that, in any case, he had painted too much. I knew too that there was this fellow Giorgione and that if I saw anything of his I could ooh and aah furiously. But there were other things I was sure I had forgotten. It was all very well for Jinny: she had been to Italy many a time and oft since our honeymoon, and dropped in on the Accademia regularly over the years; she could tell her Arp from her El Greco; and she had studied the whole business of the Renaissance and such matters at Somerville. I, on the other hand, had managed to avoid art education, most trips to Italy, and all visits to Venice for forty years, and I have great difficulty in distinguishing Whistler's mother from the Last Supper. (I have actually seen what remains of da Vinci's Last Supper, by the way, in a large and crumbling hall in Milan called, for reasons I disrecollect, the Cena, or some such. It is in perfectly appalling condition, and how anyone can tell it is a masterpiece is beyond me. Of course, I feel the same about Whistler's mother, which is, apparently, in fine condition.) In view of these facts, I had been planning to bone up on the Accademia with the Blue Guide before we went there. Having our visit to the place sprung on one like this was a bit discomfiting. I decided that subterfuge was in order.

'I must just pop back up and get a handkerchief, my love,' I said, moving towards the stairs.

'I put one in your jacket pocket, Paddy.' Naturally, that stopped me right in my tracks.

As I was searching around for another pretext, Jinny came up to me and pulled the Blue Guide out of her vast handbag (this necessary I neglected to mention earlier; I assume that it was part of what marked us off as English in the way that Bernadetto had so kindly admired). 'Perhaps you would like to browse through this while we're waiting, Paddy.' What a strange thing it is to be so thoroughly known. I smiled and thanked Jinny. And in my heart I thanked her especially for not explaining to Jamie why I felt in need of a browse.

We both felt rather self-conscious as we set out to walk along the Grand Canal and through the side alleys to the Campo San Stefano and the Ponte dell'Accademia. After all, so far as we knew, we were being tailed by at least two people, one of whom was almost certainly a bona fide villain. We paid our seven thousand lire or whatever it was – ridiculous currency, the lira . . . I can't think why they don't lop off a few noughts – and slipped into the cool obscurity at the bottom of the stairs to the gallery. 'He won't follow us in,' Jinny whispered. 'There's only one way out of here and it's straight back through the door we came in.'

'Good, then we can forget about him and you can show me your favourite paintings.'

I had forgotten that there was a painter or two I myself rather liked in this place. One of them is a fellow called Bellini – Giovanni Bellini, I think; Jinny says there's another one – who does these extraordinary madonnas. Comely young women with rather attractive babies (though I suspect their heads are too small to be anatomically correct). And in the background mysterious landscapes in blue and green. I have always had a soft spot for Mary – it is a Catholic weakness. But this chap really gave one a sense of her strength and her serenity and her certainty that she was holding the Son of God in her arms. There were several of these Bellinis not far from the Giorgione painting that Virginia so admires, a picture of a rather dishevelled woman in a landscape with a flash of lightning in the background. I can't say I quite grasped what was so world-shatteringly brilliant about it, but Jinny hovered about it for a good twenty minutes. Finally she came over to me and asked whether I had seen anything I liked. And I told her my thoughts about Bellini and his madonnas.

Virginia's response was most extraordinary. She put her head on my chest and hugged me and said, 'Oh Patrick.' And when she looked up and kissed me her eyes were moist.

I wasn't sure whether I should be gratified that she felt I had had an epiphany or cross that she was so surprised that I had had a few presentable thoughts about art. After forty years, we can still amaze one another.

When we escaped an hour or so later I had made only one howler. On one occasion, I had misread Titian's name as Tintoretto and scoffed, as a result, at what was, apparently, a painting of real greatness of the Deposition of Our Lord. Fortunately I had stored up a few points where moth doth not corrupt with my Bellini remarks, and so, instead of scolding, Jinny only giggled and said: 'Titian, darling; not Tintoretto.'

As we came out into the bright sunlight, we were approached by our old friend Laurel (this time minus Hardy) who smiled in a friendly and reassuring way. 'You was not followed 'ere by dat man. Maybe 'e 'as taken what he want from your box?'

'Have you had a chance to look for fingerprints and that sort of thing?'

He nodded. 'Now you must come back to the *palazzo*, and we take your print too. Already, we 'ave the print of everyone in the *palazzo*.'

I wondered if that included Mrs Aschenheim's Sujit, but thought it better not to ask. I didn't fancy having to discuss why Sujit was visiting Paulo with even the friendliest policeman in Venice.

As we made our way back I recited in my head, like one of those mantras that Indian gurus go in for, 'Titian, good. Tintoretto bad.'

When we got back to the *palazzo* it was time for aperitifs and luncheon. Having satisfied the spiritual man, it was the turn of the physical man. I had worked up quite an appetite.

12

But first we had to have our fingerprints done. This is not a new experience for me. If you have hung about as many murders as I have, the police have a way of wanting to have your fingerprints on file. Nowadays there are computerized central records of these things; but when I started out, it was usually easier for the local chaps to take your prints again. Virginia, on the other hand, has only had her fingerprints taken once before: and that was when my chum Inspector Fanshaw of the Cambridgeshire Constabulary showed her how it was done for one of her books. It seemed unlikely to be helpful to tell the Italian police that both of our fingerprints could be acquired through Interpol. Better not to have to explain why we were on file in England. They probably had their suspicions about us already.

If you ever want to know why being fingerprinted, even for the purposes of excluding your prints from consideration, makes everyone feel like a criminal, you should volunteer at your local police station to have it done. Police officers always press your fingers into the ink with the same unkindly vigour, whether or not you are a suspect; and they always use an ink that stains your fingers (and anything else they touch while wet). It's my theory that if this were a procedure that was regularly undertaken by the law-abiding, they would have found a less staining ink by now.

It took us only a minute or two to get our fingers and thumbs completely filthy with ink and another twenty minutes or so to scrub them clean. The result was that the cocktail half-hour from half-past twelve until one was almost over by the time we were able to join Bernadetto on the terrace.

'And how are I Scotti?' he asked us cheerfully.

'Hungry and thirsty,' I said.

'Elevated by all those marvellous paintings,' Jinny added, completing the picture.

'My friends at the *posto di polizia* tell me that they'll know by this evening if there are any fingerprints in your room from anyone outside the house. But they're not optimistic. They think that a professional thief would be likely to have been wearing gloves.' Bernadetto looked down for a moment. 'I'm really so sorry that you're having such a ghastly time.'

'Really, old man, you can't feel responsible for any of it. If it *was* the same chap who stole the briefcase on the train, then we brought him with us.'

'How could he have stolen the papers if he was following us last night?' Bernadetto's question was a perfectly sensible one. I had a vague memory that Jinny had raised the issue as I was falling asleep.

'You're right,' Jinny said. 'So, either he had nothing to do with the theft, or we're the victim of some sort of plot. It's all very puzzling.'

It did not seem wise to challenge this rather overdrawn picture of the situation and so I tried to move us along. 'Speaking of puzzles,' – this was not, I agree, the most subtle way to conceal a change of subject – 'where's Jamie?'

'He went back with Melissa to Peggy's. He should be here in a moment.'

'I'm sorry we missed her. Did she come while we were at the Accademia?'

Bernadetto chuckled nervously and I detected just a hint of a blush. 'Actually, she spent the night here.' I was very glad that Giorgio arrived at this moment and announced that lunch was ready in the dining-room. 'Saved by the bell.' Our host plainly shared my relief. 'Jamie asked us not to wait for him. Let's go ahead.'

As we reached the end of the meal, Jamie had still not got back from chaperoning Melissa; from which we concluded that he had stayed with Peggy for lunch. The official magistrate investigating the death of Gary Mitchell appeared at the *palazzo* as we were finishing. He was a youngish man, not much over forty-five, I should have said, dressed in a very elegant suit. Bernadetto invited him to join us, offering him coffee and a slice of one of Teresa's exquisite little apple tartlets. He accepted the former and declined the latter; a policy that may have accounted for a svelteness rather uncharacteristic of Italian men in their middle years.

Unlike Laurel and Hardy, Signor Valentino Montenari spoke excellent English. 'I am sorry to have to trouble you,' he began, after Bernadetto had introduced us all. (Excellent that, I thought; not 'to trouble you' but 'to have to trouble you.') 'The police tell me that you have been very helpful' – a slight tremor of guilt passed through the old conscience as I thought of the delay in reporting the theft from my briefcase – 'but they are not, as you saw, entirely fluent in English. So they may have missed something.'

He reviewed what he knew so far. Mr Montenari proceeded with great efficiency, glancing occasionally at a little black, leather-bound notebook, recounting precisely all the details we had passed on. 'As you know,' he went on, 'Mr Mitchell's briefcase was stolen from his cabin on the journey from London. You told the police you had exchanged cabins with him. It is natural to wonder whether his briefcase could have been mistaken for yours.'

'Indeed. We wondered that too. And now that a chap whom we saw on the train has turned up here in Venice round about the time the contents of my briefcase were stolen, it seems more likely.' Clever fellow, Signor Montenari, I was thinking as I spoke. You'll get to the bottom of this.

'I'm afraid the small trap we set for the gentleman from the train did not work. He did not follow you this morning. But perhaps he took your papers after you returned home from dinner; perhaps he was following you to get to the briefcase?'

'We telephoned you about the chap who was following us about half an hour after we returned. But then one or other of us was in the room until I found the papers gone this morning.'

'But you were asleep much of the time?'

'I am a very light sleeper.'

'You slept with the windows open?'

'Yes.'

'Over the Grand Canal?'

'Yes.'

'I do not think you are as light a sleeper as you think,' he said, smiling. 'The Grand Canal is mezzo-forte even in the night. It is never pianissimo.' Our one lie was beginning to catch up with us.

Bernadetto interrupted. 'I do not think it is possible that the papers were stolen while they were asleep. I asked Paulo, one of the servants, to spend the night on the balcony. I was worried about this sinister stalker.' He turned to Jinny. 'I should have told you, my dear, but I didn't want to disturb you any more than was necessary. One can get on to your balcony from the bedroom next door. Forgive me.' I noticed that Giorgio slipped out of the room during this last little speech. I suspected he was going to brief Paulo on what he should say if asked about his movements last night.

'It was very thoughtful of you, really,' Jinny said. Naturally, she was wondering, as I was, if what Bernadetto had said was an invention designed to cover our lie or the literal truth. He was so plausible.

'Good. Then, if he stole it, it was probably after you came back, but before you went upstairs.'

'It could have been someone else. Someone working with him.' I was curious to see what Mr Montenari would make of this possibility. But he only nodded, in acknowledgement of the suggestion, and took a sip of his coffee.

'Mr Mitchell was a lawyer,' he offered.

'Really? What a coincidence.' My remark only seemed inane after he had allowed it to hang in the air for a moment or two. 'I mean, so am I.'

'I understand you had some conversation on the train.'

'Yes. He was very grateful to us for swapping cabins so he could be next to his friends. He gave us drinks.'

'So you said.' Mr Montenari paused for a moment and took out a packet of cigarettes. *'La disturbo se fumo?'* he said to Bernadetto, who shook his head. 'Do you mind?' We did not. He offered the packet to each of us, bowing his head slightly as each of us declined. He lit his own cigarette and inhaled deeply. 'Perhaps he told you why he was coming to Venice.' It was not a question, I suppose, from the point of view of a grammarian; but the intonation was interrogative.

'*He* didn't, actually. But his friend, Mr Miller, did say that they were coming to Venice to meet a beautiful and mysterious woman who held the key to his destiny. I'm afraid I didn't take it very seriously.'

For the first time in our brief acquaintance Mr Montenari's interest was piqued. He sat up straight and put out his cigarette in the saucer of his coffee cup. He had taken only two or three puffs. 'Now, this I think you should have told us. It was Mr Miller's destiny not Mr Mitchell's? You are sure?'

'Mr Miller's,' I said, 'definitely Mr Miller's.' He scribbled a note. 'Look, I'm sorry. As I say, I wasn't sure he was serious. And it really slipped my mind. I didn't even mention it to my wife at the time.' Virginia confirmed this outrage with a vigorous nod.

'Is that all he said?'

'It's all I can remember of any interest. It was their first trip to Europe. He was travelling with his wife, his friend, Gary Mitchell, and *his* girlfriend, and a whole load of other Australians who were going on to Turkey.'

'And you, your ladyship?'

'I talked to Gerald Miller's wife. Actually I spent most of the time explaining to her about English titles. She seemed rather riveted. Though it's not nearly as interesting as Italian titles.' Our magistrate smiled politely at this little compliment to his country. 'To tell you the truth, I was rather preoccupied on our journey. I am writing one of my novels.'

'A new Bella Sharpe,' he said, to the total astonishment of us all. He savoured our surprise for a moment or two before he went on. 'I spent two years at Cambridge doing an MA in criminology. And at Cambridge, *everybody* reads Bella Sharpe.'

'Which college?' Bernadetto and I said in unison, in that boring way we Cambridge men have.

'Clare Hall.'

'Really?' I said. 'You know, I'm an honorary fellow of Clare. Bernadetto here misbehaved at King's. Clare Hall, eh? Do you know, I was involved in setting Clare Hall up in the first place? Well, well.'

'You must know Sir Leon Radzinowicz,' Jinny said. 'Such an interesting man. Patrick and he are always swapping criminological lore.'

'A very great scholar. He is, for me, one of the great heroes of criminology. A great man. It was an honour to study with him.' Mr Montenari said nothing for a moment and then chuckled. 'Have you ever read a poem by Sir William Schwenck Gilbert called "Etiquette"?'

'Can't say as I have,' I volunteered quickly, knowing perfectly well that Virginia, who has read everything, would be able to recite it from memory.

> '*The Ballyshannon foundered on the coast of Caribou,*
> *And down in many fathoms went the captain and the crew*
> *Greedy men, whom hope of gain allured*
> *Oh dry the starting tear, for they were heavily insured.*'

My dear wife recited in unison with our new friend.

'It's about these two Englishmen who are cast away on a tiny desert island. They've not been introduced, so naturally they don't speak to each other. Then one day, after many years, Smith overhears Jones mentioning, as a friend, someone he also knows. So they can talk to each other, at last, because they have a mutual friend.' Jinny's explanation was breathlessly efficient: I gathered Mr Montenari thought that it was typical of the English that we had warmed to him only when we discovered a mutual acquaintance.

'Unfortunately, at the end of the poem, they see their friend on a passing convict ship. And so they have to *stop* speaking to each other.' Mr Montenari was smiling a good deal less broadly now. 'This has been very enjoyable, but, alas, I am on duty. I'm afraid I still need to go through what you know of the papers that were in your briefcase, Sir Patrick. Perhaps we do not need to disturb the others. We could talk in another room?'

'Why don't you use the library?' Bernadetto said. 'Sir Patrick knows the way.'

After twenty minutes in the library with Mr Montenari, I felt as daft as I had known I would feel when I was asked about the papers. I told him the little I had found out: the ranch in Bolivia and the illegitimate children; the endless details of financial holdings. 'And then,' I continued, 'there was his Australian marriage certificate and his son Alexander's birth certificate, which is British, of course.'

'Don't you think the Australian connection might link your papers to Mr Mitchell?'

'Well, to tell you the truth, I really don't see how,' I said. And then I explained about the late Lord Hawksworth's bee in his bonnet and how he had put it behind him. 'So you see, he stopped worrying about these Australian details some months before he died.'

'But why?'

'I think it was because he had proof that Alexander was his son.'

'Did he ever tell you he doubted that the boy was his son?'

'No. But he wouldn't have. I mean, it would have suggested he thought his wife had been unfaithful in the first year of their marriage.'

'But you think he did doubt her.'

'Mr Montenari, Lady Hawksworth was – and is – a very beautiful woman.'

'How did he come to be sure the boy was his?'

'Ah, now that's very interesting. I wish Jinny was here, she could explain it better than I can. Apparently they did some sort of genetic test.'

'DNA matching.'

'That's it. There was a report in the file. It said that Alexander's tissues were those of Milo's son.'

This seemed to satisfy him. 'Do you think there was anything else of importance in the file?'

'I have absolutely no idea. As soon as I get back to London, I shall go through the originals and see.'

'And you will pass on to me anything . . .'

'. . . anything I find that is of the slightest possible relevance. Of course.'

We walked together out into the hall. There were voices in the drawing-room opposite. I said goodbye to the good Signor Montenari. 'I do not want to disturb you all further,' he said. 'Please just convey my thanks.' A moment later, he turned around as he reached the doorway of the *palazzo*. 'Oh, Sir Patrick. I don't think we have any further need of these.' He handed me our passports. 'You are free to leave Venice. You can go back to England. I have your London address and phone numbers.'

'Thank you so much, Signor Montenari. We were actually planning to go to Lake Como for a few days. Hotel Serbelloni. I've got the address somewhere upstairs.'

'Bellagio. I can look up the phone number if I need it. Have a wonderful time. It is a beautiful spot.'

'I know. I went there on my honeymoon.'

When I entered the drawing-room, Bernadetto was standing by the fireplace and Virginia was seated in one of the large, comfortable armchairs. Jamie was regaling them from the centre of the room with a tale and a fair amount of pantomime that was clearly amusing them enormously.

'So there was Melissa, her face practically invisible under this enormous hat, her eyes covered with a pair of those huge dark glasses that Jo-Ann Bouncer wears, going on in her Texas accent about roof gardens, when Sujit appears and says in a very loud voice: "Mrs Aschenheim, de Bouncers are here." ' Jamie produced a pretty good facsimile of Sujit's accent, I thought. He paused to allow it to be properly appreciated and, in the silence, noticed that the others were staring at me. 'Ah, hallo, Patrick. I was just telling

Bernie and Virginia how we nearly got caught out being rude about the Bouncers. Peggy was frightfully nervous. She thought that if they'd got the faintest whiff of what we were up to, that would have been the end of the paintings for the Met. But actually she handled herself magnificently. Poor Melissa had had no time to remove her fancy dress; so Peggy said the hat and glasses were because Melissa had developed photosensitivity.'

'How was your meeting with Montenari?' Bernadetto asked.

'Fine, fine. I'm afraid I didn't have much for him. But he's doing a very thorough job.'

'You look quite exhausted, Patrick.' Jinny was more solicitous than I hoped my looks warranted.

'Do I look *that* awful?' I smiled. (Jinny told me later the effect was 'frankly wan'.) 'Well, I think I shall take a siesta, then.'

'I'll keep you company.' Jinny kissed Bernadetto and waved at Jamie. 'We'll see you for tea.'

'Half-past four. In here, I think. It's rather sunny outside.'

'Good,' I said. And then I added: 'By the way, he gave us our passports. We can go.'

Bernadetto and Jamie both seemed genuinely pleased that we had been released by the Venetian police. 'I'll call the Hotel Serbelloni for you. Tell them you'll be there . . . when?' Bernadetto was ever the perfect host.

'Why not Wednesday? Just a day late. It'd be nice to have one more day here when we were completely relaxed and not worrying about this murder business. And then we'll take ourselves back off down memory lane.' Jinny had spoken for us, and she looked at me, to make sure I was happy with the suggestion, too. I nodded in agreement.

'Very good,' Bernadetto said. 'I shall do it right away.'

We made our way upstairs.

'We *could* have gone off to Bellagio tomorrow,' Jinny said as we arrived back in the bedroom. There was a slight afternoon breeze stirring the canopy of the bed: between them the marble floor and the breeze left the room refreshingly cool. 'But I would like to visit the Carpaccios in the Scuola di San Giorgio degli Schiavoni again; and there are just a few things I think we should clear up before we go.'

'What sort of things?' I probably sounded as suspicious as I felt. We were in a foreign country: here was a murder with which we were connected only by the briefest of chance encounters with the victim. Best, I thought, to leave well enough alone. The theft of Milo's papers *was*, obviously, something we – or, at least, I – had to worry about. But it was clear enough that the fellow who had followed us the night before, the one Jinny recognized from the train, had come with us from England. That meant he was quite likely to follow us back there; and in England I should be better placed with my police connections to catch him. *If*, that is, now that he had the papers, he was still interested in us. To find out why the papers were gone would in any case require me to get at the originals again, something I could basically only do in England. As I say, Milo's originals were in a sealed deposit box in London. I had left the key in a safe at our offices in the Inns of Court. By the time I could arrange for someone to get the key and a power-of-attorney, recopy the papers and post them, we would be back in England anyway. And, in any case, there was not much to be said for committing anything to the Italian mails.

'Well,' Jinny began, 'for one thing, I'd like to know why Mrs Bouncer might have lied about being up near the station on Saturday afternoon.'

'Really, darling, what business is that of ours? In any case, I thought you said I was wrong when I told you I saw her.'

'I did. But when she reacted like that on Saturday night, I realized that you might have been right.'

'But why should we care about it?'

'Because Peggy Aschenheim is a very nice woman and if she is dealing with someone... shady, we ought to let her know.' By Virginia's standards this was, I thought, a pretty feeble pretext. But then I knew exactly what she was thinking.

'Virginia, my love, let us entertain, just for a moment, an hypothesis. Let us suppose that it *was* Mrs Bouncer on the bridge when we returned from the Punta di San Vigilio. Let us suppose, too, therefore, that she was lying when she said she had never been up there. If she was returning from the ghetto, that would mean she was there in the late afternoon at about the time when Mr Mitchell was stabbed to death. At that time on a Saturday, according to Bernadetto, there are very few people about in the ghetto. If I hadn't happened to have glimpsed her, perhaps no one would have noticed she had been up there.'

My wife looked at me with that serious, expectant expression which means that we have an inescapable obligation to do something.

'There isn't the slightest reason to think that she had any connection at all with the man.'

My wife remained mum.

'Perhaps you should pass these suspicions on to Signor Montenari, who will, I am sure, give them the consideration they deserve.'

'Sarcasm does not become you, my sweet,' Lady Scott pronounced, sounding for all the world like an English Jean Brodie. 'At any rate, it would be very unfair to Jo-Ann Bouncer to suggest to the police she might have committed a murder, if there's a perfectly innocent explanation. I think it would be better if we found out a bit more, first.' She paused. 'Besides, there's another thing.' I'm afraid I sighed a little louder and more impatiently than I should have, because Virginia cast a stern Medusan glance in my direction. 'It's all very well for you to sigh because you want to shirk your obligations. But the fact is you know perfectly well that there are things about this whole business that you are better placed to find out than the Venetian police.' I noticed the 'you' in that sentence. It was rather unusual. Normally, *I* am the one who has to get Jinny's permission to pursue one of my investigations without her.

'I'm sorry, Jinny. I'm just a little tired. What was the other thing?'

'We must find out from Melissa if there's anything about Milo's time in Australia that might connect this dead Australian lawyer to your papers.'

'Why don't we just ask her that? After all, we know she couldn't have had anything to do with Gary Mitchell's death: she twisted her ankle long hours before he was stabbed, and wasn't out of Peggy's sight until after he was found.' It was the first time I had really begun to think about whether anyone *we* knew in Venice could have done the murder. The very idea was rather unnerving.

'What a funny thing to say, Paddy, my love. Of course, *she* didn't kill him.' But I could see that Jinny, too, had begun wondering whether anyone we knew was a suspect. The thought stopped her for a moment, but then she went on. 'I don't think we should alarm Melissa. After all, if there *were* a connection, she might feel in danger.'

'If there is a connection, she may *be* in danger.'

'And then we should certainly tell her, my love.'

We made our plans. And then we slept. A firm resolve, I find, almost always makes the journey to Nod a little easier.

13

When I awoke and looked at my wrist-watch, I discovered that I had been asleep longer than I had intended. It was a quarter past five and Jinny was nowhere to be seen. I got up hurriedly, tidied myself up a bit and made my way downstairs. In the drawing-room, Virginia, Bernadetto and Jamie were having tea with Melissa and Georgie Bishop.

We made our salaams to each other and Jinny asked me brightly if I was feeling more rested.

'You don't look it,' Jamie said bluffly. 'You look as though you'll need a few more minutes to surface.'

'And in the meanwhile,' Bernadetto offered, 'what you need is a good cup of Earl Grey.'

'I', Melissa pronounced archly, 'am being mother.' She poured me my tea and offered me some of those delicious almond biscuits. In view of their addictive character and the presence of the hawk-like oversight of my beloved wife, I decided that the best thing was not to start. I declined. This produced barely suppressed amusement, masquerading as astonishment, among our party.

'I say, Patrick. Maybe you'd better lie back down,' Jamie said with what can only be described as a snigger.

'Really,' I said peevishly. 'We had a very good lunch and I just don't happen to be very hungry.'

'Melissa was telling us about life in the outback, when you came in.' Jinny's aim was plainly to move the conversation away from her irritable spouse.

'Sydney is not really the outback, my dear. But in those days it was a very long way away from civilization. One felt . . . one felt as if one was on another planet. But of course, all those colonials were desperately trying to preserve a British façade. Floral print dresses, chintz, gloves at tea: rather like Bournemouth, I imagine.'

'I suspect that even in Bournemouth gloves are a rare sight at tea parties these days,' Jamie said. 'Any day now there'll be a *Disappearing World* television documentary about the vanishing tribe of Bournemouth's glove-wearing tea-partiers.'

'Speaking of vanishing tribes, we did go out to the outback for a few days, before we set off back to England. And we met some Aborigines. Milo was frightfully impressed with their tracking. He loved hunting, you know. Big game, that sort of thing. He was planning to buy a few thousand acres in Botswana, once, so he could hunt leopards or something on his own land.' I wondered, as Melissa rattled on, if I ought to mention that he had probably done just that. One of the accountants told me that ten per cent of the cattle in Botswana seemed to have belonged to a company of Milo's. I don't know if you've ever looked up Botswana in an encyclopedia; when I did, I discovered, among other things, that there are a good many more cows than people. 'I went there once. Extraordinarily beautiful place called the Okavango Delta. Every imaginable bird and beast; flame trees everywhere. Fabulously unspoiled.'

'Did you go with Milo?' Jinny asked.

'Good lord, no. Milo and I haven't been out of the country together for twenty years. . . . Hadn't, I should say. It's frightfully hard to get used to his not being about.'

'What did he do in Australia before you met?' I spoke quietly, thinking that it was best to move away from the topic of Milo's death. Whatever their relationship, they had stayed married for nearly forty years, till death did them part.

Melissa looked thoughtful for a moment, and seemed about to say something when Jinny broke in: 'Do you *mind* talking about Milo, my dear?'

'Of course not. Much better to think of what people were like when they were alive, than to mope about because they're gone. Besides, it wasn't as if we were what you might call a conventional married couple.' Melissa looked up at Bernadetto as she spoke. 'And I've never been sentimental. Not British,' she laughed, looking away from Bernadetto towards a corner of the ceiling, remembering something: 'When Father died, I asked Nanny whether Mother was going to cry, and she said: "Why on earth should she?" '

'So what *was* he doing in Australia?'

'Sowing his wild oats, I suppose, as far away from his father as he could get. I never met the fifteenth Baron Hawksworth of Hawksworth, and Milo never said more than two words about him. "Fine man . . ." ' Melissa made no attempt to mimic Milo's tone or accent. ' "Of course, I knew him, he was my father." That was the sort of thing he said. I couldn't ever get much more out of him. Actually, I couldn't get much out of him about what he'd been doing in Australia either. Lots of hunting in the north.

Crocodiles, that sort of thing. We brought back endless crocodile skins... you two must have seen them strewn about at Hawksworth.' I nodded. 'He'd been up in Melbourne until just before I arrived: so he didn't really know anybody very much in Sydney. We had a very quiet wedding and an enormous party when we got back to London.'

'Milo wasn't much of a one for self-disclosure,' Jinny said ruminatively, remembering, no doubt, some of our pleasant evenings at Hawksworth. There had never been much female company at Hawksworth, after Melissa left. Even when Melissa was staying with Alexander, she and Milo kept themselves to themselves, and Alexander would shuttle between them, lunching with one, dining with the other. So that when we were there, it was often just Milo, Jinny and I.

Milo was a scintillating and energetic host. He amused us with stories of glamorous people and exotic places. But he never told us much about how he knew these glamorous people, or what – save the occasional hunting – he was doing in these exotic places. Dinner with Milo was always fun: but one never felt that he had taken one into his confidence. Even when Alexander was with us for a meal, Milo treated him, too, as another, somewhat less sophisticated, person to be entertained. I suppose I should have been less surprised than I was when I started to discover his hidden life in Bolivia and a massive set of financial entanglements of which I had not been remotely aware when he was alive, even though I was a legal adviser and a friend.

'Alexander tells me that we keep discovering more and more secret possessions of Milo's. All over the world.' Melissa raised an elegant eyebrow.

'In fact, Melissa, he did buy a ranch in Botswana.' (I thought it best not to go on to mention Bolivia. I wasn't sure that Melissa would be pleased to hear of those girls in La Paz, and, somehow, mentioning Bolivia and leaving them out seemed more dishonest. But Milo had, after all, effectively ordered me not to tell Melissa anything that might upset her. Another conundrum to take up with Monsignor Galsworthy.) 'That alone will bring Alexander a pretty substantial income... and it will be somewhere to visit, if he wants. Sounds like that delta...'

'Okavango...' Melissa spoke lazily, with her eyes closed, lengthening each vowel. She made it sound like the most mysteriously attractive place on earth.

'Exactly... that delta sounds like Alexander's sort of place.'

Melissa shook her head as if to waken from her reverie, and

glanced, again, at Bernadetto. 'What a strange man my husband was.'

'What is your dear son going to do with all that money?' Jamie asked. 'Does he have ambitions to go with all those riches?'

'He's fond of some of the same things Milo was: big-game hunting, shooting, travelling to exotic places. As Patrick says, he'd adore Okavango. And he loves vintage cars. He'll probably start collecting those, once he realizes he can. He's such a happy person.' Melissa smiled maternally, and, just for a moment, her social mask slipped; the persona of a woman who had been gliding, gracious and beautiful, through European 'society' for more than forty years, fell away. I thought, suddenly, of the Bellini madonnas. Melissa in her make-up was as smooth-skinned as they; she had finer features than these peasant girls: but her slight smile, the smile of the mother contemplating her son, was as luminous as any in the Accademia.

We chatted on for another half-hour or so, until Bernadetto asked Melissa if she would care to stay for dinner.

'Thank you, Bernadetto, my love, I should love to. We must telephone Peggy and make sure it won't put her out. We're going to have a drink at midnight with the Bouncers at the Danieli. Perhaps we could *all* go.'

'Well, while you make all these exciting plans,' Jinny said, 'we must go upstairs and get ourselves tidied up for the evening.'

'We don't know any more about Milo's doings in Australia than we did before,' I told Virginia as she came back from turning on her bath.

As usual, however, she pursued her own line of thought, appearing to ignore what I had said. I knew she would circle back to it eventually. 'How old do we think Gary Mitchell was?'

'Thirty-seven. Remember we celebrated his birthday on the train.'

Jinny did some mental arithmetic. 'So he would have been born a year or two after Milo and Melissa left Australia.'

'Indeed. He'd be a little younger than Alexander.' I was sure that this was leading somewhere, and so I went on waiting patiently.

'On the other hand, he was a lawyer, Mr Montenari said.'

'That *is* what he said.'

'So he might have been acting for somebody else.'

'If I might interrupt the flow here? Might I ask what, apart from the fact – the *coincidence*, some might say – that Australia figures in the biographies of both the man who gave me the stolen papers and the now sadly deceased man we met on the train, leads you to think we should be trying to find other connections between them?'

'We agreed that we needed to get Melissa talking about Australia to see if there *was* any connection.'

'That was the plan; but she didn't say anything at all that helped.'

'That's not quite true.' Jinny put her head at an angle, and tossed her hair in a gesture that was cleverly evocative of Melissa. And then she said, in Melissa's accents: 'He was sowing his wild oats.' She paused. As the light dawned on me my dear wife half sang, in the words of Angela Lansbury on our recording of *Sweeney Todd*, 'If you get it . . .' She paused until the Scott eyebrows rose on the wrinkled brow, before continuing tunefully: 'Good, you got it.'

'We already know that Milo had *some* illegitimate children.'

'Good.'

'And he was off in the wilds on the other side of the world as a young man, kicking up his heels, disappearing off into the swamps after crocodiles and, who knows, the occasional young woman. If he had had another son, then that boy wouldn't have put Alexander's inheritance at risk unless he had been born before Alexander and to a woman to whom he was married. English titles go to heirs male of the body.'

'Maybe that explains all the fuss last winter about Alexander's succession. Perhaps the boy turned up suddenly, out of the blue . . . wrote to Milo or something; perhaps Milo had never known that he'd fathered him. And that was why he was worried about Alexander.'

'He wouldn't have worried about the title. If Milo had been married before he met Melissa, that extremely expensive Australian private dick would have found it out. So if there is an older son, he's illegitimate: and Milo certainly knew that titles only pass to legitimate heirs.'

'That's true. But he could have used the pretence that he was worried about the title to get you to investigate what rights another child would have had apart from the right to the title.'

'It doesn't make any sense, though. Alexander's rights to the house and the earlier trust have been secure for years. So the only doubts would be about the rest of the estate. And if he was *really* worried about that, why did he make the beneficiary of the trust "my eldest son"? It would have been easy enough to change it to designate Alexander by name.'

'It's all very puzzling, I agree.'

14

We had a long, late, leisurely dinner. Everything was light and summery, though not terribly Italian. A gazpacho, sharpened by a little more onion than usual and some coriander, was followed by an excellent cold trout dish with lovely little boiled new potatoes, doused in butter, sprinkled with an Italian parsley and just a touch of pepper, and served with a delicious salad of leaves and – an interesting idea, this – flowers. Then just a little lime sorbet, followed by a quail each, cooked with oodles of rosemary, and served, very simply, with a purée of turnips. And finally an *île flottante*, with the most elegantly wispy egg-whites, in a brilliantly light and creamy custard. Bernadetto offered us a whole series of Italian wines that I didn't know, each of them the perfect accompaniment to its course: and then ended (appropriately enough) with a little Beaumes-de-Venise.

By eleven o'clock, as the coffee arrived in the drawing-room, I was in a splendid mood and so I was all for going along for the midnight rendezvous at the Danieli. When Jinny gave me one of her looks, I reminded the company that unlike the others I had slept long and well this afternoon. When she announced that she was probably too tired to come, I urged her to reconsider (without, I admit, a great deal of enthusiasm, since I knew that if she did come, I should be dragged back early). Finally I heard the words I had hoped for: 'Why don't you go by yourself, darling?'

'Oh, do you think I should?'

'Of course you must,' Melissa said. 'Sweet of you to lend him to me, Virginia. I promise to return him to you at a reasonable hour in good working order.'

And so it was arranged.

Behind its gothic façade, the Hotel Danieli is, of course, an extremely grand affair. The hotel faces over one the busiest of the city's pedestrian thoroughfares: the Riva degli Schiavoni that runs from Saint Mark's, along the basin (with San Giorgio Maggiore at the mouth of the Grand Canal in its centre) towards the eastern tip of the main island of Venice. Even late in the evening the quay was crowded with noisy tourists, strolling hither and thither. But once one stepped into the cool opulence of the lobby, all was calm. Melissa – who seemed to be well known to the staff, all of whom addressed her with a bilingual *'Buona sera, milady'* – hobbled on my arm into the bar, where we made our rendezvous with the Bouncers, a little early, at about a quarter to midnight.

Philip Bouncer appeared to be dead to the world. He was settled deep in a comfortable armchair, a glass cradled in his vast hands, which were resting, loosely clasped together, in his lap. Given his passivity, it was natural, I thought, that Mrs Bouncer should have been particularly happy to see us, hugging Melissa enthusiastically and settling her into a chair with a glass of champagne. Without anyone's quite asking for it, a foot-stool appeared, and Melissa was able to rest her leg. I accepted the offer of a glass of champagne myself.

'Well, Mrs Bouncer,' I said, 'your very good health.'

'Jo-Ann, please; please call me Jo-Ann.' Our transatlantic cousins have a charming way of assuming that after a couple of dinner parties one is an old friend. 'Cheers.' She knocked her elegant Venetian fluted glass against Melissa's and mine and then leaned over to bump the glass of whisky settled in her husband's lap.

Mr Bouncer responded by lifting his head from its resting position slumped on his chest and gazing across at all of us. 'Hah,' he drawled, 'I see we have comp'ny. Melissa. Sir Patrick.' He was struggling to keep his eyes open. Suddenly a great surge of resolve coursed through him and he drew himself out of his slouched posture and waved at the waiter who was hovering a little distance away. 'Mineral water, *per favore*. And lotsa ice.' He returned his attention to us. 'So, how's that cute ankle of yours coming along? Did you give it a little rest this evening?'

'No dancing tonight, Philip; we just came over from the Longhi in Bernadetto's little motor-boat. All things considered, it's doing rather well.'

'Glad to hear it.' He nodded slowly and looked over to the door of the bar. 'Peggy should be here in a while. She's bringing Georgie. They say that Claudio isn't feeling too good.'

'We had a great trip today. Phil took me over to Murano and we ordered just the neatest chandelier for the place in San Antonio.' Jo-Ann spent the next few minutes enthusing over this object, which sounded less and less like the sort of thing that would go down well in Chewton Ampney. 'Sort of purple-pink sea-horses . . . you know, big ones . . . and they're holdin' up this sort of crown. Gee, Phil, I didn't reckon it would be so hard to describe it.'

'Why don't you show 'em the picture, honey?'

'Now why didn't I think of that?' Jo-Ann said merrily, removing from her handbag a Polaroid photograph of two smiling Italian men in aprons holding up a chandelier whose adoption in the main hall of the old homestead would certainly have led to my expulsion from the National Trust.

Melissa did her best to combine honesty with amiability. 'Yes,' she began sceptically, drawing the word out to a good two or three syllables, 'I can see that that might rather stun the neighbours in San Antonio.'

Jo-Ann look pleased and I mustered what I hoped was a genial – if non-committal – smile myself. 'Murano has a long tradition of very fine glass-making.'

'That's right. We went to the museum: do you know . . .' – Jo-Ann's voice dropped to a conspiratorial whisper – 'do you know they used to kill anyone who tried to tell the secret of how they made the glass?' She shuddered. I was contemplating trying to cheer her up by pointing out that this practice had stopped some time in the sixteenth century, when the Aschenheims, *mère et fille*, swept in.

'Claudio has retired to bed. He's nursing a headache. How *is* everyone?' Peggy Aschenheim beamed at all of us. (Her tone and manner put me in mind of Queen Victoria's remark about her Prime Minister: 'Mr Gladstone speaks to me', the Queen-Empress opined, 'as if I were a public meeting.') 'Melissa . . . how's the ankle?'

'Lovely, darling, lovely. But I'm sure everyone's bored of hearing about it. Let's talk about something jolly.'

Naturally, this was a bit of a conversation-stopper (as Melissa no doubt intended). Philip Bouncer raised his tumbler of mineral water thoughtfully in the pause and then, his mind made up, addressed Peggy Aschenheim. 'I don't know if this will count as jolly, Melissa. But I guess you'll be pleased to know, Peggy, I've decided to give those pictures to your museum.'

Peggy Aschenheim is an accomplished woman, a suave and much-travelled sophisticate, who has spent much of her adult life in the civilizing (if mildly decadent) air of this Most Serene City. But in moments of extreme excitement one's background shows through. She rose from her seat with an enormous whooping sound and engulfed the blushing Philip Bouncer. At home they would probably have called it a Texas holler. 'You wonderful man. That's the best news I've heard in years. It's the best news, in fact, since . . . I don't know when. Jo-Ann, you are married to a wonderful guy. I'm just gonna have to give you a squeeze as well.'

As Philip Bouncer's blush retreated, a great pleased smile settled on his face in its stead: Peggy's response had been just the thing. While Bouncer beamed, I divided my attention between my companions and the other occupants of the bar: as svelte and cosmopolitan a crowd as you could see in a vermouth advertisement. It was fascinating to watch them manage the conflict between the urge to gawp at the Americans' fantastic performance and their conviction that it was infra dig to take any notice of anyone else. Philip Bouncer and Peggy were plainly the topic of conversation at more than half a dozen nearby tables; sly sidelong glances were being cast from every direction.

The Bouncers and the Aschenheims were much too pleased to take any notice of the notice that was being taken of them. There was only one jarring note. As Melissa congratulated Peggy for persuading Philip Bouncer to divest himself of his paintings and then praised Philip for his generosity and public-mindedness, I noticed that Jo-Ann Bouncer was having some difficulty in maintaining her equilibrium. Finally, after several minutes of silence and a fixed and implausible grin, she excused herself. 'Women's room,' she said to the air above the table, and stalked off.

Melissa cast me a look whose meaning was not clear to me. But the others were still immersed in their excitement at Mr Bouncer's news. When Mrs Bouncer returned, she had recovered her composure and was smiling more plausibly.

'See, honey,' her husband said as she returned, 'I told you I had something excitin' to tell you this evenin'. Do you forgive me for keepin' ma little secret?'

'Course, I do, hon. And I just know you've made Peggy here just really, really happy.'

'Well, I don't know about the rest of you folks, but I'm gonna need some sleep tonight. Why don't we all have one more round to celebrate? And then we can call it a night.' Philip Bouncer snapped his fingers to summon a waiter.

It was, it turned out, an offer we could not refuse. Once each of us had been equipped with a glass of Veuve Clicquot, Philip Bouncer raised his glass: 'To old friends and new.'

'And to generous donors,' Peggy added before taking a sip. 'We'll have a wonderful dinner at my place tomorrow night to celebrate. You must bring everyone from the Palazzo Longhi, of course,' she said to me. 'It'll be such fun.'

'I'm afraid we're setting off for Bellagio on Wednesday morning. I don't know how late we shall be able to stay. At my age, I'm afraid...' I was making sure that if Jinny thought this wasn't a good idea, the groundwork had been laid for us to withdraw.

'Don't be silly, Patrick,' Peggy Aschenheim said firmly. 'You can't leave without a farewell dinner with me. You can snooze all the way to Bellagio; it's a four-hour drive.'

'I'm afraid that we shan't both be able to snooze. One of us will have to keep an eye on the road, especially the way these Italians zip about.'

'Don't be ridiculous. You can't drive yourselves. Take my car. The chauffeur has nothing to do most of the time, he'll enjoy it. He loves to show off on the *autostrada*.'

'It's very generous of you, Mrs...' I amended myself in response to a wagging finger, 'Peggy. But we shall need a car while we're there.'

'Keep mine. How long are you going for?'

'A few days.'

'There you are.'

'Where will your man stay?'

'Bruno will be all right. He has a cousin in Como.'

I smiled gratefully at Mrs Aschenheim, but said nothing, wondering if Jinny would feel I should demur. This endless generosity was becoming rather wearing.

'Do say yes, Patrick, my dear, or Peggy will never forgive you,' Melissa said cheerily. 'We English', she went on, addressing the four Americans, 'know how to deal graciously with adversity. It's good fortune that stumps us.'

Georgie, Mrs Aschenheim's daughter, who had sat almost completely silent for an hour or so, abruptly broke out in hysterical laughter. 'You are *so* funny, Melissa', she said, between gasps. I must say I didn't see it at all, but I was grateful for the diversion.

Not long after this, Melissa hobbled off with the Aschenheims and I bade farewell to the Bouncers. I decided to stroll back to the Longhi, so I marched towards Paulo, who had brought us over in Bernadetto's boat. 'I say, Paulo, I'm sorry to have kept you up all this time, but I think I'm going to walk back to the *palazzo*. So why don't you just make your way home alone?'

Paulo smiled beatifically and offered me a hand on to the boat. He was still expecting me to join him. I made a few feeble attempts at putting my ideas into the tongue of Garibaldi, concluding eventually that our knowledge of each other's language was probably not sufficient to communicate the necessary information without a good deal of pantomime. There followed a moment or two of resorting to gestures – I tried communicating the thought of walking by marching two fingers of my right hand on my left palm, and then tapping my chest. Paulo mirrored my gesture and then slapped me heartily on the back and laughed. I was reminded that I have never been much good at charades – and I had no reason to think that Paulo was any better than I am – and so I resolved reluctantly to accept his invitation and step into the boat. Then a thought struck me.

'*Aspetti*,' I said to Paulo, hoping that this was a suitably imperatival form of the verb. I stepped back out of the boat and made my way back up to the Danieli: since the staff all seemed to understand English, any of them would do as an interpreter.

Two minutes later, one of the gentlemen in livery was a few thousand lire richer, Paulo was waving to me from out in the basin, and I was able to set off on the twenty-minute walk home. A brisk constitutional in the night air is just the thing at the end of a boozy evening.

As I walked through St Mark's Square, I noticed a crowd of rather louche young men gathered at the foot of the bell tower. I wondered for a moment whether it was wise to walk towards a crowd of youths in the middle of the night in a strange city, and looked around to reassure myself that there were other people about. There were, indeed, a few young people strolling through the vast square in groups. And so I approached the bell tower, intending to turn left towards the exit from the square that leads to the Accademia bridge. As I drew closer, I noticed one of the group – a stocky, long-haired young man in a dark windcheater – dive into the shadows, as if trying to avoid me.

At first, in my befuddled state, I thought nothing of it. But then it struck me that the only person in Venice who had any reason to avoid *me* was the man who had been stalking us; the man Jinny and I were convinced had also stolen Gary Mitchell's briefcase. And this man fitted Jinny's description. I circled back round the bell tower to see if I could catch a glimpse of the fellow.

I crept stealthily round one corner and was about to turn the second when a hand descended on my shoulder from behind. My heart lost a beat. I leapt an inch or two in the air and let out a small cry, 'I say, you really shouldn't creep up on a chap like that.'

'You need a frien' tonigh'?' He was a boy of about twenty, wearing what looked like a slightly grubby sailor's uniform.

'I beg your pardon?' This was frankly rather puzzling. There was something slightly threatening in his tone; despite the friendliness of what he was saying, he made it plain he wanted something from me. I wondered if he was after my wallet. Involuntarily I reached to see if it was still in my jacket pocket. After all, Italy is full of pickpockets. It was still there.

'I show you good time.' If he wasn't a thief, was he, perhaps, a tout for some local tourist trap?

'I had no idea any of the sights were open at this hour. But we're staying with friends, so we're in good hands.'

'You no lonely?' Now he sounded like a moderately unprofessional social worker.

'Not really.' This was one of the most peculiar interrogations I had ever experienced, but it wouldn't do to be rude. 'Actually, I'm on my way home to bed.'

His face lit up with a lascivious leer. 'I come too.' He sounded as though he thought this was what *I* had intended. I looked at him in puzzlement, at a loss for words.

His tone now became impatient. 'Little money, no espensive.' And this time, after he spoke, he took hold of himself in a suggestive way and licked his lips. Finally, I grasped what he was proposing.

'Oh, I see.' I laughed nervously and almost immediately thought better of it. 'No, thank you,' I said sternly. '*Grazie*. Good-night.' I gave him a reproving look and shooed him off with a manly wave of the hand. When he held his ground and started to blow me little kisses, I decided that it was time to be firm: 'Do you want me to call the police? *Carabinieri*.'

'F — off, queer,' the disagreeable youth said. He strutted off into the shadows whence he had come.

By the time I extricated myself from this distasteful encounter and made my way once more around to where I had seen the figure hiding in the shadows, at most thirty seconds had passed. But even so, the man was no longer there. I caught sight of a figure with his long hair and stocky build trotting off towards the basin; but he was moving with more agility than I can muster and there was little point in following him.

'Excuse me,' I said to a pair of young men who were leaning

against the tower, smoking a shared cigarette. 'You don't happen to know that man, do you?'

They laughed. "E is *inglese*, like you. But you are too ol',' the taller man said. "E like young boy.'

I decided I had better give up.

To my surprise, Jinny was still awake when I got back to the bedroom. When I entered, she was propped up on a pile of pillows, a copy of a book called *The Great Train Robbery* folded on the sheets in front of her, peering at me over her glasses. On the bedside table was a notepad. She had been thinking about Bella Sharpe.

'Fun?' she said briskly, raising her eyebrows. I should have felt less wary if she had first said hallo.

'Yes. No. Well, I mean it was fun at the Danieli, but I've just had a rather disconcerting experience in the square.'

'Oh darling, are you all right?' Virginia made to sweep back the bedclothes and leap to my aid.

'Fit as a fiddle.' She settled back.

'Why didn't you come back with Paulo?'

'I thought a brisk stroll would do me good.'

'Accelerate the alcohol metabolism,' my wife said drily. 'So, what happened in the square?'

I told Virginia my story. She seemed to find the whole thing very amusing. 'You've obviously stumbled upon a homosexual trysting place.'

'Well, that's easy enough to say after the event. But how on earth was I supposed to know?'

'You would have known what was going on at once if it had been a girl.'

'That's completely different.'

'Well, there's a discovery: the campanile in St Mark's at two in the morning is not a place for a gentleman of ordinary tastes to loiter.'

'So what about the chap who was hiding from me?'

'A dark windcheater and long hair and a stocky build?'

'Couldn't see anything else.'

'And English. Sounds like our man. Would you recognize him again?'

'I don't think so. But I'm sure the two young men I talked to would.'

'Would you recognize *them*?'

'Absolutely. I saw them from up close.'

'I think you'd better telephone Mr Montenari in the morning.'

I wandered off to the bathroom to prepare for bed and remembered, while I was brushing my teeth, that I hadn't yet told Virginia any of my news from earlier in the evening.

'By the way,' I said, upon my return, after kissing Virginia good-night, 'Peggy has insisted we take her car up to Bellagio.'

'Oh, you didn't say yes, did you, Paddy? How are we going to get it back?'

'It will get itself back. It comes with a driver.'

I could tell that my good wife was having to struggle with her English conscience. On the one hand, this was obviously going to be an enormous convenience. And, on the other, it involved putting ourselves in somebody's debt. We had been able to accept Bernadetto's generosity only because he was an old friend and he insisted. But we barely knew Mrs Aschenheim – Peggy – and Jinny had not been present to confirm the vigour with which she had pressed her offer. This delicate moral crisis kept Jinny quiet for a good half-minute. Then she asked: 'Are you sure she meant it?' I knew at once that Bruno was going to be our chauffeur. I had merely to go through the formalities.

'She was relentless in her insistence. I did my best to get her to retract. I only gave up when it became quite clear that she would have been very upset if we had declined.'

'Well, in that case, we must accept. One mustn't be ungrateful, must one?'

'Indeed.' I paused. 'It was in the same spirit that I accepted her invitation to a farewell dinner tomorrow night,' I hurried on. 'We are also to celebrate Mr Bouncer's decision to give his paintings to Peggy's museum.'

'It's not Peggy's museum, it's the Metropolitan Museum of Art in New York.'

'So, we have a busy day ahead.'

'I wouldn't call a day filled with incident after seven in the evening all that busy, darling.'

'I have to telephone Montenari in the morning. We still haven't been to your Carpaccios. And then we must go and see the Jewish ghetto.'

'Does that mean you've had some more ideas about that poor boy's murder?'

'Not really. I'd just like to have a clear picture of where it happened. You never know, we might see something helpful.'

Virginia sighed deeply. She did not believe I had no new ideas. And, as usual, she was right.

15

By the time I woke up, Jinny had flown the nest. When I got downstairs to breakfast, Bernadetto informed me that she had gone off for a walk and had promised to be back by ten o'clock so that we could visit the paintings of Carpaccio.

Jamie perked up at the mention of this particular painter. 'It's a rather wonderful place, if you haven't been there, Patrick. I go there fairly often.' Jamie's artistic side was a complete revelation to me. 'They're open from about ten until lunch.'

'Jinny has a German copy of one of them in her study at home – it was given to her by one of the dons at Somerville,' I put in. 'It's a picture of a chap in his study and there's a tiny dog sitting there, which apparently is a sign that it's St Jerome.'

'A lovely painting. Carpaccio', Jamie went on, 'is really one of the first Venetian masters of perspective: all his buildings are frightfully good. Didn't you say you liked Giovanni Bellini?'

I refrained from repeating the stuff that had gone down so well with Jinny the day before, responding only with an enthusiastic nod. I wasn't sure Jamie would be as appreciative.

'Well, I think Carpaccio was trained by his brother, Gentile. And you can see signs of Giovanni's influence as well. You should like them.'

'When did these chaps live?'

'Turn of the sixteenth century. The stuff at the Scuola you're going to was done in the first decade of the century for the Dalmatians.' (I'm a good enough Catholic to know that he was referring to a religious order not a variety of spotted dog.) 'Actually, there's a rather good series of paintings of St George, too. The dragon's frightfully convincing. Enough to warm the heart of any red-blooded Englishman.' Jamie laughed. 'Didn't the Curia decide that he was mythical, not so long ago?'

Jamie has never taken our religion very seriously – I myself am inclined to blame this on his having been sent to Eton rather than Ampleforth – and he has always had a tendency to mock those of us in the family who have stayed with Rome. Over the years, I've found that in this mood the best thing to do is not to take him on. I nodded, in the sort of way my father used to nod in the Commons when he wasn't listening to the socialists, and mentioned to Bernadetto that I had some news for Signor Montenari.

'Really?' He looked up from buttering his toast.

'Yes. I wonder when he'll get to the station.'

'Couldn't say. But you might want to telephone about now' – it was a little after half-past nine – 'and tell them you'd like him to call.'

'Good idea.' I paused. My own experience in telephoning Italians had been rather limited and I was not convinced that I could communicate even this simple message. 'I wonder if you could do that for me?'

'Of course. What shall I say your news is about?'

I had slept well enough that the old grey matter had done a fair amount of reorganizing of last night's doings. I found, as I spoke, that the affair of the campanile had shaped itself up into rather a good anecdote. The first part of the story revolved around my obtuseness about the indecent proposal of the young man in the sailor suit. The creeping round the bell tower, the hand on the shoulder and my own rather nannyish rebuke – 'I say, you really shouldn't creep up on a chap like that' – were received by both members of my audience in a hushed and appreciative silence. But then Jamie raised a quizzical eyebrow when I referred to my interlocutor as a 'young sailor'.

'I don't think he will have known too much about the naval sciences,' my cousin pronounced. The tone and the smile were roguish.

'Someone you know, perhaps?' Bernadetto enquired evenly.

This little exchange rather put me off my stroke, as it forced me to revise once more my notions about, shall we say, the degree of intimacy of my cousin's, shall we say, relationship with our host. Still, a good anecdote is not to be wasted, and I think I recovered pretty well and pulled off a fairly good account of the second stage, in which the two young men mistook my motives in asking after the stalker.

'If he *is* the chap that followed you and Jinny, it seems awfully strange that he's established himself as a familiar figure in the square after only a few days,' Jamie said.

I had had the same thought myself. 'Exactly. It suggests, does it not, that, though he's English, he's actually based here and was dispatched to join the train.'

'But if he was following you and Jinny, whoever sent him would have had to have known you were coming.'

'My dear Jamie, I can see you have the makings of a very fine sleuth.'

'How many people would have known which train you were taking?' Bernadetto said, as much to himself, it seemed, as to the rest of us. Since I had been planning to ask him this very question, I was glad to have been anticipated. 'At this end, it would have been everybody here at the Longhi, and all the Aschenheim ménage. The Bouncers were told you were coming last week. And any of us might have mentioned it in passing to somebody. It's a pretty large group, but not too enormous to stop Signor Montenari interviewing them all.' He looked at both of us. 'Anyone else you can think of?'

'I fear that a fair number of the good folk of Banbury will have been informed by Sheila Nipper at Thomas Cook's. And lord knows who Jinny might have told.' The list Jinny and I had made before dinner on Sunday night contained quite a few others. People I had talked to about Milo's business, for example. A couple of lawyers; some of the senior staff of Hawksworth Holdings Ltd.

But given Bernadetto's relationship to Melissa, anything I said to him would be likely to be passed on to her, and would likely be received with alarm: if someone was after me, it would not necessarily be good news for Alexander. I did not want to worry Melissa with any of this, especially since I knew how extensive were the arrangements that Milo had made for Alexander's security.

Jamie had been looking pensive while I spoke. When I finished he said: 'Well, I would be the last one to encourage the *polizia* to go charging off after everyone in the circle that gathers under the campanile. The *carabinieri* can be very tiresome about that sort of thing. But a couple of the boys who work here are not averse to . . .' He paused and looked first at me and then at Bernadetto. I am glad to say that he saw that it was not necessary to be more explicit. 'And if your – what is it you call him? – your stalker had met up with them and they had been talkative . . . well, it might have slipped out.'

This was not, I confess, a possibility that had occurred to me. I took my notepad out of my pocket and jotted down this new line of enquiry to offer to Montenari.

At this point Jinny arrived, bearing a bouquet of flowers, which she presented to Bernadetto. 'I found them just over the Rialto bridge in a wonderful flower stall. I couldn't resist.' She waved gaily at Jamie and came round and kissed me on the cheek. 'Are we ready to go off to the Scuola di San Giorgio degli Schiavoni?'

These names just roll off her tongue. Since it had taken me a good while to get to the point where I could say 'Basilica di San Marco' with a plausible lilt, I continued to find my wife's grasp of Italian impressive.

'I do love the way you say that.'

'Don't be silly, Paddy. That's like telling an Italian you love the way he says "the Palace of Westminster".'

'Don't you want to have a go at Signor Montenari before you set off?' Jamie asked.

'Good idea. I'll do that right away,' Bernadetto said. 'But why don't you two go off? I'll tell him you'll be back here for lunch.'

'We might as well at least wait and see if he's there.' I hoped I didn't seem too insistent. But the last time Bernadetto had urged me not to hurry about passing on some information to Mr Montenari, the result had been the embarrassment about the timing of the theft of the papers from my briefcase. Bernadetto shrugged in that Italian way – as if to say 'I'm quite happy to conform to your demented whims' – and set off for the library.

Two minutes later he was back. 'Your man will be here at about one this afternoon. I passed on the general gist and they seemed to be writing it down for him.'

It was time, once more, to take the pilgrim's path with my good lady in search of culture: and this time, after my tutorial from Jamie, I felt equipped to look for occasions to feign a grasp of the fine arts.

The route to the Scuola di San Giorgio degli Schiavoni involved retracing the path I had taken early that morning from the Danieli to the Palazzo Longhi. In the bright sunlight of a busy day, the Piazza San Marco looked very different. The vast square, which had been largely deserted save for a few scattered young people and the small crowd at the base of the bell tower, was now filled with tourists making their way to the cathedral and the Palace of the Doges. A score of languages – and a good many accents of English – assailed our ears as we made our way through the piazza to the Riva degli Schiavoni. A sturdy and peremptory German woman of indeterminate age, with a mop of blonde hair rather carelessly coiffed, was busy organizing a group of teenagers in jeans and T-shirts emblazoned with the word *'München'* and the phrase *'Christus lebt'*.

'Bavarian Catholics,' I opined to Virginia, as *sotto voce* as was appropriate in the hustle and bustle of the square. 'Overtaken by a fit of evangelicalism four hundred and fifty years after Luther.'

'Rühig, Konrad. Wir warten noch ein paar Minuten nur,' Brünnhilde said sternly, grabbing hold of the arm of a rather-too-lively boy, who was busy chasing after pigeons.

'Bloody Krauts,' an English voice murmured to my right. I turned to see a man of my own age, with a handkerchief-sized Union Jack, knotted at its corners, atop his pate, in the company of a much younger woman in a cotton frock. They were both rather reddened by the sun, and they did not seem particularly pleased to be there. Was I more embarrassed by my co-religionists or my fellow countrymen? I asked myself uncharitably as I raised an eyebrow or two in Virginia's direction.

'You realize, don't you darling, that you're going to have to confess the thoughts you're having at this very moment when you next visit Monsignor Galsworthy?' Virginia laughed. 'Venial sins, perhaps. "Embarrassment at the presence of an Englishman letting down the side." '

'You're right. It's absurd to care about such things. Especially with people of all the nations of the world misbehaving all about one.'

Two or three minutes later we passed the Danieli. The young man in the hotel's livery standing at the door looked vaguely familiar and, thinking he might be the chap who had helped me explain things to Paulo, I waved at him and cried out, *'Buon giorno.'* He looked not so much startled as slightly discomfited by this gesture of *bonhomie*. 'Odd,' I muttered to Jinny, who was now eyeing me somewhat quizzically, 'I thought I recognized him from last night.'

'I don't suppose that the gentlemen of the campanile are in the habit of acknowledging each other in the full glare of day.'

'At the Danieli,' I explained crossly. 'Of course, I shouldn't wave cheerily if I thought he was . . .' It was at this moment that the ageing grey matter had one of its occasional epiphanies. 'Do you know, my darling,' I said to my good lady, 'you are absolutely right.' It was, I realized, one of the two young men who had warned me of the stalker's preference for the young. 'Come on, my love.' I took Virginia firmly by the arm and strode over to the door of the Danieli. My acquaintance of the previous night had utterly disappeared.

I walked up to the nearest member of the Danieli's fine staff and addressed him: 'There was a chap in your uniform standing outside the door just now. Do you happen to know where he's gone?'

The fellow looked absolutely blank. Since every one of the members of staff I had talked to the night before had had a pretty good mastery of the language of Wordsworth and Milton, this came as a bit of a surprise. 'Jinny, would you mind asking him in his own tongue?'

My wife obliged. He uttered some words in response. She passed on their general gist to me. 'He doesn't know what you are talking about.' He shrugged at me and smiled, as if to confirm Virginia's words.

'Ah well,' I spoke clearly to him, smiling and shrugging myself, 'I shall just have to take the matter up at lunchtime with the police.'

The Scuola to which we had made our way was not especially brightly lit. Not a great deal of light came in through the windows, and there was a fair number of people crowding the space. The paintings, which told of major episodes in the lives of St Jerome, St George and St Tryphon – who was, I admit, a new one on me – were crowded next to each other on the walls. They were finely detailed, and each character's clothes, each building, even St Jerome's books, were brightly and accurately painted. 'Rather like good illustrations,' I whispered to Virginia. As the words came out of my mouth, I realized that this might well be a *faux pas*. I know from visits to Duke Street to buy paintings with the art expert of our family that people in the smart art world are rather inclined to chuck the word 'illustrative' about as a sort of malediction. But for some reason, in this context, Virginia only nodded her head.

'That's what they are, really. They're telling the lives of the saints. Quite brilliant illustrations.'

In some of the more crowded scenes one could see figures in the background with the same sort of colouring as the Bellini madonnas. I was working up to formulate this *aperçu* – which I will admit at once might not have struck me without Jamie's fairly strong hint over the breakfast table – when I felt a firm tug on my right sleeve. Since I had just seen Virginia take my left arm, in order to move us on to the next painting, this was somewhat unexpected. I wondered, in a brief moment of panic, if this was one of those distractions that precede the attentions of a pickpocket, and wrenched my right arm sharply away to check on the security of my wallet. Reassured by the discovery that it was still in place, I turned to see who might have been clutching at me. It was the young man I had just seen outside the Danieli.

'Escuse me, Signor. I 'elp you. You don' call police. Yes?'

I turned to Virginia. 'I think we had better conduct this conversation outside.'

We took him to a little café not far from the Scuola and sat down with him. 'Coffee?' I asked.

'Si. Grazie.'

We ordered a couple of cappuccinos and he had an espresso.

'I'm sorry to trouble you,' I began.

Jinny interrupted. *'Parla inglese?'* He nodded. 'If you don't understand anything my husband says, just say so and I'll try to translate it into Italian.' He nodded again. 'By the way, I'm Lady Scott. This is my husband, Sir Patrick Scott.'

'Giovanni Branco.' He looked at us nervously, his eyes growing larger by the minute. He was plainly surprised by the notion that a fellow should come prowling about in the middle of the night at the campanile and then entertain one with his wife for espresso the next morning. I couldn't say I blamed him.

'I'm sorry, as I say, to trouble you. But I wondered if you knew where to find the Englishman who was with you last night in the piazza. He travelled down from London with us on the train and left something on a seat that we'd like to return to him.' It seemed best to keep our new friend in the dark about our real interest in the stalker. (Somehow, I found it easier to lie to someone with a loose grasp of English: it occurred to me that it was perhaps because one was less likely to be caught out. Another problem to address to Monsignor Galsworthy.) 'I was so pleased to see him when I walked by last night. And then, unfortunately, he rushed off.'

'You're talking much too fast, Paddy.' Lady Scott offered Mr Branco a paraphrase of my remarks in Italian. Immediately, I could tell that he was as impressed by Jinny's command of his language as I am. And then, as he took on board that my interest in the Englishman of the campanile was purportedly benevolent, relief flooded his features. The stiff and formal official smile with which he had first approached me was replaced with an expression of genuine good humour. Virginia and Giovanni gabbled at each other for a while and I sipped my cappuccino and admired the passing show. At some point, I felt sure, one or other of them would explain.

Eventually the mutual admiration society meeting drew to a close, and Jinny gave Signor Branco a scrap of paper from her capacious handbag on which to write. She looked up at me. 'Name and address. Of the stalker.' When Mr Branco finished she picked up the paper, with a gracious *'Grazie,'* and read aloud what he had written. 'James Pritchard. Pensione Scarpia.' She held his gaze once she had finished as if seeking to confirm that she had read his handwriting aright. The young man nodded vigorously. 'I've told him we'll keep his name from the police when we go to them with Mr Pritchard's package.'

'What . . .' I realized a moment too late that this was an elaboration of my own little untruth and stopped before I gave the game away. 'Thank you so much. I'm sure he'll be very grateful.'

We paid for the coffee and said our farewells. As we walked away, I asked Virginia if Mr Branco had volunteered how he knew the name and address of the man we were seeking.

'I think, Paddy dear, that we can assume that Giovanni Branco was young enough to appeal to Mr Pritchard, and Mr Pritchard was rich enough to appeal to Mr Branco.'

'I rather doubt that the Danieli would employ someone who had a second career as a call-boy.'

'I was merely speculating. But if I'm right, I rather doubt that the Danieli knows about Giovanni's other string.'

Now we had some real news for Mr Montenari, I was keen to get back to the Palazzo Longhi and talk to him. If we could find this Mr Pritchard we might well be on the way to sorting out the mystery of the briefcases – either poor Gary Mitchell's or mine. 'If we're really lucky,' I said to Virginia as we stepped into a water taxi near the Danieli, 'Mr Pritchard will tell us what has happened to Milo's papers *and* help Montenari find his murderer.'

16

Signor Montenari arrived at the *palazzo* at almost exactly half-past twelve. This struck me as faintly unusual, since Italians are not known for arriving on time, let alone for showing up early at a rendezvous. Once more he was stylishly apparelled. Today he was dressed in a white linen suit and a very relaxed pink shirt, open at the neck, allowing the dark curly hair on his chest to peek out in the Mediterranean manner. He kowtowed slightly when Virginia and I entered the library, where Giorgio had left him waiting, and came over and swept up my wife's hand to receive a gentle bussing. 'Signora,' he said quietly, his voice falling to a rough bass. Not, I thought, the sort of chap one would meet beneath the campanile on a midnight stroll.

Jinny and I settled down on the sofa – its gold-painted scrolls of wood and elegant red silken upholstery almost radiant in the sunlight – facing the great stone fireplace, with its carved lions and a gryphon rampant. Mr Montenari settled on the armchair, next to us, and took out his notebook.

'Good. I am ready, Sir Patrick. What have you got for me?'

It took me only a few moments to tell him where and when I thought I had seen my stalker. (I decided that the importunate sailor was not essential to the police investigation.)

'So,' Mr Montenari summarized, 'you saw a young man who resembled your wife's description of the person who followed you the other evening.'

'That's right. Well, as you know, he was also on the train. And so, of course, as you suggested, he was probably the fellow who took the briefcase . . . thinking it was mine.'

'Exactly.'

'Well, this morning we found his name and address.'

'Astonishing.'

'Yes. I happened to bump into one of the other young men who had been taking the night air in the piazza, and he was able to provide us with a name and a *pensione*.'

'This name would not happen to be James Pritchard? Of the Pensione Scarpia?'

I was unable to conceal my surprise. 'Astonishing, indeed.' I chuckled. 'Of course, it's Mr Pritchard. Your people certainly know their business.'

Mr Montenari tipped his head slightly in acknowledgement of my compliment. Jinny and I both looked at him expectantly and when he said nothing, my wife asked: 'Well? What did he say?'

'We only received his name ourselves a little over half an hour ago. The boys are bringing him in. I was wondering, Sir Patrick, if you would care to join me for the preliminary interrogation?'

'I should be honoured,' I said. 'Honoured.'

Virginia coughed somewhat artificially and smiled at the good magistrate. 'And I shall, of course, need you to join us, Lady Scott, since you saw him on the train and again the other night. I shall need you to identify him for us.'

'Very good. We'll just need to tell our host that we shall be missing lunch.'

'That won't be necessary. It will take some time for the paperwork to be done for the arrest. And then I find it is always better to leave a suspect alone for a period to reflect on his sins . . . or, at the moment, in this case, let us say his alleged sins. Perhaps you would join us at the police station at about four.' He smiled. 'I shall, of course, have tea waiting for you.'

We rose and walked together to the library door. As we entered the hall, Giorgio announced that lunch was ready in the dining-room.

'I wonder if I might ask you a question, Signor Montenari?' I said, as we reached the entrance of the *palazzo*.

'Of course, Sir Patrick.' He looked at me thoughtfully, obviously trying to decide if he knew what I was going to ask.

'Would you mind telling me where you found the body of Gary Mitchell?'

'You have only to read the newspapers, Sir Patrick. He was in the Rio della Misericordia.'

'Yes, I know. But where exactly? I looked at one of Bernadetto's maps of the city this morning: the Rio della Misericordia runs a long way.'

'It was at the north-western end, near the old ghetto.'

'Behind the Jewish museum?'

'Exactly, Sir Patrick. You must have studied the map very carefully.' He bowed again to Virginia and shook my hand. 'There isn't something more you would like to tell me?'

'Not really. I just thought I would go and have a look at the spot before we talked to Mr Pritchard. Doesn't do to talk to a suspect without examining the scene of the crime.'

Montenari shook his head and smiled the slightest of smiles. 'For an amateur sleuth, Sir Patrick, you are a real professional.'

It was my turn to make a modest and appreciative obeisance.

We had only the briefest of siestas and then we set off on the number 1 vaporetto up the Grand Canal towards the railway station. The boat was not especially crowded and we were able to find seats for the ride. There are scores of grand buildings on every side: Renaissance masterpieces, Gothic fantasies, endless ornamentation. Even the most modest houses – the ordinary dwellings one can see up the rios that split off to right and to left – are covered in a stucco painted with a palette of jewel-like colours. The multiple panes of glass of the loggias that hang precariously over the canal, overlooking the human comedy of Venice, cast bright reflections in the afternoon sun, scattering the light that reached them from the blue brightness of the Venetian sky on to the turbid waves of the canal. As we approached the Ca' d'Oro, with the elegant Gothic tracery of its façade, Virginia squeezed my arm: 'Isn't it gorgeous? Look at the stonework. It's so sad to be passing all this beauty on the way to the scene of a horrible murder.'

'We shall have to come back one day and stay in a quiet little *pension* by ourselves: and then you can show me all these marvellous buildings properly.'

Jinny laughed. 'It's *pensione*, my love. *Pension* is French.'

'I never could keep track of my romance languages.'

'Perhaps we should come for our fiftieth anniversary . . . a jubilee tour of the Serenissima.'

'I'm not sure I want to wait that long.'

Once we reached the station, we walked back along the crowded streets of the Lista de Spagna, filled with tourist knick-knacks. It was now a little after two o'clock. (Venice practically invented tourism, of course, and so they know that many of their northern visitors are silly enough to forget the siesta.) We followed the map in the Blue Guide and made our way over the Cannaregio canal, slipping through a small alleyway on its northern side into the Jewish quarter. In the square of the Ghetto Vecchio there were Jewish shops, with messages in the window in Hebrew, Italian and English. One of these announced: 'Messiah is coming.'

'Now there's a note that might be misunderstood in a Catholic city,' Jinny observed. 'It ought to say: "Messiah is coming . . . for the first time." '

There was something sombre about the atmosphere of the ghetto. 'I wonder if it's only because we know what has happened to the Jews in our own time,' Jinny said when I mumbled something to that effect. 'Or perhaps it's just because we're thinking of poor Gary Mitchell.'

We walked past the Jewish museum and through an archway that led out of the quarter. And there, muddy and still, was the Rio della Misericordia. This is the Venice of the ordinary Venetians: a quiet canal, with no tourist sights and no tourists, the only sign of life an occasional cat basking in the sunlight. We crossed the canal and turned left, walking towards the other entrance to the ghetto.

'Well, according to Bernadetto, there's not much activity in the ghetto on a Saturday. And there are plenty of spots out of view where you could stab a chap and let him fall into the canal. Look up there,' I said to Virginia, pointing to the crumbling plaster walls that rose above us, facing the ghetto. 'The shutters on all those windows are closed.' I picked up a brick and dropped it into the murky water. There was a loud plop. But there was not a peep from any of the tenements. 'All in all, I'd say this was a pretty good spot for a murder.'

17

James Alexander Pritchard's long brown hair was tied behind his head in a pigtail. His face was much as Jinny's drawing had shown it: broad, crudely handsome, with the lips of a voluptuary. He couldn't have been more than about thirty-five or six. Both of us had noticed that he was stockily built, but we had not seen him close enough to notice how well muscled he was. He was dressed today in a T-shirt so exiguous that one could not ignore the ample diameter of his upper arms, or the marmoreal firmness of his abdomen. Not a chap you would want to tangle with, really.

Virginia and I looked at him through the small observation hole in the door of the room in the police station where he was being held. He was seated on a wooden chair, his arms folded on his chest, leaning backwards and humming tunelessly. He did not look like a man reflecting on his sins.

Mr Montenari took us back into his office and offered the tea he had promised. He also had some almond macaroons; light enough, I felt, to count for almost nothing in the great calorific scale in the sky.

'So, Lady Scott, you are sure that's the man?'

'Positive. He was on the train and he followed us home the other night. No doubt about it.'

'I haven't talked to him yet but, as you can see, he doesn't look very troubled. He has a police record in your country: petty thievery to support a heroin addiction. But he's pretty healthy now, so he must have kicked the habit. His family is pretty well off, it seems.'

'Perhaps he's a remittance man: paid off by his family on condition he stays out of the country,' Jinny said.

Montenari nodded. 'Perhaps. The people at the Pensione Scarpia say he's had a room there for six months. He has a few young friends: Venetian working-class boys. Never causes any trouble: they were very surprised when the police arrived to arrest him.'

'Any sign of any papers in his rooms?'

'They found about eight hundred English pounds, some Australian dollars and a receipt for the train ride on the Orient Express . . . and a kit for picking locks. But no briefcase and no papers.'

'May I look at his police record?'

Montenari shrugged. 'Just as long as you don't tell Scotland Yard.' Only a slight twinkle in his eyes attested that this was a joke.

I scanned the piece of paper he handed me. 'Educated at a decent enough school; went to York University for a year or so.' I glanced at Virginia. 'Not much here.'

'Well, let's go and see what the gentleman has to say for himself.'

If Pritchard was surprised to see us, he certainly concealed his feelings pretty well.

'Good afternoon, Mr Pritchard. I am Montenari. I am a magistrate here in Venice. These two gentlemen are policemen who will record our conversation. And I believe you know my two English friends, the Scotts?'

'Never seen 'em before in my life.' He affected one of those spurious 'working-class' accents that seem these days to indicate a public school education.

'You travelled down from London on the train with them last week.'

'There was a lot of people on that train. I can't say I remember most of them.'

'May I ask what you were doing in London?'

'Visiting friends.'

'For twenty-four hours?'

'Short visit.' He smiled cheekily at Montenari. Montenari smiled back.

'Mr Pritchard, let me be frank with you. Ordinarily, I wouldn't much mind a small lie of this sort. But I am investigating a murder. And I have reason to believe that you had something to do with it. The more you lie to me, the more convinced I shall become that you have something to do with the murder. If, therefore, you had nothing to do with this murder, you would be well advised to start telling me the truth.'

James Pritchard's manner changed somewhat abruptly when Signor Montenari first uttered the word murder. He brought his chair down on to all four legs and uncrossed his arms. Suddenly he was all ears. 'I've got nothing to do with any murder. Nothing at all. I don't know what you're talking about.'

'Very well, then perhaps you would like to rethink your answer to my earlier question. Do you recognize these two people?'

'What have they got to do with the murder?'

'Mr Pritchard, I am asking the questions. Do you recognize them?'

'Maybe.'

Montenari raised his eyebrows expectantly but that was all the young man was going to say. 'Let me remind you, Mr Pritchard, that you are in serious trouble and I do not have unlimited patience.'

'All right, I did see them on the train.' The young man smiled.

'There. That wasn't too hard, was it?' Montenari's mild sarcasm froze the smile off Pritchard's face.

'What's that got to do with any murder?'

'Nothing. At least, not yet. Where else have you seen them?'

'I saw Sir Patrick last night in the square.'

'And his wife?'

'Just on the train.'

'I wonder, Signor Montenari, if I might say a few words to my compatriot.' This was the moment, I thought, for me to play the "good cop" to Montenari's "bad cop".'

Montenari sighed. 'Of course, be my guest.'

'Mr Pritchard, let me help you with what *I* know. Somebody asked you to follow my wife and me from London and to steal my briefcase on the way. This you did. Then the same person asked you to follow us again while we were here.'

Pritchard said nothing.

Montenari tapped the desk lightly with his pen. 'Is that so?' The magistrate waited for perhaps half a minute and then repeated his question. 'Is that so? Mr Pritchard.' He had not raised his voice, but there was more than a hint of menace in it.

'All right, all right. Yes.'

'Why were you asked to follow them again?' Montenari spoke coolly, as if barely interested.

'I don't know.'

'Speculate for me,' he said, doodling ostentatiously in his notebook.

'I *don't* know.'

'Could it be because you are incompetent: because you took the wrong briefcase the first time?'

Once more, Mr Pritchard seemed caught off guard. 'Could be.'

'Who was the owner of the briefcase you stole?'

'It had a monogram on it: G. M. But I didn't look into it. I just passed it along.'

'To whom?'

'A man by the campanile, late at night, the night we got in from London on the train.'

'Who was this man?'

'I don't know.' He shrugged.

'Who asked you to steal the briefcase?'

'I don't know that either.' He looked piteously at Virginia, expecting, I suppose, more sympathy from the feminine than from the masculine principle.

This was not a successful tactic. He was rewarded by my good wife with a stern: 'Mr Pritchard, you will have to do better than that.'

He sighed and shook his head. 'I know it sounds stupid, but I really don't know.' This was now addressed to the magistrate. 'It was all done by notes, you see. And the guy in the square had his face covered with one of those carnival masks. He was dressed like a sailor.'

'Weren't you curious?'

'He told me not to follow him. He sounded as though he meant it.'

'You're a strong fellow.'

'Muscle's no match for a knife.'

'Did you see a knife?' Montenari asked. He did not sound as though he would have believed an affirmative answer.

'No. But . . . I don't know, he just seemed like someone not to fool around with.'

'Which way did he go?' I asked.

'Towards the Riva degli Schiavoni.'

'And you can't think of any way of identifying him?' Montenari was sounding bored again.

'He was Italian. No obvious accent. Deep voice. Probably in his twenties.'

'Any tattoos?' Virginia and I kept mum as Montenari continued his interrogation.

'It was dark . . . and, anyway, his arms were covered. I said he was wearing a sailor's uniform.'

'How did he identify himself?'

'The note said he'd say, "Hallo sailor," like a password. And I was to reply, "Land ahoy." '

'Ah yes, the note. Who wrote the note?'

'Look, I don't have any idea.' I think we all conveyed by our expressions that we found this rather hard to believe.

'Where is it?'

'I was told to destroy it.' This remark was received by all of us with more frankly sceptical looks. James Pritchard raised his hands and buried his head in them. 'Oh shit.'

'Perhaps, you would like to be left alone for a while to recollect?'
'I promise you. I never saw anyone.'
'Then how did you get the job?'

James Pritchard's story was simple enough. The question, of course, was whether it was true.

He had, he said, been contacted by a letter left at his hotel. The unsigned note had been written in capital letters. 'I can't remember the exact wording,' he told us, his voice almost devoid of expression, 'but basically it said: "Here's five hundred pounds. Go to London and come back on the Orient Express next Thursday. Find Sir Patrick Scott's cabin and steal his briefcase during dinner. You'll be contacted when you get back. If you've got the briefcase, you'll get another thousand quid." Then it said: "Destroy this note now." So I did.'

When he got back from London, Pritchard went back to his *pensione* with the briefcase and there was another note waiting. 'It said: "Be at the campanile at midnight. Give the briefcase to the man who gives you the password." Then it gave the passwords I told you. And at the end it just said: "He'll give you another thousand pounds. Destroy this note now." I just did what I was told and I got my money.' He sighed loudly. 'So you see, I didn't have anything to do with the murder business.'

'If you didn't have anything to do with the murder, then there's no reason to lie about whether you looked into the briefcase,' I told him. Montenari had let that one pass earlier, but it was crucial to know everything we could about the briefcase. And it was inconceivable that a petty crook like Pritchard would have been able to resist the temptation to see what in the briefcase made it worth fifteen hundred pounds to somebody.

Of course, so far as we knew, Mitchell's death might have been a simple robbery, but I didn't think so. And if it was a premeditated murder then the briefcase might give us the key to the motive. Pritchard took his time responding to my enquiry. 'Come on, old chap, where else would you have got those Australian dollars? What else did you see?'

'There was all these papers about a chap named Gerald Miller. Had to do with a lot of money he would get if he could prove he was the son of this English lord.'

'Was there anything else?'

'Some photos, taken in one of those booths they have at railway stations.'

'Did you recognize the people in them?'

'There was only one person: a man. His picture was in the paper on Sunday. It was the man that was mugged up by the ghetto.'

'That wasn't Gerald Miller,' Montenari said. 'That was a man named Gary Mitchell.' And he wasn't mugged, either, I thought.

'I know. I saw that in the paper. But whoever he was, his picture was in the briefcase along with all these papers about Gerald Miller. It didn't make any sense. I thought you must have got his name wrong, actually. Of course, once I recognized him, I thought maybe the briefcase business had something to do with his murder. That was the only reason I lied about opening it. But I promise you, I didn't have anything to do with what happened to him later.'

Pritchard had certainly solved one mystery for us. But until we knew who had asked him to get the briefcase, we would still be a long way from understanding Gary Mitchell's murder. As I thought about this, I remembered something else that we needed to ask him: 'Why were you following us the other evening?'

'When I saw the picture in the paper, I began to wonder whether what I had done had anything to do with the murder. I followed you because I wanted to find out more about you, to see if I could work out what was going on. When you got back home I was hanging around outside for a while. Giorgio, who works at the *palazzo* where you're staying, came out a little later. He's a friend, someone I know. I asked him what he was doing. He said he was off to tell the cops that you had been followed home. That scared me off. So I gave up.'

'Didn't he tell you that I had drawn a picture of you?'

'Oh, that's how you found me. I was wondering. No. Giorgio was carrying an envelope, but I didn't ask him what was in it and he didn't mention it.'

'If he'd looked at the picture, he'd have known it was you. If we hadn't put Jinny's drawing in an envelope, we'd have found you a good deal earlier.'

'So you never entered the *palazzo*?' Montenari asked.

'Course not. Why would I do that?'

'To get Sir Patrick's briefcase . . . or at least its contents.'

'What are you talking about?' Unless young Mr Pritchard was a brilliant performer, there was no doubt he knew nothing about the theft from our room the night before.

I asked Signor Montenari if we could have a bit of a conference out of Pritchard's hearing before we went on.

'I'm sure you know your business, old man, but it seems to me it might be worth recapping where we are.'

'By all means, Sir Patrick.'

'First of all, I believed him just now when he said he didn't know about last night's theft. So we're still no further forward on that one. But we do now know what happened to poor Mr Mitchell.' I paused for a moment to collect my thoughts and looked out of Mr Montenari's window over the roofs of the city. It was a lovely sunny day, with a light breeze flitting over the red-tiled roofs. 'Gary Mitchell, as we know, was Gerald Miller's lawyer. Whoever put this Pritchard on to me was plainly interested in Lord Hawksworth's estate. From what Pritchard says, it's clear enough that Gerald Miller is – or thinks he is – Lord Hawksworth's illegitimate eldest son. If that's so, then when they happened on Gary Mitchell's briefcase, marked with his initials G. M., and found all this stuff about Mr Miller in it, they may have assumed, as Pritchard did, that the chap in the photograph was not Mitchell, but Miller.'

'So now,' Jinny added, 'we have a motive for the killing: it may have been done to keep Gerald Miller from claiming his father's fortune.'

'Who would receive Mr Miller's portion, if he dies?'

'The present Lord Hawksworth.'

'I think I should ask the British police to talk with this Lord Hawksworth,' Montenari said. He had been scribbling notes vigorously as we spoke. Since neither Virginia nor I said anything for a moment – we were both, naturally, thinking how unlikely it was that Alex, who could barely count to a dozen, should have organized a murder in Venice by remote control – he looked up at us expectantly. 'You look sceptical,' he said.

'The present Lord Hawksworth is a very nice young man with an IQ that doesn't much exceed his collar size,' I began.

Jinny cut me off. 'My husband is exaggerating wildly, as usual, Mr Montenari. Alex isn't very bright, it's true; but his IQ's certainly more than sixteen and a half. It's just that he really isn't at all ambitious or competitive. Actually, he'd probably be rather delighted to find he had a brother.'

'Exactly. My wife is quite right. But there is another possibility. Remember we told you that Gerald Miller joked with us about being on his way to meet a beautiful woman who held the key to his destiny?'

Montenari nodded.

'Well, the obvious candidate is Lord Hawksworth's widow, Melissa, Lady Hawksworth,' I went on.

'And she has a motive, too: to protect the interest of her son.' The Italian magistrate was catching on fast.

'She has a perfect alibi. She was at Peggy Aschenheim's with a doctor binding her ankle when the murder was done,' Virginia reminded us.

'If she could find someone to steal the briefcase, couldn't she find someone to do the murder?' I was thinking out loud, really. Finding a petty thief in a foreign country is an achievement; but finding a professional assassin would require real genius. 'If you were trying to find an assassin, Mr Montenari, in the city of Venice, whom would you ask?'

'I hesitate to confirm your English stereotypes of my country, but the answer is, of course, the Mafia.'

It will not surprise you that a moment later my wife and I whispered in unison: 'Bernadetto di Montebello.'

I began to explain to Montenari what Jamie had told us about Bernadetto's father, but he stopped me almost immediately. 'The career of Signor Armando di Montebello is familiar to me.'

'Well, of course, it would be,' Jinny said, smiling ruefully.

'Allow me to observe, too, that you were not quite correct to say we were no further forward with the matter of your stolen papers. If Pritchard was hired by Signor di Montebello, then the theft from your briefcase would have been a very easy inside job.'

If this theory was right, our Mr Pritchard had been hired by Melissa, with Bernadetto's assistance. That would also mean it probably wasn't just a coincidence that the Australians came down on the same train as we did. Bernadetto, and therefore Melissa, knew what train we were travelling on; they had also probably instructed Gerald Miller when and how to come to Venice to meet Melissa, the woman who held the key to his destiny.

If Pritchard knew anything at all about them, that would confirm the hypothesis. Even if he didn't, he must know *something* that would help lead us to them. Montenari and I agreed on a few questions we wanted to ask him and we returned to the room where he was waiting.

'What are you going to do with me?' His face was drawn with worry. 'I didn't know they meant any harm.'

'We're going to have to hold you a little longer,' Montenari said. 'You may have become involved in a Mafia hit. If they know we have interrogated you, you will not be safe alone here in Venice.' The magistrate was not going to try and mollify our stalker's anxieties.

'Oh shit!' He looked at us mournfully.

'We need to ask you just a few more questions,' Montenari said, pointing towards me with a jerk of his head. He took a packet of cigarettes from his pocket and gave one to the young man, who mumbled his thanks and accepted a light from the magistrate's lighter.

'We need to try and work out who might have sent you the notes you spoke of,' I explained. 'Were you told anything about the Australians on the train? Were you to follow them or take something of theirs?'

The question clearly surprised him; but he thought about it for a bit. 'No,' he said finally. 'There was nothing in the notes about them.'

It occurred to me suddenly that Melissa might have thought that the presence of Gerald Miller on the train would provide a natural suspect for the theft of my briefcase. I jotted down a note in the silence that followed Pritchard's response. Something to discuss with the others later. 'Let's try another tack,' I said. 'Do you know who, in Venice, would have known of your past brushes with the law?'

'God, I don't know.'

'Have you mentioned it to anyone?'

'Maybe.'

'Who?'

James Pritchard looked uneasily about him.

'Didn't you ask yourself that question when you got the note?'

'Yes. I thought maybe one of my friends might have mentioned me to someone who needed a job doing.'

'What friends?' Montenari asked.

The same uncomfortable look descended once more on his features. I thought I knew what the problem was. I leant over to Virginia: 'It's his friends of the campanile. I expect he doesn't want to discuss it with ladies present.'

Jinny smiled at him. 'I may look like your granny, Mr Pritchard, but I am certainly not squeamish. So you may talk freely about the young men you meet below the bell tower in the Piazza San Marco without any fear of upsetting *me*.'

For the first time in a long while, the young Englishman laughed. It was one of those staccato cough-like laughs of embarrassment or surprise. 'All right. I met a lot of young men. Eighteen, nineteen, that sort of age. I probably told some of them I'd been in the nick. That sort of thing impresses 'em.'

'How many might you have told?' I asked.

He was quiet for a moment as if he was thinking through the list of his acquaintances. 'One guy asked me about the tracks on my arm . . . I told him I used to be a junkie till I went to jail. Another boy was boasting about stealing some money from a rich American he'd picked up.' He sighed. 'I don't know, maybe half of the guys I've slept with in the last six months. Maybe fifty or sixty guys. But then, you know, they gossip with each other.'

This last remark rather passed me by. I was busy calculating that if 'fifty or sixty guys' was half his total for six months, he must have had a new companion almost every night (assuming he took weekends off to recover). I must say I wondered if the fellow had heard of Aids.

'So you would guess that anyone in the circle of young homosexuals who pick each other up around San Marco might have known?' Montenari was not concealing his distaste.

'I suppose so.'

'That doesn't really help very much, then, does it,' I said to Montenari. I turned back to Pritchard. 'I don't suppose you asked the people at your *pensione* who left you the letters?'

'Of course I asked. But they were just pushed under the door at night when everyone was asleep. They put them into my box.'

'I'll get my policemen to ask around again,' Montenari said. 'See if anyone remembers anything. But it sounds as though they're not likely to come up with much.'

'I already asked,' Pritchard said irritably, as if wounded by the magistrate's lack of confidence in his skills as an investigator.

None of us said anything. Montenari took us back to his office to debrief.

18

We now knew who had taken Gary Mitchell's briefcase. We had confirmed that it was taken in error. And we could be pretty sure that if the briefcase had ended up with the people who killed him, they had every reason to think he was Gerry Miller, Milo's natural son. I remembered that Gary had told us that he was lucky not to have lost his passport and all of his money. Ironically enough, if he'd left them in the case, he might now be alive. If he'd not removed all these identifying documents, whoever had the briefcase would have known that its bearer, the man in the photograph, was the other G. M. And so, if all this was right, the obvious local suspect, with motive if not real opportunity, was Melissa.

I seem always to be getting involved in murders where the obvious suspects are old friends of mine. Unfortunately, these suspicions sometimes turn out to be well founded. So I have long ago given up assuming that someone whom I know and like can be ruled out. I realized, as I spoke to him after our long interrogation, that Montenari was surprised at how easily Jinny and I discussed the possibility that my old friend and host had conspired with his mistress to contrive a gruesome murder. Still, not ruling them out wasn't the same as ruling them in, if you follow my meaning. And the evidence against them so far was too flimsy even to count as circumstantial. To begin with, neither Melissa nor Bernadetto could actually have carried out the murder. Melissa, as Virginia had reminded us, had twisted her ankle and was being fussed over throughout the period when the crime must have been committed and Bernadetto was miles away with us. True, if they had employed James Pritchard for one purpose, they could also have engaged a murderer. But that was still an entirely speculative possibility.

The question was: could we connect James Pritchard with Melissa or with Bernadetto? Obviously, if Bernadetto was able to draw on his father's Mafia connections, he could simply have asked them to find him a suitable crook. Montenari's policemen had the resources to follow up this possibility, and he had said that they would be asking their informers if they had heard anything. But Pritchard had said he knew Giorgio – in the circumstances I presumed carnally – and that meant there was a connection both to Giorgio's master, Bernadetto, and to *his* mistress, Melissa. As Virginia and I walked back to the *palazzo*, each of us communing with our own thoughts, I decided that a little *conversazione* with Giorgio might be in order.

It was close to a quarter past six when we reached home; we found Bernadetto and Jamie having a drink on the terrace, dressed in their evening togs for dinner with Peggy. Jamie was actually in a dinner-jacket, and Bernadetto was dressed in an elegant collarless black silk jacket and a white polo-neck shirt. I explained that we had been busy at the police station with our stalker. We promised a fuller account later and went immediately on up to change ourselves for the evening's entertainment.

'Well,' I said, as we prepared for our ablutions, 'it's not going to be much fun chatting with Bernadetto and Melissa while secretly suspecting them of murder.'

Jinny looked at me with a look I know well, the look of a woman hatching an idea. 'I don't see that it makes much sense. I mean, as you said, Alexander is frightfully well off without this extra money; and Bernadetto's absolutely rolling in money. Why should they want to risk murder?'

'Who else might have done it?' I sounded more sceptical than I meant to.

'A whole host of people.' Jinny was insistent. 'It might still be that the theft of the briefcase was one thing and the murder just a mugging.'

'Well, we'll just have to wait and see what else turns up.' I was thinking about Mr Montenari's police investigation: one of his people might uncover just what we needed.

'And what are we going to tell them about our new chum James Alexander Pritchard?' Jinny was adjusting her coiffure as she asked the question, and I was admiring the fetching little shake of her head she goes in for at the end of the process. I did not, as a result, entirely grasp her point.

'No need to tell them anything much. Police investigation ongoing. So far no clear indication of why he was after us. That sort of thing.'

'Darling, we might *want* them to know we're on to something...' My dear wife's tone was mildly exasperated.

'Ah, I see.' I paused a moment to reflect, and took the opportunity to do up my black tie. 'I'm not absolutely sure we should do that.'

'Why not?' Jinny said. 'Why not rattle 'em a bit? After all, if they're innocent it won't upset them a bit to think we know who organized Pritchard; and if they're guilty, we might flush them out.'

'Flushing out someone who has already organized one murder is... well, it might be a bit risky; especially if you're staying with him.' It always comes to this. At some point, solving a murder means putting yourself in the line of fire.

'We shall just have to be careful, my sweet.'

'Next time Sebastian complains about our taking risks, I shall refer him to his mother.'

'Don't be silly, darling. By the time Sebastian knows anything about this, it'll all be over.'

'Well, if we're going to fib, let's agree on the same lies,' I said.

It took only a few minutes to construct a tale. We went down to join the others on the terrace, decided to hint darkly from time to time that Pritchard had led us close to finding his pay-master.

'So, do tell,' Jamie bellowed enthusiastically as soon as we had settled into our cocktails, 'who *was* the mysterious stalker?'

'A young Englishman,' Jinny said. 'Rather good family, actually, but he seems to have come unstuck over drugs. So his family has pensioned him off over here.'

I thought I caught just a glimpse of anxiety in Jamie's eyes as Jinny spoke. 'Why was he following you?' This question was considerably more restrained.

'One can't really explain *that* without telling you why he tried to steal my papers on the train,' I said.

'I thought your papers were stolen here.' Jamie's anxious frown was now replaced with puzzlement. His face was becoming a positive kaleidoscope of emotions.

'Patrick and Jinny changed cabins with that fellow Mitchell before his briefcase was stolen.' Jamie still looked blank, so Bernadetto continued: 'The magistrate was here while you were at Peggy's. He suggested Mitchell's briefcase might have been stolen in error. Apparently, he thought the thief might really have been after Patrick's briefcase all along.' Bernadetto's tone was calm and matter of fact. He did not have the air of a man burdened with guilt.

'Ah, so this Pritchard fellow stole the papers last night?' Jamie asked.

'He denied it, of course,' Jinny said, 'but' – this was part of our story, since we didn't want Bernadetto knowing we suspected anyone in the household – 'he would, wouldn't he?'

'So: he stole Mitchell's briefcase from what he thought was our cabin. He'd been commissioned to do this by somebody here in Venice who paid him fifteen hundred pounds for the job.'

'Who was that?' Jamie was doing his best to seem idly curious, but his voice cracked as he finished speaking and he coughed nervously into his hand. Lord Leith was plainly far from relaxed.

'Well, that's a little unclear as yet.' I smiled at the two of them. 'You see, he was commissioned in a series of anonymous notes left at his *pensione*. And nobody admits to having seen who left them.'

'Why the hell did the little idiot agree to do it, if he didn't know who he was working for?' Jamie sounded now like a cross uncle.

'He's not really terribly thoughtful, our stalker. And besides, for a remittance man, fifteen hundred pounds is a lot of money.'

Jinny took over the tale. 'Then, when he got back here with the briefcase, he had a little look in it before he passed it on. There was a photograph in it of Gary Mitchell and a certain amount of Australian money, which he stole. There were also a lot of documents about a chap named Gerry Miller and an inheritance to which he was entitled in England. Naturally, he made the inference that the man in the photograph was Gerry Miller, especially since the briefcase had G. M. monogrammed on it. Then he handed the briefcase to a masked man, who'd been sent by the people who had commissioned him. Of course, at that point, he thought he'd heard the last of it.'

Jinny looked at me expectantly. She had passed the conversational baton. I took up the relay. 'Imagine his surprise, then, when, two days later, on Sunday, he sees a photograph of the same man, dead, on the front page of the daily paper. Imagine his surprise further compounded the next morning when he discovers that the police think the body's name is Gary Mitchell. Now he begins to wonder if the death has something to do with the briefcase he stole: and so he follows the only lead he has. Us. He was commissioned to steal my briefcase and given pictures of us to help him. So he follows us home to the *palazzo*.'

'Why didn't he come back the next day, when the police were waiting to catch him?' Bernadetto asked.

'Because Giorgio inadvertently gave the game away.'

'What *do* you mean?' For the first time, Bernadetto's cool veneer slipped away. '*My* Giorgio?'

'I'm afraid so,' I said. 'But he didn't know what he was doing. Apparently, they're ... they know each other. Giorgio and the stalker, I mean. So the stalker asked Giorgio what he was doing and Giorgio, of course, passed on the excellent gossip: someone had followed the English couple home and Lady Scott had seen him and he was off to tell the police.' Bernadetto looked extremely cross. 'That put the wind up him,' I added.

'He was packing when the police found him at his *pensione*. Now Montenari is busy going over everything Pritchard remembers about the notes that came to him.' Virginia shook her head. 'The whole thing was very cleverly done. Pritchard was told to destroy each note after he'd read it. Fortunately, he kept the last one. Montenari thinks the forensic people should be able to come up with something.' I listened as Virginia spun the web we had plotted. There must be nothing implausible, nothing that would make Bernadetto think we suspected either him or Melissa. 'And the police are trying to follow up his associates to see if they can find someone who suggested his name for a job. Their theory is that the petty criminals he hung around with won't want to be involved in murder.'

'Well, let's hope that works,' Bernadetto said. 'I'd hate to see anyone get away with murder.' He looked at his elegant wristwatch. 'And now, I think we should make our way to Peggy's for dinner.'

As we were walking through the drawing-room to the hall, Jamie turned to me. 'You said he was English.' His studied casualness was less than artful. 'You don't, by any chance, remember his name?'

'James Pritchard,' Virginia said, stopping and looking him straight in the eye. He blanched. 'You don't happen to know him, do you?'

'Good lord, no,' my kinsman said, turning away from us to stiffen his drink from the tray. There was no doubt Jamie Leith was lying.

On the other hand, our Mr di Montebello was completely unruffled by this story. Since Giorgio was driving the boat, Bernadetto set to quizzing his manservant about his meeting with Pritchard. Naturally, Giorgio was deeply embarrassed to discover that he had passed on our plans to the person we had been aiming to trap. (We were grateful, at least, that he'd not mentioned Jinny's sketch: that would have had Pritchard leaving the Pensione Scarpia a good deal more swiftly, and then the police might have missed him.) Giorgio glanced often at Jamie as Bernadetto spoke to him, as if seeking a reassurance that Jamie was in no state to provide. It occurred to me that the interview I had promised myself with Giorgio had better happen soon: if something was going on between them, I didn't want Jamie telling him what to say. As we tied up at the Palazzo Aschenheim, Bernadetto stepped out first to give Jinny a hand up on to the wharf. Jamie looked as though he was hanging back for a tête-à-tête with Giorgio.

'So, Giorgio,' I said, smiling at Jamie and waiting for him to get out of the boat and join me, 'your friend James Pritchard is in a lot of trouble.'

'He's no' my frien',' Giorgio said sulkily. 'I justa know 'im from drinkin' bar.'

'I think Sir Patrick is teasing you,' Jamie said, an unhappy smile forced upon his visage. 'We'll see you later.' And then he muttered something I couldn't quite hear over the slapping of the water against the piles. It sounded to me as though he might have said *'Ciao, bellow.'* And it seemed to me that he winked slightly and that Giorgio responded with a more cheerful smile.

As Jamie and I walked up together to the *palazzo*, I asked him if Giorgio was a proper Venetian.

'As proper as they come,' Jamie laughed. 'His father's people have lived in the same rio here for two hundred years; his mother comes from an old Murano family. He's very proud of his Venetian ancestry. Melissa once made the mistake of saying something to him about 'you Italians' and he said: 'Excuse me, my lady, but I am a Venetian.' Very touching, don't you think?'

19

We were the last to arrive at Peggy's celebration dinner party. The Bouncers were already ensconced, seated side by side in front of the great fireplace under the enormous Occampo 'action painting'. Mrs B. had her sun-glasses on as usual, and was wearing a vast black and white dress, with enormous puffed sleeves, and a hooped skirt that it must have taken several minutes to arrange about her. I gathered from something Melissa murmured in response to a muffled query from Virginia that it had been made by a Frenchman by the name of La Croix. The diamond choker around her neck sat above a décolletage even more daring than usual, and was matched by a bracelet at her right wrist: the combined value of these two items would probably have paid off the national debt of Lesotho. Claudio and Melissa were seated facing this stunning sight; neither of them, however, seemed particularly keen on it. Lady Hawksworth was having difficulty concealing her disdain for the flamboyance of Mrs B.'s outfit, but her own dress was also stunning (if in a rather less showy way), and it was *her* décolletage that was drawing the Chilean painter's frankly libidinous attention. The dress was of dark blue silk, and it clung close to her form: I wondered how easy it had been for *her* to sit down.

Georgie, Peggy's daughter, was hovering about in a simple dark red velvet dress, directing one of the Tamils, who was serving drinks. Bernadetto had draped himself elegantly as usually, this time against the fireplace.

Everyone save Mr Bouncer (and the Tamil) had champagne glasses. Mr B. was nursing his customary tumbler of spirits and looking distinctly less cheery than he had the night before. As we arrived he was engaged in an unlikely conversation with Claudio, with Melissa as translator, which seemed to be about buying some of the painter's work. Claudio was trying, without much success, to look pleased. At least, I thought, the fellow cared that his work was going to a philistine.

We said our hallos and I moved over to stand by the armchair in which Jinny had settled. 'Mom will be here in just a moment,' Georgie said. 'She's on the phone to New York. Would you like a drink?'

'I think a glass of that champagne would be just the ticket,' Jamie said.

I seconded the motion.

'So, Peggy has persuaded you to part with your wonderful collection,' Bernadetto said. 'Here's to you, to her, and to it.' He raised his glass and took a sip.

Mr Bouncer acknowledged the toast ... and then grimaced painfully, heaved his great body with remarkable energy out of the sofa and hurtled towards Georgie. 'Bathroom?' he shouted, planting his glass on a small table in front of Claudio Occampo.

'I'll show you the way,' Georgie said; and she was as good as her word. They disappeared down a corridor.

Jo-Ann smiled apologetically at us all. 'I'm afraid my honey has tummy trouble. He's been runnin' to the john every five minutes for a couple of hours. I said we maybe oughta tell Peggy we'd come by tomorrow, but he insisted a date was a date.' Jo-Ann's frankness was, I suppose, refreshing; but it did not seem the ideal conversation with which to begin a dinner party.

I was about to try to change the subject when Melissa spoke. 'Have you eaten out much while you've been here? You couldn't have picked anything up at the Danieli.'

'Oh, sure. We've been eating all over. But, to tell you the truth, Phil never did have a strong stomach. Why, I remember ...'

I was delighted to see Peggy arrive at this moment. Jo-Ann Bouncer stopped, no doubt because she was as stunned as we all were by the splendid (and sizeable) scarlet evening dress in which our hostess sailed into the room. Peggy Aschenheim was in festival mood. She beamed at all of us. 'Welcome, welcome,

welcome. Too awful of me not to be here to greet you, but I have been trying to calm the firestorm of excitement at the Met. Everyone is just thrilled with . . .' She paused, noticing for the first time that Phil Bouncer was not with us. 'But where is the man of the moment?'

'I'm afraid that Phil's tummy is playing up,' Melissa said quietly. 'Georgie offered to show him the way to the loo.'

'Oh, the poor dear man,' Peggy said. 'Jo-Ann, what can we do for him? Shall I get that lovely doctor who was so good with Melissa's ankle to drop by?'

'I don't think that'll be necessary, Peggy. Phil just has a weak stomach: it's his only weakness. It'll pass. It always passes. He'd be happiest if we just didn't take too much notice, if you know what I mean.' There was a tremor in her left cheek, as if she might be winking from behind those vast dark lenses, and Jo-Ann smiled sweetly at us all.

Georgie returned at this moment and had a whispered exchange with her mother. 'Good, good,' Peggy Aschenheim said. 'I'm sure he'll be back with us soon. And then we can all go in to dinner. There's kind of a breeze on the roof today, so I thought we'd eat in the big old dining-room overlooking the canal. Al liked us to keep it just the way it always was: it's like a bit of Venetian history.'

'Now, Patrick, do tell, what's happened with all the murder investigations?' Melissa turned to Peggy. 'Wherever Patrick goes people just drop dead like flies. His life is as thrilling as a Bella Sharpe novel.'

I was busy recounting the story of James Pritchard when Mr Bouncer returned. He waved cheerily as Peggy came over to greet him. 'I'm just fine. Nothin' to worry 'bout. You just don't mind me and my belly.'

'Come sit down with me, hon. Sir Patrick is right now in the middle of tellin' us how they found the guy who stole the briefcase from that Australian who was murdered last week.' Jo-Ann patted the sofa beside her hoops. What with the space occupied by her skirt, Mr B. was not going to be able to get within a foot or two of his wife.

'Nobody tol' me 'bout no murder,' Phil Bouncer said. Then he looked around for his drink. Claudio passed it to him with a friendly smile. In the five minutes before dinner was announced, the company brought him up to date. When we set off for the dining-room, everybody knew the story we had told to Bernadetto and Jamie earlier.

*

We crossed the marble floor of the great hall to the dining-room on the other side. Melissa hobbled along briskly on Bernadetto's arm, limping now only slightly. Obviously, her ankle was improving. To our left rose the great stone staircase, its walls embellished with stone carving, and hung, rather incongruously, with pictures from Mrs Aschenheim's collection of modern art. The combined effect of carved putti and abstract expressionism was striking. Since we had entered the house from the terrace on our first visit and gone to the roof in the lift, Jinny and I had not seen this strange sight before. 'Rather peculiar combination,' Lady Scott murmured in my ear as we glanced up at a large well-lit canvas which seemed at first to be painted a uniform white, hung below a baroque angel, his stone cheeks blowing for ever into his little trumpet. As one stared more, the canvas turned out to be covered with little squares in many slightly different shades of off-white. I looked away: too long studying this one and I would have had an attack of vertigo.

After this eclectic mixture of ancient and modern, the dining-room itself came as rather a surprise. Peggy had told us that it was part of old Venice, but I had not anticipated how exactly true that would be. Murky portraits of Venetian merchants hung on the wood-panelled walls. Enormous dark red curtains floated from great brass rods above the windows, twenty feet of heavy velvet-like material, girdled with a braided band that held it back to reveal the canal, glistening in the moonlight. Over the ancient oak table – set now with china that looked as though it could have come back with Marco Polo, intricately wrought silver candelabra, and a glittering cascade of gilded glasses – was a vast and ancient chandelier in the style of Murano. I almost gasped as we entered the room. 'Peggy,' Jinny spoke for both of us, 'after our last dinner party here, I didn't think you could surprise us, but this is absolutely stunning.'

She laughed her cheerful gurgling laugh. 'Glad you like it. But the real test is gonna be the food.' There were place-cards set and Peggy guided us into her placement. 'Bernadetto, you're gonna have to stand in for Al as usual. Jo-Ann, honey, you go right over there next to Bernadetto; and Phil, I'm gonna have you right here beside me.' She beamed at us all as Sujit pushed her chair in behind her and the other four Tamils offered the rest of the ladies the same service.

Once they were seated, we gentlemen took our places.

*

It was only a few minutes into our soup – a delicious and surprising confection of wild berries in a light mushroom broth – that Mr B.'s face took on once more that pained look and he muttered to Peggy. He got up, trying this time to move in a more dignified way, and waved at us all, essaying a pained smile as he left: 'You guys go on, I'll be back.' But then he was taken with a spasm: he clutched at his stomach and speeded up. Sujit accompanied him on his precipitate exit from the dining-room.

I turned to Melissa, who was on my right: 'Glad to see your ankle's so much better.'

'Actually, Patrick darling, it hurts like hell. I've overdone it today. But I'm sure it'll be fine in a day or two more.' Melissa smiled at me, her beautiful smile. 'I assume, from what you were saying earlier, that it can't be long before I get a visit from Signor Montenari.' I raised a querying eyebrow. 'Don't be silly, Patrick. I'm not a half-wit. If he thinks that Mitchell was killed because he was mistaken for Milo's son, then I'm an obvious suspect.'

'You were closeted with Peggy, a doctor and a twisted ankle when he died. Montenari knows that.'

'Of course, *I* didn't kill him: but I could have had him killed.'

'Motive, by itself, isn't sufficient. He has nothing that connects you to the murder.'

'Unless he thinks I hired the English boy to steal your briefcase. Whoever mistook Mitchell for Milo's son, remember, was misled by the briefcase.'

'Well, you needn't worry about that for much longer. They've enough evidence to identify the source of the last note that Pritchard got from the person that employed him.'

'Why are they sure Mitchell's death wasn't just a mugging? I mean, if his briefcase hadn't been stolen . . . ' Melissa's voice trailed off.

'They *aren't* sure yet,' I said truthfully. 'But murder in the course of a mugging is pretty unusual here in Venice, so they'd like to believe that there's some other explanation. But, as I say, I don't think you need to worry. Once they've worked out who had the briefcase stolen, you'll be in the clear.'

'Let's hope they do work it out, then. Are you sure that they will?'

'Pretty sure. The note will have sweat from the hands of the person who put it in the envelope; the envelope will have traces of the person who delivered it. Salivary proteins and all that. All they'll need to do is to check that none of your proteins are there and you'll be in the clear.' I couldn't help noticing that, far from seeming reassured, she had paled somewhat at this last invention. And yet I felt oddly guilty leading Melissa on like this.

The next course arrived, to a buzz of excitement: on each of our plates was a large scallop, a pair of prawns, a shrimp, and a small langouste, all peeled, and each accompanied by a sauce of its own. The elements had been combined differently on each plate to produce a picture: mine was the face of a woman with long hair; Melissa's was a little cat (or was it a vast lion?) stretched out on the ground; and Jo-Ann, to my left, had a cornucopia, drawn in red and green sauce, out of which the seafood tumbled. 'Marinella has absolutely outdone herself,' Bernadetto said.

Claudio Occampo looked at his plate vaguely, as if he couldn't see it at all, and then patted the front of his jacket. *'Ah, mes lunettes. J'ai laissé mes lunettes dans ma chambre. Je m'excuse. Il faut que je voie cette merveille de Marinella.'*

'Oh, Claudio. Mais tu es impossible. Rentre aussitôt.' She paused as the Chilean left the room. 'Well, I dunno. Everybody seems to be running away from the table. I do wish Phil was here to appreciate it. It's meant for him.' Peggy sounded very unhappy.

'He's been away rather a long time. Perhaps I should go and check on him.' Jo-Ann began to push back her chair and one of the Tamils sprang to her aid.

'Don't you worry. I've got to go anyway,' Melissa said and her Tamil stepped forward.

'Do you want an arm to lean on?' Bernadetto asked.

'Good lord, no. You mustn't all treat me like an invalid. If I just go carefully, I'm fine. Don't fuss. I'll be back in a jiffy.'

We all made a good effort at injecting a more cheerful mood into what was, after all, meant to be a festive occasion: the celebration of the Met's latest acquisition. As Melissa left, waving away the attentions of one of the Tamils, all of us returned with a sort of false gaiety to the task of amusing our companions. It was probably no more than a couple of minutes later that the sound of our chatter was broken by a thud and a piercing scream. I leapt to my feet and made my way swiftly into the hall, following the direction from which the sound had come, accompanied by Bernadetto and Jamie and followed by the rest of the party. Claudio appeared from the drawing-room, his glasses now on, and joined us as we made our way.

As we entered the passageway behind the stairs from which the scream had come, Melissa came towards me, dragging her sprained ankle but moving as fast as she could, her face pale, her eyes filled with terror. She threw herself into Bernadetto's arms. 'I think something awful has happened to Philip.'

Together we all hurried down the corridor to the door of the loo. I was leading the way. As soon as I reached the door I shouted: 'Phil. Mr Bouncer. Are you all right?' I listened for a reply but there wasn't a sound. I tried to open the door, but it was firmly locked. 'Is there another way into the room?' I asked Peggy.

She nodded. 'Sujit.' The Tamil went back down the corridor and opened a window. He climbed out. 'He can walk along the ledge over the canal,' Peggy explained. 'The bathroom window's probably open.'

While we waited I looked at my watch. It was a quarter to nine. Twenty seconds later a chastened-looking Sujit opened the door. He let Bernadetto and me in and then closed the door firmly behind us. 'Not good for the ladies.'

He was right.

There, face-down on the floor in front of the lavatory, was Philip Bouncer, his trousers about his ankles, his body unnaturally rigid, like a kneeling statue, fallen forwards. I knelt down beside him and felt for a pulse in his neck. There was none. His skin was already cooling. There was no doubt he was dead.

With Bernadetto's help I turned the body over. Philip Bouncer's muscles were as stiff as a board. And so, as we turned him over, his legs stayed at the same angle to his body, fixed in a strange mockery of a foetal position. The muscles of his face were frozen in his last grimace; his mouth contorted in a rictus of agony; his eyes were wide open, staring emptily; a stream of mucus dripped from his nostrils. One didn't have to be a forensic pathologist to see that Philip Bouncer had been poisoned.

'It's poison. We must call the police,' I said to Bernadetto. 'And we must leave everything as it is.' Sujit – who had been pinching his nose fastidiously – made to flush the bowl and I grabbed his arm. 'No. Don't touch anything.'

As we came out of the room, Jo-Ann stood between Peggy and Melissa. And when she saw our faces, she began to wail hysterically.

Long before the police arrived, Melissa had told us her story. It didn't amount to much. She had come down the corridor, she said, and knocked gingerly on the door. Philip Bouncer said, 'Occupied.'

'So I said: "Phil, it's Melissa, are you okay?" He sounded quite relaxed. He just said, "Fine, fine. Be right along." And so I came back down the corridor to go to the loo on the other side of the sitting-room. But then I heard Phil say loudly, "What the f— ?" And so I stopped and turned back and went back down and I said, "Phil, are you all right?" Then he said: "Shit, Melissa. The f—er's got me. I'm gone." ' Melissa broke down again in sobs. 'He sounded . . . ' She sniffed. 'He sounded more surprised than scared. And then there was this sound like a body falling over, not very loud. And a sort of grunting noise . . . That's when I screamed.'

Jinny and Peggy concentrated on trying to calm Jo-Ann. 'Go get some of your Valium, Georgie,' Peggy said to her daughter. 'Jo-Ann's gonna need all the help we can give her. And Sujit, you get Mrs Bouncer a nice warm toddy and tell Obi to bring us a blanket from off of my bed. And somebody bring up some warm water and a towel.'

Jo-Ann's face was streaked with tears and she lay on the sofa, pale and still, sobbing occasionally. 'I told him. I said: "Phil, if you need a bodyguard in Dallas, you sure as hell need one in Venice." I mean, Italy is the home of the f—in' Mafia. But he says no. And what the hell do I know? I mean, I'm only a f—in' cop.' This last piece of intelligence struck me as fairly startling. My surprise must have shown, because Jo-Ann looked at me and said: 'Yup, that's right. We met when I was detailed to protect him, after some sicko started sendin' him threatnin' notes.' She laughed humourlessly. 'You know what? Phil took one look at me and said: "I think I better hire me a bodyguard." So I told him: "Excuse me, Mr Bouncer. But I am a highly qualified police officer, and if you don't think I can do my job, I'd like to know the hell why." I was pissed. Course he *loved* that.' She sighed and then the memory seemed to pain her, because she shook her head as if to shake off a vision. And then she burst into sobs again. It was a pitiful sight.

One of the servants arrived with the bowl of warm water and the towel that Peggy had ordered. She reached across to remove Jo-Ann's glasses, but Jo-Ann held on to them. Peggy insisted. 'Come on, Jo-Ann. I need to clean your face.'

'I'm okay.'

Peggy shrugged and gently wiped Jo-Ann's cheeks with a dampened corner of the towel. Then she pushed up under the glasses to wipe around Jo-Ann's eyes and as she edged the glasses up she gasped. Firmly she removed Jo-Ann's fingers, which had returned to grasp the frames, and lifted off the glasses. All around her eyes were the most terrible bruises. Jo-Ann winced as Peggy bathed her eyes. 'What happened, sweetie?' Peggy cooed.

'I guess he just liked to knock me around,' she said simply.

That moment made it hard fully to mourn the passing of Philip Bouncer.

It took the police about an hour to get around to interviewing us. Mr Montenari arrived at about half-past ten and greeted us all. 'Have you given your statements, Sir Patrick?'

'Indeed.'

'Then you should feel free to go.' He paused. 'I'll drop by tomorrow morning for a chat. Are you still planning to leave for Bellagio?'

'May we?'

'It might be better if you stayed for a little. The investigation of this murder has only just begun and, alas, you are prime witnesses.'

'Of course.' We looked at each other for a moment and then I added: 'Looks as though he was poisoned.'

Montenari nodded. 'It looks like it. And the fact that he already had stomach ache when he arrived suggests he was poisoned already before he came here.'

'Well, your forensic people should be able to tell you when he must have ingested whatever it was.'

'Right,' Montenari said. It was clear that he was not in a mood for a chat.

'We'll see you tomorrow, then,' I said; and he nodded distractedly and moved off into the hall, which was full of policemen.

Jinny looked at Peggy, who was seated next to Jo-Ann on the sofa, but before she could say anything Peggy spoke: 'You guys go along back to Bernadetto's place. We'll be all right.'

'I think I'll stay here, if you don't mind,' Bernadetto said to us. 'Melissa's had rather a shock.'

'Of course, we'll be fine.'

'Jamie knows how everything works. He'll look after you.'

'You worry about Melissa,' Jinny said. 'Don't think about us.' We said our adieus.

'Where *is* Jamie, by the way?' Melissa asked as Jinny kissed her good-night. I looked around. Jamie was, indeed, not in the sitting-room with the rest of us. Jinny and I glanced at each other, as we had the same thought.

'I expect we'll find him at the boat,' Jinny said.

She was right.

The second murder didn't seem to have anything to do with the first one: but we couldn't be sure until we had a few more answers about both of them. And Giorgio, who knew Pritchard, and, of course, Bernadetto and Melissa, might have a few of those answers. Since Jamie and Giorgio had now had time to commune, there was not much point in trying to talk to Giorgio on his own.

I explained these thoughts to Jinny as we walked down to the water.

'How did you get to know Mr Pritchard?' I began, as Giorgio steered the boat out into the canal. It's funny how someone who speaks perfectly good English can lose it all in an instant, if he doesn't want to answer your questions.

'I beg pardon?'

'Mr Pritchard. How did you meet?'

'Meet?'

Jinny took over. I understood nothing of the conversation that ensued. Jinny seemed to say a good deal more than Giorgio did, reducing him eventually to a sulky series of '*si*'s and no's'.

'He's not feeling very helpful,' Jinny said. 'Perhaps you could ask him for us, Jamie?'

'What do you want to know?'

'If he introduced Pritchard to anyone who might have had a connection with Milo.'

Jamie shook his head: 'Giorgio didn't know Milo.'

'But he does know Melissa.'

'I doubt that he introduced Pritchard to Melissa. I mean, what possible interest could they have had in each other?'

'Let's ask.'

Jamie shrugged and burbled at our driver; and Giorgio looked crossly at Jamie as he answered in the negative.

'Of course, if *I* count as someone who had a connection with Milo, he might have introduced him to me,' Jamie said.

'Well, we wouldn't need to ask *him* that, would we?' Jinny said lightly.

'He'd say no, if you did.'

'And would that be true, Jamie, my dear?' I could tell that Jinny's playfulness hid a good deal of irritation.

'Yes.' Jamie's archness was also becoming a trifle irritating to me.

'You met Mr Pritchard without Giorgio's help.'

Jamie looked at me for a moment. It was an empty and uncommunicative expression. And then he said: 'Shall we talk about something else until we get back to the *palazzo*? It's rather breezy out here. One's words might carry.'

When we got back to the Palazzo Longhi, Jamie and I had a short conversation in the library. I learned only one thing of importance: how Melissa came to hear of the life and career of James Pritchard.

20

Nobody ever believes me when I say it, but the fact is that the main instrument in the solution of crimes is not the intellect, or the memory, or the senses: it is the imagination. Once you have the main facts before you, what you must do is spin yarns with those facts (remembering that every fact may turn out to be an illusion, and every act of imagination may as easily mislead you as uncover the truth). In all my murders, there comes a point when I let my imagination loose. And so long as I remember what is fact and what imagination, at some point the answer bursts through.

The other essential – and this I do not ordinarily mention – is my wife. I don't mean, of course, that every sleuth in the world needs to contact Jinny at some point in his labours. But talking through the facts with her at the end of the day, as I make my notes, prepares me for the task of imagining: a task that begins, as often as not, as I sleep. Philip Bouncer's death had naturally disrupted my thinking about Gary Mitchell's murder and all the complications about his briefcase and mine.

But Philip Bouncer's murder seemed like a straightforward thing. Until the forensics had been done, we wouldn't know what sort of poison had killed him: and so we wouldn't know when it must have entered his system. But the most likely hypothesis was that a hired assassin had killed a hugely rich man. Hugely rich men always have enemies. Some of their enemies – themselves hugely rich – can always afford assassins. That was why Milo Hawksworth had had bodyguards and arranged bodyguards for his son. It struck me as rather odd that Phil Bouncer hadn't taken the same elementary precautions. Maybe being married to a former police officer had allayed his anxieties. Maybe he really thought he was safe in Italy, away from the people who hated him. It was, I thought, something Mr Montenari should reflect upon.

On the other hand, it was not really the sort of thing I should meddle in. Solving the Bouncer murder would need policemen in America, tracing out the deals in Bouncer's life, finding motives. Hired assassins are often hard to find: the trick is to find the person with the motive to engage their services. No, what I needed to do was to think about the death of Gary Mitchell.

And so, as we prepared for bed, Jinny and I talked about what we now knew.

'Why was Jamie making all that fuss about whether or not he knew Pritchard?' Jinny asked, when I joined her upstairs.

'Can't you guess?'

'He picked him up under the campanile.'

'That sort of thing.'

'Why didn't he tell us that in the boat?'

'It appears that he doesn't want Giorgio to know.'

Jinny eyed me sceptically. 'Jamie's having an affair with Bernadetto's manservant?'

I nodded.

'And Jamie is under the impression that the boy would be upset if he were unfaithful?' Jinny's tone suggested that she thought I had had my leg pulled.

'Not exactly. I don't think Jamie's under any illusions about Giorgio's feeling for him. He was just worried that Giorgio would be cross if he knew Jamie's told us. I mean, if Bernadetto finds out, it'll put Giorgio in a very awkward position with his employer.'

Jinny nodded. She made it clear that this was not something she found easy to believe. 'Did he tell you anything else?'

'Yes. Something very important . . . though not exactly salubrious.' My wife having a robuster moral sense than I do, I don't have to keep anything from her. But that doesn't make these things any easier to discuss. 'Apparently, Jamie enjoys discussing his conquests with Melissa – who, for some reason lets him do it.'

'I should think it's rather riveting learning about the seamier side of Venetian life. Does Melissa reciprocate?'

'That's what I asked. You know, he thought that was frightfully funny: he said it would have been terribly dull since Melissa hasn't slept with anyone except Bernadetto for years.'

'How long do you think Melissa and Bernadetto have been having their affair?'

'At least since Jamie first started spending most of his time with Bernadetto.'

'That was twenty years ago, when Anthony went up to Oxford.' I nodded. 'It's amazing that Milo never knew.'

'I can't understand why she didn't divorce him and just marry Bernadetto.'

I nodded again. I did not particularly want to dwell on these private details of our friends' lives. 'Anyway, the point is that Jamie told Melissa about Pritchard about six weeks ago. Everything he knew, including the petty criminal convictions, the fact that he was short of money. His name. Even the address of the *pensione*.'

'Why did Jamie tell you this, do you think?'

'I think he's jumped to the same conclusion as we have.'

'Very loyal, your cousin,' Jinny said in that dry way she has.

'I think he's scared, actually. I think he's wondering whether Melissa might not have him bumped off, too.'

'Do we think she's capable of that?'

'No. Of course not. Arranging the murder of a stranger who threatens Alex's welfare is one thing; killing an old friend is something completely different. Melissa's tough, but she's not cold-blooded. But Jamie's not thinking very clearly. He's shocked at the thought that she might have arranged a murder; he thinks she couldn't have done it without Bernadetto's help; and so he's worried about what Bernadetto is capable of, too.'

'He has a point,' Jinny said, her eye glancing towards the door of the bedroom.

'I'll prop a chair under the handle, if it would reassure you.'

Jinny's response surprised me: she laughed. 'Don't look so solemn, Paddy. Paranoia always sets in eventually. Why lock the door, when they could poison the food? So far, we can't prove a thing against Bernadetto *or* Melissa; and if they killed us they'd only draw attention to themselves.' She paused and looked me in the eye: 'Besides, old thing, do you really think that Melissa's capable of organizing a murder?'

I made the best case I could: 'Fact: Melissa had motive and opportunity to arrange the theft of my papers from the train. Fact: Gary Mitchell was probably mistaken for Gerry Miller, and only someone who had looked into his briefcase would have been likely to make that mistake.' Jinny's scepticism was still firmly entrenched in her features. Frankly, I wasn't even convincing myself. I went on without much conviction. 'Fact: Bernadetto, Melissa's lover of at least twenty years, has the Mafia connections to arrange the murder.' I stopped because something new had just struck me. 'Wait a minute, Jinny. Melissa was here in the house when we were out at dinner on Sunday night.'

'What are you talking about? Bernadetto telephoned her when we came in. She must have slipped in later.'

'He *said* he telephoned her. And Giorgio, recognizing that Bernadetto didn't want us to know Melissa was spending the night, would have kept quiet. But for all we know, he just went upstairs to his bedroom.'

Virginia nodded. 'All right.' There was a rising tone here, suggesting diminished scepticism.

I ploughed ahead. 'So *she* could have taken those papers from my briefcase. All she had to do was take them to Bernadetto's room where she was going to sleep and then she could get them out of the house at her leisure.'

'If she did that on her own, and she was able to find Pritchard on her own, are we sure she couldn't have found someone to kill Mitchell without Bernadetto?'

'When I told Bernadetto over the phone that Gary Mitchell was the name of the dead man, there was an almost audible gasp of shock. That's how he would have reacted if he realized they'd had the wrong man killed.'

'That's how he would have reacted if he knew that was the name of the lawyer who was coming to visit Melissa about Milo's Australian son.'

'Point taken. Good. So we don't yet have anything against Bernadetto.'

'We don't *really* have anything against Melissa.'

In the silence that followed, I jotted down a few notes. 'Time for bed, I think.'

Jinny kissed me good-night and picked up her copy of *The Great Train Robbery*. 'I'll join you in a little while. I've a chapter or two of this thriller to finish.'

'Good-night, my dear.' I closed my eyes and listened to the sounds of the Grand Canal. And I prepared to set my imagination to work.

I rehearsed *in pectore* what we had learned over and over again. For one thing, I knew that the awful sight of Philip Bouncer's face would keep me awake for a good while: and if I was awake I wanted to have something else to keep my mind on.

Melissa knew about James Pritchard; Jamie had told us that. She could, therefore, very easily have arranged for him to steal my briefcase; certainly, she is an extremely intelligent and practical woman. Once she saw what was in the briefcase that Pritchard took in error, she had reason to think that the man in the photograph was Milo's son. So, *if* she had opened the briefcase, she had a motive to kill Gary Mitchell: and what looked like a meaningless mugging was, in fact, a premeditated murder.

But who, then, actually carried out the *actus reus*? Finding a petty criminal is one thing. Finding a murderer is quite another. Here she would have needed help: and that is where Bernadetto would have been useful. *If*, that is, he really was able to draw on the Mafia connections that Jamie thought old Montebello had been able to rely on.

Could we think of anyone else who might have a reason to kill Mitchell – not because of a mistaken belief that he was Gerry Miller, but in his own right? Hard to say. Certainly Gerry Miller didn't seem to have any reason to kill him. His disappearance was, of course, suspicious. But it was easy to see why he might have been frightened of turning himself in to the Italian police when his lawyer was killed. He was an intelligent young man: he would, of course, see that the police might imagine that someone, like himself, with a connection to Mitchell, was the most likely suspect. Interpol would probably find him some time soon, if he didn't have the sense to give himself up. Montenari had seemed confident that they would have him soon, when we discussed the matter after interviewing Pritchard.

Frustrated by the unsatisfactory nature of this line of thought, my mind turned again to the murder we had witnessed this evening. The horror of the corpse never quite ceases, however many you see. And there is an especial shock to seeing the body of someone you know distorted in death. The shock had been compounded by the revelation of Jo-Ann Bouncer's battered face. If anyone had a reason to kill Phil Bouncer, I thought, it was Jo-Ann Bouncer. Whether she had the opportunity would depend on what the poison was. I would have to wait for Montenari to tell me exactly how Mr Bouncer had died.

I tried, once more, to put Philip Bouncer out of my mind. It was time to concentrate on what I knew about Gary Mitchell and let my imagination loose.

A young man walks up to Gary Mitchell near his hotel – the Firenze, just off the Piazza San Marco – and hands him a note. 'Please come at once to the Ghetto Vecchio.' It's signed: 'Lady H.' There's a map, an arrow. Naturally, he doesn't go back to the hotel. She says 'at once' and there's no reason to fear her; no reason to go for reinforcements or to tell anyone where he's going. Besides, it will be a bit of a coup to be the first to make contact with Gerry's father's widow. He makes his way up through the island towards the railway station, following the map, the sap rising in his veins.

It is quiet in the ghetto at the end of the Jewish Sabbath: nobody is there. He waits for a while in the deserted old square of the Ghetto Vecchio, looking expectantly this way and that; noticing, perhaps to his amusement, the signs in the window announcing the imminence of the Messiah. (It's a clever spot to choose: where else would be quiet on a Saturday in early summer in Venice?) Then, a man approaches him and beckons him to follow through the gate into the deserted alley, along the edge of the Rio della Misericordia.

I stopped.

Why should he follow a man? He has come at the behest of Melissa, Lady Hawksworth. He is surely expecting Mr Miller's 'beautiful and mysterious woman'; the woman with 'the key' to his client's 'destiny'. I remembered our conversation on the Orient Express, the bright, gay looks in their eyes as they spoke of the mysterious lady at the end of their journey. He and Gerry Miller had constructed a romance around the meeting with Melissa: the note, the strange location, the air of intrigue would have fitted easily into his expectations. But didn't it have to be a woman?

I tried again.

A woman approaches him and beckons him to follow through the gate into the deserted alley, along the edge of the Rio della Misericordia. Almost certainly, he has seen a picture of her: in the process of researching Gerry Miller's rights to Milo's estate, he would certainly have had someone send him one of the many photographs of Melissa from the society pages.

But, of course, it isn't Melissa. It can't be Melissa – she has the perfect alibi; but Gary Mitchell, Gary Mitchell mistaken for Gerry Miller, has to believe it is.

The woman – the assassin – is wearing a veil; she is dressed, as he might imagine Melissa would dress, in the clothes of a 'beautiful and mysterious woman'. Or perhaps not a veil: that would be conspicuous coming in and out of the ghetto. Perhaps, like Jo-Ann, the assassin wore sun-glasses.

Like Jo-Ann. A strange thought struck me. Since Jinny's light was still on, I turned over and tried it out on her. 'Just had a ridiculous thought. You remember we thought we saw Jo-Ann near the ghetto, when we were coming back from that wonderful picnic with Bernadetto, at about the time when Gary Mitchell was killed?'

My wife peered at me over her pince-nez and nodded slightly.

'So the fact is, Jo-Ann, who has no motive at all to kill Gary Mitchell, had the opportunity; and Melissa has the perfect alibi for the Mitchell murder, for which she alone has a motive.'

Scepticism was written all over the fine features of the good Lady Scott.

'I wasn't seriously suggesting it. It was . . .' I paused, seeking the right formulation. 'It was only an irony.'

'An irony,' Jinny said, offering me one of her bleak smiles: a smile at the hopelessness, utter and complete, of the man to whom she has been married all these years. She returned to her reading for a minute or two: she had reached the last pages of the book. As I lay and watched her she finished and placed the book gently on the bedside table.

'Any good?' I enquired.

'Useful. For Bella Sharpe.'

'Ah, I see.'

'Good. Well, I think it's time to try and sleep, don't you?' A question expecting the answer: Absolutely. The pince-nez travelled to their elegant little case on the bedside table. Jinny settled down, removing the second pillow, which props her up for her reading, and kissed me with great ceremony. 'Good-night, Paddy. Don't stay up all night cogitating, my sweet. We don't want to be out of sorts all day tomorrow.' She turned out her light and we were left in the semi-darkness, bathed in the light filtering through the half-open curtains of the window over the canal.

'You know,' I said, as Virginia settled down for the night, 'Montenari thinks Philip Bouncer's tummy upset suggests he was already poisoned when he got to Peggy's.'

'Indeed,' Virginia said, yawning wearily.

'But the sort of poison that kills you an hour or two after you take it wouldn't normally produce that sort of muscular paralysis.'

'Really.'

'So, I wonder if he wasn't actually killed by one of those fast-acting poisons?'

Virginia grunted non-committally.

'But that would have had to have been administered while he was actually in there.'

This last insight produced no response at all.

Perhaps, I thought, if I deliver the conclusion of my argument, I might get more of a rise. 'And that could have been done with a blow-dart from the window. That would be why Philip said, "The effer's got me." Otherwise, why would he have said that?' Virginia was still silent, unappreciative of this *aperçu*, but she was too quiet for someone who was really asleep. 'Of course,' I added recklessly, 'it could also have been done through the keyhole of the door by Melissa.'

Virginia sat up sharply and turned on the light. 'Patrick, darling, I *was* listening. But it's half-past one in the morning. I'm tired. You're obviously not thinking your best. Let's go to sleep.' She kissed me firmly. 'Anyway, there wasn't a keyhole.'

'I know, my sweet, I know.'

The woman has followed Gary Mitchell: she knows that he hasn't talked to anybody, knows that he is alone. She looks around one last time. She approaches. Her right hand is stretched towards him in a gesture of greeting. And then, when she gets close, she reaches down into her bag and, standing there, her body warm against his, she draws out the knife. He has no time to see what she is doing. No time to parry. No time to escape. She stabs him – once only, Montenari had said – towards the heart. He feels the blade entering his abdomen, stabbing upwards, piercing his diaphragm. But Gary Mitchell has almost no time to be surprised. The blood is pulsing out of his body. He loses consciousness almost at once. As he slides earthward, the woman searches his pocket for the note, with the incriminating signature, and removes it. And then she pushes him unceremoniously into the canal.

'Impossible, of course,' I murmured to myself as sleep finally took hold of me. 'Anyone who had done that would have covered herself in blood.'

It was Gary Mitchell's blood, imagined, that I was thinking of as I fell asleep; but Philip Bouncer's face, remembered, pursued me into my restless dreams.

21

The sunlight streamed in and woke us early in the morning. I staggered over to the window and pulled the curtains shut; but, by then, of course, I was wide awake.

Jinny addressed me as I made my way back to the bed. 'We shan't get back to sleep, now. Let's just get up slowly and go down to breakfast.'

'Very odd business last night. I'm afraid that Mr and Mrs Bouncer must have had a most peculiar relationship. Did you notice that she said he loved her because she was drunk?'

'Not drunk, darling. Pissed. In America that means angry, not drunk. It's that Hollywood cliché: you look lovely when you're angry.' Virginia's encyclopaedic knowledge of the idiosyncracies of our transatlantic cousins never ceases to amaze. 'Come on, Paddy, up we get.' The elegant feet of Lady Scott slipped out from under the bedclothes and she padded across to the bathroom.

'I'm pretty sure it's going to turn out that Bouncer was killed with one of those fast-acting poisons. The assassin must have been following him about waiting for an opening,' I shouted to Jinny through the bathroom door, when I returned from my ablutions. 'I suppose he'd have got him somewhere eventually.'

'Still, he managed to pick a peculiarly undignified moment.'

'Perhaps that was part of the aim: these sort of Mafia killings often have a sort of vendetta aspect.'

Jinny said nothing – I wasn't sure that she had heard me, actually – and so I set about picking a shirt to wear, waiting for her to join me in the bedroom.

'Most frustrating,' I said a little later as we were dressing. 'We simply don't know enough to work out what happened.' Normally, if I can wait long enough to let my imagination loose, when I finally do, it comes up with something. This time it didn't seem to have produced anything at all. I thought I might mention to Montenari that he shouldn't rule out a woman as Mitchell's assassin. But that simply added to his list of potential perpetrators the other half of the human race. And I would have told him my thoughts about the poison, too, if I hadn't known that the forensic people would get there before me. Not much profit from a night of tossing and turning. I descended grumpily to breakfast, irritated, I have to admit, slightly, by Jinny's generally cheerful demeanour.

'Are you all right, my love?' I asked as we descended the grand staircase to the hall on the way to the dining-room. 'Very upsetting business last night.'

'One can't let things like that put one off one's stride,' my dear wife said in that schoolmarm's tone she adopts occasionally. 'I mean, we hardly knew him, and he was obviously a rather unsavoury character. The person I feel sorry for is his wife.'

'If we're being consistent, shouldn't we feel that she has been relieved of a great burden?' I asked tentatively.

'Consistency is the hobgoblin of the small-minded.' Jinny produced one of her rare misquotations. I savour them. (On the whole, it is best not to point them out, unless the moment is right: I let it pass in silence.)

We found Jamie in the dining-room, chatting with Giorgio, who stopped his animated Italian immediately and adopted a stony-faced demeanour. He bowed slightly to each of us with his *'Buon giorno.'*

'Hallo. Good morning, Jinny, Patrick. Bernadetto appears to have stayed with Melissa last night. There's a note here, which Giorgio has just brought in, telling us he'll be back later this morning.' Jamie perused the notepaper, which lay beside his place at the table. 'He says: "I shall be bringing everyone here home for lunch. Naturally enough, they'd rather get out of the Palazzo Aschenheim." Et cetera.'

'I think we might go for a walk after breakfast, Patrick, mightn't we? Do you know' – Jinny turned to Jamie once more – 'when they're likely to arrive?'

'Mr Montenari told us he would pop in this morning, too,' I pointed out. 'Perhaps I should wait for him.'

'I don't think Bernadetto expects us to stay in to wait for them, though,' Jamie said genially. 'Perhaps Jinny and I could wander over to the market by the Rialto and browse through the cured meats.'

Jinny was clearly torn between the feeling that time indoors on a sunny day in Venice was wasted and the desire not to miss Montenari's bulletin from the front line. 'You go, my sweet,' I urged. 'I promise to try and keep Mr Montenari here if he comes before you get back.'

Montenari was extremely businesslike when Giorgio let him in an hour or so later. 'Good morning, Sir Patrick.' As usual he was elegantly attired, this time in a dark olive summer suit.

'Good morning, Signor Montenari.' We shook hands.

'Your wife is out?'

'Indeed.' I nodded. 'Can't keep Lady Scott away from the treasures of Venice.'

'Perhaps we may talk alone.' With a tiny tilt of his head, he indicated Giorgio, who was still standing by.

'Why don't we go into the library? And perhaps Giorgio would bring us some coffee.'

Giorgio acknowledged my request, and Montenari and I walked together into the library and settled, facing each other across the fireplace, our conversation watched over by the angry stone gryphon and the rather more pacific-looking lions.

Quickly, he brought me up to date. 'Mr Bouncer's autopsy was very interesting. There was a small puncture wound in his thigh. Sort of thing that means he might have been injected with a poison. From the condition of the wound, they said it might have happened any time in the hours before he died. So, of course, they looked for a fast-acting poison that could be delivered that way. So far, we haven't found anything. But my people are pretty sure that's what happened. We think he was killed by a poison injected in the thigh.'

'No sign of a syringe or a blow-pipe . . . some means of injecting the stuff?'

'We've been dredging through the silt below the window. We haven't found anything yet. But it could have been done in the open, on the way from the hotel to the *palazzo*.'

Montenari paused, and I thought for a moment.

'That's more likely. If it was done in the bathroom, through the window, the dart would still be there. But if it had happened elsewhere it could have been done by stabbing him in a crowd almost anywhere. In any case, wouldn't it be very odd for an assassin to go round to the back of the *palazzo* and to happen to be there when Bouncer wandered into the . . . ? Unless . . . ' We looked at each other, plainly having the same thought.

'If somebody knew . . .'

'That Bouncer's stomach was upset . . .'

'And knew which bathroom he would probably use if he needed a toilet during dinner . . .'

'Somebody inside the *palazzo*?' I had already said to Jinny that Mrs Bouncer seemed to have a motive. Montenari, who would know by now about her bruises too, must have had the same thought. 'Perhaps Mrs Bouncer? You might want to have the chap who's doing the autopsy look to see if his stomach upset was brought on by poisoning of some sort. I mean, his wife might have deliberately made him sick, so he would have to go back to where the murderer was waiting.' I stopped. 'This is all rather speculative, isn't it?'

'Sir Patrick, even if all this were true, how could I prove it? She had a motive: but the wives of most men have a motive to kill their husbands.'

'I'd say that was a bit of an exaggeration, old chap.' I chuckled but Montenari remained stony-faced.

'I meant, most women, and especially the wives of rich men, would gain something financially from their husbands' deaths.'

'Well, she was in full view when he died. And I'd say she put up a pretty convincing display of grief.'

'I suppose we should say that your friend Lady Hawksworth had the opportunity to commit the murder.'

'The door was locked from the inside.'

'There is the ledge.'

'Lady Hawksworth was wearing an evening dress that would have made walking along the ledge very difficult indeed.'

'You're right about the dress.' Montenari, however, was prepared with a new piece of information. 'But I did a little experiment last night. The lock of the toilet was one of those buttons you push in, in the middle of the handle, probably something Mrs Aschenheim brought from America. There was no keyhole. So I pulled in the button, with the door open, and pushed it shut. It locked.'

I saw, at once, what he was thinking. 'So, if the door had been open when Bouncer died, Melissa could have locked it behind her after killing him?'

'Exactly.'

'But why would he have opened the door to her?'

'Why would he have locked the door?' I looked a little puzzled at this question. In my experience, the custom of locking the door to the loo when you're in it is, shall we say, one of the elementary courtesies of civilized life. 'That bathroom was not used by the servants. And everybody else in the house, all the guests, knew that Bouncer was there. You told me he was in a hurry. So, I repeat: why would he lock the door?'

'Why on earth would Melissa kill Philip Bouncer?'

'Ah, now *that* I cannot tell you. You have known her for a long time. I was hoping *you* might be able to come up with something.'

I was stumped. For a moment neither of us said anything. I thought about the lock on the lavatory door. 'Did you find any fingerprints on the handle?'

'Wiped clean.'

'That fits with your theory.'

'I know, Sir Patrick. But we are still without a single definite piece of positive evidence.'

'And if it wasn't Melissa' – it felt strange, now, contemplating the possibility that Melissa was responsible for two deaths – 'it could have been practically anybody: until we know what the poison was and how long it takes to act.'

'There are thousands of possible poisons, my man says, some of them very hard to detect. And often the dosage determines how fast they act. I'm afraid there is no guarantee that the chemists will solve our problem.'

At this point Giorgio arrived with the coffee and I was reminded that I owed Montenari my new discoveries about the other murder. He still didn't know about Giorgio's role in connecting Melissa to Pritchard. As he sipped his espresso and nibbled at the almond *biscotti* that Giorgio had produced, I brought him up to date.

Montenari had a good deal to tell me in return. 'We have found Mr Mitchell's companions, in London. Gerald Miller has an Australian police record, so we were able to send the British police a photograph. It was only a matter of time before one of your bobbies recognized him.'

'Are they going to extradite him?'

'No need. He's agreed to come here. He seems to regret having flown the coop' – I kept being amazed by Montenari's grasp of English idiom – 'when they heard Mitchell was dead. He told them he wanted to help find the murderer.'

'If he *did* have anything to do with the killing, that's a very clever line to have taken.'

'Well, we'll soon see how clever he really is. He's coming back with a couple of our people this afternoon. And the two girls who were with them, too.'

'Miss Marilyn Rimmer and Miss Rita Spender – or perhaps we should say Mrs Miller?'

Montenari flipped through a page or two of his little black notebook. 'Yes. Rimmer and Spender, his wife. Exactly. They will be in my office by about four.'

'Did they have any ideas about what might have happened?' I asked.

'Not really. They assumed he'd been mugged. They ran, they say, because they thought they'd be suspected.'

'That doesn't make a great deal of sense, does it? Perhaps they really thought that the person who killed Mitchell was after them.' It was an idea. 'Did they mention the business of meeting somebody here in Venice?'

'Not yet.'

'Did he say he was Lord Hawksworth's natural son?'
'No.'
'Then I'd say you two have a good deal to discuss.'

When Montenari made to leave, a little later, I explained to him that Jinny had hoped to join our conversation. 'She'll be very sorry she missed you. But it's hard to stay in on a lovely sunny day in Venice. Pity she wasn't here, though – she often comes up with rather good ideas,' I went on. 'Perhaps between us we'll think of something and telephone you later on.'

Montenari shook my hand and then looked up awkwardly. 'I hope I can ask you for another favour.'

'Of course, of course. Anything.' I had an idea what he was going to say.

'It will be helpful when I am discussing the Hawksworth will with Mr Miller if you are there to help me. After all, you probably know more about Lord Hawksworth's affairs than anyone else alive.' I had rather hoped that Montenari would make me this sort of offer. This business was becoming more and more puzzling and I was frankly longing to see if I could work it all out.

I made an effort to seem surprised by the magistrate's invitation. 'Really? Do you think I might be able to help? Then I'd be very glad to do so.' I paused, wondering if I should lay it on quite so thick. 'It will be a great honour to work with a real professional.'

Montenari smiled. 'Thank you, Sir Patrick. It will be an even greater honour to work with a great amateur.'

22

By about eleven o'clock, I was beginning to wonder where everybody was. There was still no sign of Jinny and Jamie, and no hint of Bernadetto and the party from the Palazzo Aschenheim either. So I was hovering about the hall, wondering whether I ought to go out on a search party for my wife (and reassuring myself that, after all, she was escorted by Jamie, who knows the city well), when the bell rang at the front door. I rushed across to open it, and found myself face to face with an embarrassed Sujit.

'Very sorry, Sir Patrick. I am looking for Paulo.'

'Help yourself,' I said. 'I expect he's . . .' I realized I had very little idea of the geography of the servants' quarters. But Giorgio appeared at this moment, scowled fiercely at the Tamil, muttered to him in Italian, and began to drag him back towards the door to the kitchen, behind the great staircase. Before they could quite disappear, I addressed Mrs Aschenheim's manservant: 'Ah, Sujit. How is Mrs Bouncer this morning?'

He stopped. 'Very, very sad. She is crying and crying. Her husband was beating her. Now he is dying.' A fine couplet, I noticed, made finer by the melodious Indian sing-song.

'And Lady Hawksworth?'

'She, too, is sad. Everybody is sad. It is a sad house where a man is brutally murdered.' I wondered if this was a piece of Tamil proverbial wisdom. 'Signor Occampo is sad because the policeman told him he cannot leave Venice. And my lady is sad because her guests are not happy. But they will all join you here for lunch, yes? Maybe you can give them some jolly good cheer?'

Giorgio was looking crosser and crosser throughout our exchange. I wasn't sure whether it was the familiar tone of our conversation or the fact that Sujit was passing on household gossip that rankled. But it was clear that he thought Sujit's cheerful and open responses to my enquiries unprofessional.

Sujit ploughed on, oblivious to the storm-clouds. 'How is Lady Virginia? She is well, I am sure.'

'I hope so. Actually, she's disappeared for the moment. I was waiting for her when you rang the bell.'

'Here I am, darling.' I spun round to see Jinny, radiant in the Venetian sunlight, framed in the portal of the *palazzo*, her arms filled with flowers. 'Jamie and I have had a wonderful time shopping for fruit and flowers. This great big bunch of roses was a gift from a most gallant florist. I'm sorry we took so long. Has Montenari been?'

'And gone, I'm afraid, darling.' Giorgio and Sujit had rushed to unburden Jinny of her purchases.

'Pop them in vases for the moment, would you, Giorgio?' Jamie said, appearing from behind Virginia, laden himself with bags overflowing with peaches, grapes, and plums. 'Lady Scott wants to arrange them later.' Giorgio piled the flowers into Sujit's arms, and disencumbered Jamie of the fruit.

'*Si, milord*,' Giorgio said (rather archly, I thought). Jamie tapped him easily on the bottom. If Sujit had infringed Giorgio's notions of decorum, he and Jamie were making a fair shot at going the Tamil one better.

'I think I need a little lie-down, Paddy. Perhaps you'd come and keep me company.' Lie-down, my foot. What Jinny wanted was the latest news from the front.

Once we were upstairs, I was happy to pass on to her the substance of what I had learned from Montenari. She listened attentively, interrupting only occasionally.

When I began to explain why Montenari and I had wondered if the assassin had an accomplice, she said sharply: 'Jo-Ann, of course. He beat her. He probably threatened to beat her or worse if she tried to leave him. So she thought the only way out was to kill him. It happens all the time.'

'There's absolutely nothing else to connect her to the murder.'

'Quite, darling. Do go on.'

I explained about the door to the loo: and told her how Montenari thought Melissa could have entered the room, jabbed Bouncer with the poison and then locked him in.

Jinny looked meditative. 'She's a very cool customer, Melissa. But there isn't the slightest reason to think she had a motive. Melissa would hardly kill Philip Bouncer for beating Jo-Ann.'

It was my turn to say: 'Quite, darling.'

By a quarter to twelve, I had told her all. My invitation to the interrogation of Gerry Miller produced an excited response. 'Good, he must know something that'll help. We'll be able to find out if they really had come to Venice to see Melissa.'

The 'we' here drew to my attention the fact that I had neglected to ask Montenari whether Jinny was to come, too. Gingerly, I brought the topic up. 'I'm afraid he said he wanted *me* to come, Jinny, my love. I shall have to ask him if you can come, too.' I paused. 'But you'll understand if he says no. I mean, it's already a bit irregular letting me in on it.'

My wife smiled sweetly at me. 'Why don't you just ask him, Paddy? You can be very persuasive when you want to.' It was clear who would have to bear the blame if Montenari declined the offer of Jinny's invaluable assistance. 'Well, there's not much more to be thought out until we talk to Milo's son.' Lady Scott yawned, covering her mouth with a graceful hand. 'I don't think I want to snooze before lunch. I think I'll just read for a bit. We'd better get back to England soon, or I shall run out of books.' From the top of the chest of drawers she collected one of the two remaining novels. Another train book, I noticed: it was, I thought, a very odd way to organize one's reading. This time it was one I had read myself years ago: Patricia Highsmith's *Strangers on a Train*. I couldn't remember much about it.

When the gong summoned us for lunch, we went down into the hallway and found the whole party making its way across the hall from the drawing-room to the dining-room. Jo-Ann was simply dressed, in black jeans and a plain white shirt, with a dark scarf over her head. Her eyes were no longer covered – though I noticed that her sun-glasses poked out of her breast pocket. It was as if she had only ever hidden her bruises to save her husband embarrassment. Her eyelids were puffy, not so much from the bruises as from a night of weeping, and the whites of her eyes were streaked with red. She mumbled a greeting when Jinny kissed her. While Jo-Ann was in a worse condition than any of the others, none of them had an exactly cheerful countenance. Sujit was right. The inhabitants of the Palazzo Aschenheim were indeed a sad lot.

Melissa was hobbling a good deal less than she had the day before, no doubt, in part, because she was on Bernadetto's arm. But she looked very pale, as if she had hardly slept at all: and Bernadetto's solicitude reflected an even greater concern for her health than when she had been more obviously physically injured. Peggy Aschenheim, normally so robustly cheerful, was oddly shrunken, as if the diminishing of her spirits had compressed her body, and I could see that her daughter was distressed that her mother was in such an uncharacteristically sombre state.

Claudio Occampo was the least affected by the whole business. This wasn't too surprising. He barely knew the Bouncers. He had only recently met any of the others. He was a stranger in their midst, a professional humouring one of his major patrons. Over lunch, as I tried to talk with him once more in French – the only language he had admitted to having in common with me – I gathered that he felt highly discommoded by the fact that the Venetian police were not going to permit him to leave for a day or two.

After a particularly unsuccessful exchange, it occurred to me that, since Chileans were, as I gathered, mostly Catholic, he might know some Latin. *'Non intellego, triste, quod dicas. Linguam latinam loqueris?'*

'Comment? Excusez-moi.' Mr Occampo's look of utter surprise was clear evidence against my hypothesis.

'J'ai pensé que peut-être vous parlez le latin,' I explained. *'Mon français est, malheureusement, execrable.'*

'Mais, non. Vous parlez très, très bien. Le latin?' He laughed heartily. 'Mais quelle drôle d'idée.' He set about explaining to the table what had just occurred. The mood was sombre and the tale of my mistimed foray into the language of Cicero produced only a polite smile from the Aschenheims.

'Avez-vous faites des peintures pendant votre séjour ici?' I enquired in the unhappy silence that followed.

'Mais non,' Peggy said. 'Il a absolument refusé. Je lui ai offert l'atelier de mon mari. Il a parlé des fantômes.'

'Les vacances sont les vacances. On ne travaille pas en vacances.' Mr Occampo smiled mysteriously, as if to say that only a true artist could appreciate the deep insight he had offered us.

Jo-Ann, who had sipped her wine and nibbled the odd piece of bread, suddenly spoke up. 'Can you tell Mr Occampo for me, that I'm gonna go ahead and buy those paintings of his that Phil was gonna buy. Maybe Phil didn't know much about art, but he sure knew what he liked. And he loved those sheep you did a few years ago.' She was speaking to him now, as if she'd forgotten that he wouldn't understand. Georgie Bishop, who was seated next to Claudio, translated softly into his right ear and he bowed his head to Jo-Ann as he listened and said: 'Merci, madame, merci.'

We proceeded in this dismal manner through the rest of the very light luncheon that Bernadetto's cook had produced for us. As we rose from the table, Claudio Occampo announced that he was going for a walk and would meet the Aschenheims back at the *palazzo* later. My wife cast me a glance that suggested that we might retire at once. But there were a few questions I wanted to ask Peggy Aschenheim, and so, as we crossed the hall, I whispered to Jinny: 'You go on up, I'll be along in a jiffy.'

'I think, Bernadetto my sweet, that, if you'll excuse me, I shall go up and lie down,' she announced. She kissed Melissa and Jo-Ann. 'See you later.'

It took only a few minutes to get the answers I needed from Peggy Aschenheim. I was frankly very glad when I was able to excuse myself from the drawing-room. Peggy had given me some more grist for the old imagination. Before I went upstairs, I crossed the hall to the library and made a telephone call to London.

'Jamie?'
'Patrick?'

I was talking to Jamie Fitzgibbon in our chambers in London. 'Yes, it's me.'

'I say, what *is* going on down there? There's a lot of stuff in the newspapers here about a murder in Venice during a dinner party you were at.'

'You really must stop reading the *News of the World*, Jamie.'

'It was in the *Independent*.' My colleague assumed the tone of one aggrieved.

'Look, I need your help.'

'How thrilling. Are you solving this murder, too?'

'Not really, Jamie. It's a different murder I'm really interested in.'

'Do you mean to say there've been *two* murders in the week you've been in Venice? Really, Patrick, you're a dangerous chap to have in the vicinity. Remind me not to follow in your footsteps on my next holiday.' I am used to this sort of thing, even from Jamie Fitzgibbon. I try not to be irritated by it.

'Murders occur with regrettable frequency in all cities,' I replied loftily. 'The only difference *I* make, Jamie, is that I solve some of them.'

'I say, don't get on your high horse, Patrick. I was only teasing. Now, what can one do to help?'

'Somebody's pilfered the contents of my briefcase. Could you do me a favour and ask Smedley to rustle up a copy of Milo Hawksworth's will?'

'What's Hawksworth's will got to do with the murder?' I have tried in the past to explain to Jamie that one shouldn't ask questions of this sort. To no avail. When I sighed heavily into the telephone, one of these lectures obviously came to mind. 'Oh, all right. Mum's the word. What do you want done with it?'

'I'd like to telephone you back in about an hour and have you read it to me.' It was Jamie's turn to sigh sceptically. 'Go on,' I said, 'be a good fellow. We'll have you over for dinner and explain the whole business when we get back.'

By two I had completed two more phone calls; one to New York, the other to Bolivia. When I told Jinny what I had been up to, she was not impressed.

I managed actually to snooze a bit, but Jinny was clearly aiming to stick with her reading. When I woke up from my siesta it was about a quarter past three. I turned towards my wife. She had indeed ploughed on through Miss Highsmith's novel. 'Good, is it?'

'Yes, dear.'

We got up and I phoned Montenari, at Jinny's instigation, to ask if she might come along. There was a slight hesitation before he said yes, and I decided I owed him a favour. I made a small suggestion as to an enquiry he could make through Interpol.

Then I got on the blower to Jamie and he gave me the details I wanted from Milo's will. I wrote them down in my notebook. We set off at about twenty to four for Montenari's office in the police station.

I think I have mentioned that the key to the solving of murders is the management of the imagination. Of course, I had not had much luck so far with mine, but sometime soon, I was sure, the pieces would fall into place.

23

Gerald Arthur Miller was taller than I remembered him. And I realized now, looking at him with the knowledge I had not had when I first met him, that there really was something of Milo about him. Not only did he have Milo's dark good looks, but he was beginning, now in his early forties, to acquire the bulk that had distinguished his father. When Virginia and I entered the room with Montenari – the same room where we had quizzed Pritchard – he seemed only mildly surprised.

'Lady Scott, Sir Patrick. Nice to see you again.' I wasn't quite sure what to say and Miller, seeing this, laughed and added: 'I know. Not the best place to meet again, is it, in jail?'

'You are in the police station. You are not in prison. And you are here of your own choosing,' Montenari said stiffly. 'I am grateful that you are willing to help us with our enquiries.'

'If I tried to leave, you'd arrest me.' He spoke firmly with his Australian twang. Montenari said nothing. 'But I do want to help. Gary was my best mate. I'm sorry I ran off when he was killed. It was stupid.'

'Good. Well, let's get going, then,' Montenari said. He offered Jinny and me chairs, and we sat, all three of us, across the table from Gerald Miller, with a tape-recorder between us.

Montenari began by taking him through their exact movements from the time they left the railway station in Venice until the time they took the plane to London. Nothing much of note, there.

'So, why did you come?'
'Hasn't Sir Patrick told you?'
'Why should he know?'
'My father left him instructions.'

I touched Montenari's elbow and he looked at me. Without speaking, I sought his permission to ask Miller a question. Montenari nodded.

'How did you know that?'
'My father wrote to me.'
'Do you have this letter with you?' Montenari asked.
'I've a copy. I put the original in a safe-deposit box in London.'
'Why did you do that?'
'It's the only thing I ever got from him. I don't want to lose it.'

Filial piety. It seemed especially sentimental in someone so open and unpretentious.

'May I see the letter?'

Miller reached into his jacket pocket and pulled out the photocopy. It was dated 16th October 1989, nearly four months before Milo died.

My dear Gerald:
Your mother was wrong not to tell me of your existence and even more wrong not to tell you of mine. That she repented on her deathbed does not make me any more inclined to forgive her. I too am dying, now, and I do not think it would do much good for us to meet. I have enough else to do in the time I have left. You have a brother, Alexander, who will inherit my house and my title, because your mother and I were not married. You have two sisters, in Bolivia, for whom I have also made generous provision.

After I die, you should find Melissa, my wife. Take her this letter, and she will introduce you to my friend Sir Patrick Scott. If you persuade him you are my son, as you have persuaded me, he will tell you what I have done for you. He will be able to lead you to your brother and sisters.

I wish you well. I shall die regretting, above all, that I have never known you.

Your father,
Milo Hawksworth

'Sir Patrick, do you recognize the handwriting?'

'It's very convincing. May I?' He nodded and I took the photocopy in my hand. 'Yes, I'm almost sure. But a handwriting expert who had the original could certainly decide.' I asked Gerald Miller the obvious question. 'If you already knew your father meant you to see me, why didn't you make yourself known to me on the train?'

'Gary saw your name on the door of your cabin first. I must admit I was a bit stunned when I heard who you were. But my father told me to get Melissa, his wife, to introduce us. So I told Gary and the others not to say anything.'

'How did you know my wife and I were still in Venice?'

'On Monday, in London, I went to see John Ellis.'

'Lord Hawksworth's personal secretary,' I explained to Montenari.

'To begin with he didn't want to tell me anything. Then I showed him the letter. So, then he told me, if I needed to see you, I'd have to come back here.'

'How did you persuade Milo you were his son?' It was Jinny's turn to satisfy her curiosity.

Before he could answer, the truth struck me. 'He asked for some blood. He had your DNA analysed.' Now, Gerald Miller *was* surprised. 'I made a stupid mistake a little while ago,' I went on. 'I found a lab report – there was a copy in the papers stolen from my briefcase – that said that some tissue came from Milo's son. I assumed it had been Alexander's tissue. Very silly. Milo *knew* Alexander was his son. Such a stupid slip.' All the time I spoke, I was thinking: What other mistakes have I made? Is there something else obvious that I haven't seen? Is there a clue, hidden like Poe's purloined letter, in full view? I was cross with myself for missing something so obvious, and so I missed the next few exchanges between Montenari and Miller. The next thing I heard was: 'Sir Patrick?'

I turned to Montenari.

'Mr Miller was asking you a question.'

'I'm sorry, I was thinking about something else,' I said. 'What did you want to know?'

'Does that letter satisfy you that I am the son of Lord Hawksworth?'

'From what Virginia has told me about these DNA tests, they are pretty decisive.'

'If they still have the tests, they could retest a new sample and confirm that it was your blood,' Jinny said.

'But I am already satisfied, Mr Miller. You see, I spent a lot of time with your father. And you look like him. Not superficially; not in the obvious ways.'

'Then, will you do as my father asked?'

'I think, first, we should let Mr Montenari finish his interview. We still need to find the murderer of your friend.'

'Did Lady Hawksworth ask you to meet her in Venice?'

'At first, she didn't want to meet me at all. I tried to tell her as gently as possible the first time I wrote. But she got a lawyer to write back and say I mustn't contact her again.' Gerald Miller looked at each of us before going on. 'I thought for a while about whether I wanted to go on. And then I asked Gary to send her a copy of my father's letter. You see, I hadn't wanted to do that, originally. I mean, it's such a strange letter. It must have been hard for his wife to read it.' He snorted. 'Anyway, that did it. We arranged to meet here last week. She told us where to stay. She said she'd contact us.' He paused for a moment, in painful recollection. 'Then Gary was killed. The message never came.'

'Perhaps it came to him,' Montenari said.

'Why would he keep it from me?'

'I don't know. Do you?'

He thought for a while. 'No.'

'Perhaps the note said: "Meet me in ten minutes." Perhaps he didn't have time?'

'Could be . . . '

Montenari offered a new suggestion. 'Or perhaps he wanted to meet Lady Hawksworth alone?'

Gerry Miller reddened, grasped the table, and rose slightly. His jaws were clenched tight. 'I ought to sock you for that. He wouldn't do anything like that. He was my mate. I trusted him.'

'I didn't intend to suggest his motives were impure. He might have felt that you would be too emotional; that it was better for him to deal objectively with the matter.'

Gerry Miller relaxed visibly. 'Sorry about that,' he mumbled sheepishly. 'I s'pose I'm a bit tense.'

'Do you know what is in your father's will?'

'No.'

'Your lawyer could have found out. Wills are public documents.'

'My father told me to do it through his wife . . . his widow. It didn't occur to me not to do what he asked.'

'There were documents about your inheritance in the briefcase that was stolen from the train.'

'Yeah, I know.' Puzzlement crept across his features. 'Did you find it?'

'Mr Miller, I am asking the questions. Are you sure that your lawyer did not know what you were likely to inherit?'

'He explained that I only had a right to what my father wanted to leave me. He said I couldn't have the title – not that I wanted it. If a fellow knows he has a son and doesn't want to leave him anything, that's legal. That seemed right to me.'

'It's not easy for me to believe that you waited for so long to find out what your father might have left you. After all, you knew he was a very rich man.'

'I was doing what he said,' he repeated stubbornly. 'You may not understand it, but that's what I thought a son should do.' He was absolutely sure that he had done the right thing. I thought: This is definitely Milo's son.

The interrogation continued for a period in this desultory manner: we were not making much progress with the murder investigation. Still, there were a few questions I wanted to ask, and so, with Montenari's permission, I proceeded.

'Do you know anything about your brother and sisters?'

'My brother ... half-brother, really, right? ... is Alexander, Lord Hawksworth of Hawksworth. I've seen a picture of him. The girls no one seems to be able to tell me about. I asked Mr Ellis and he looked very surprised and said he didn't know what I was talking about. Good at secrets, my dad, wasn't he?' It was hard not to agree.

'When did you originally contact your father?'

'About a year before he died. I wrote to him on 17th February 1989. I remember the date. It was a week after my mother died. She left me a letter with his name and address. It took me a week to decide whether to write to him.' That accounted for Milo's sudden interest in Australian matters. 'It took about six months before he decided it was worth doing the DNA test. He kept sending me these lists of questions. He must have been a strange man.'

I stopped. None of this seemed to be helping us with the death of Gary Mitchell. We excused ourselves and stepped out of the interview room together.

'I'm afraid that your friend Lady Hawksworth has been concealing material facts from you.' Montenari's mood was gloomy.

'So it seems.'

'Why do you think she didn't tell you she knew why Gary Mitchell was here?'

'You know very well why. I was working with you: and it would link her to the murder.'

'Exactly. So, now I must go and interview her myself.' He sighed. 'I am sorry it is your friend, Sir Patrick.'

It seemed to me that it was too early for Montenari to approach Melissa. If she had done it, it would be better to wait until he had something, something that could set her off balance. All she had to do now was deny having anything to do with the murder and he could do nothing. And, if she was innocent, it would only distress her. I decided to try to persuade Montenari to hold off, for both their sakes. 'You could do that,' I began. 'Still, we don't have very much evidence, do we? I mean, she didn't tell me that the dead man had come to see her. But, as we agree, that's perfectly understandable. And it's the only fact. The rest is all conjecture. She has a motive, it's true, but not a very strong one. Neither she nor her son is going to be exactly poor if Gerry Miller turns out to be the long-lost son. It's also true that she could have arranged the theft of the briefcase. Perhaps. And she might have been in a position to find an assassin through Bernadetto. Perhaps. But there's nothing real there.'

'You think I should wait?'

'I do.'

He paused. 'I suppose I should trust the instincts of another Cambridge man.' The smile that played about his lips was thoughtful. 'Okay. One more thing, then, before you go. What will Mr Miller inherit?'

'Several hundred million pounds' worth of assets all over the world, from Bolivia to New Zealand. If he's still alive five years after Milo's death, he gets it absolutely. Till then it's in a trust of which he's sole beneficiary.'

Montenari whistled. *'Porca la miseria!'*

'Who gets it if he dies?'

'It stays in trust for Alexander and the girls for a further five years, and then they get it absolutely.'

'You didn't tell me that.' Jinny did not sound pleased. I gave her a contrite look.

'I hadn't worked it out until Jamie read me those provisions of the will just before we came over here.'

'Do you think Lady Hawksworth knew this?' Montenari asked.

'She had a copy of the will; she probaly looked at it again pretty closely after Gerry contacted her. She must have seen that, as long as the executors never heard of Gerry, they'd assume Alexander was the eldest son; and the clause that covered the girls would never come into force. I assume she thought that with Gerry out of the way, Alexander could keep everything.'

He nodded. 'Ah well.'

We left Montenari and asked him to tell Gerry Miller that I would expect to see him after dinner that evening at the Palazzo Longhi. Once he had finished his business with the police, I had trustee's business to carry out with him.

'Oh, and do give me a buzz, when the answer comes in about the other matters,' I said as I was leaving.

'Of course.'

We had been back at the Palazzo Longhi for about an hour, when Jinny announced suddenly, 'I've got it!'

She and I were seated alone together on the balcony of our room, overlooking the Grand Canal and drinking tea. Jinny had been reading her novel with great concentration and exclaiming from time to time. But this was the first time I actually heard what she said.

'What have you got?' I said, humouring her as is my wont.

'I know who killed them,' she said. 'It's clear as anything. Of course, I've no idea if it can be proved.'

'Pray proceed.'

It took my dear wife a good fifteen minutes to mount her case. She would have been an able advocate. When she was finished, I had to admit it was an elegant hypothesis. I also had to admit that I too doubted it could be proved.

'Of course it is a hypothesis,' Oscar Wilde wrote in *The Portrait of Mr W.H.*, 'but then it is a hypothesis that explains everything, and if you had been to Cambridge to study science, instead of to Oxford to dawdle over literature, you would know that a hypothesis that explains everything is a certainty.' As one who dawdled over law at Cambridge, I have always been in a muddle about exactly where I fall in Mr Wilde's scheme. But one thing I could have told him is that a hypothesis almost never explains everything: and there were gaps in Jinny's notion. Still, there were remarkably few, and I had to admit I still hadn't come up with anything better.

I tried to muster some enthusiasm. 'I'll pass your thoughts on to Montenari. But, if you're right, we'll need to flush the conspirators out, since we don't have the evidence. I think the best thing would be to gather here for dinner and have Montenari join us afterwards with Gerry Miller. Then we'll have all the *dramatis personae* in one place and we shall see if, with everyone there, we can entrap our killers.'

That was what I said. But I wasn't completely happy about it. In fact, I wasn't happy about it at all.

A few minutes later, there was a knock on the door of our bedroom. 'Come in,' I shouted from the balcony and Giorgio entered and made his way across the room towards us.

'The telephone. Is for you.' He plugged it ceremoniously into a socket by the desk and removed the receiver.

'Sir Patrick?' It was Montenari's voice.

'Yes, Signor Montenari.'

'We have found the briefcase. And I have the answers to your two questions.'

24

As you close in on murderers they have increasingly good reason to add you to their victims. That is the simple fact. But, if I was right, the person who stabbed Gary Mitchell had no reason to think we had yet established his – or her – identity. I had not publicly identified anyone with both motive and opportunity. In fact, I had done a fairly good job of making it plain that I didn't know: so far, then, Jinny and I were safe.

But once we began the game of cat-and-mouse that I had set up for this evening, the danger would increase. It was essential to proceed with the greatest caution. After Montenari's call, I went downstairs and found Bernadetto. I explained to him that we were closing in on Gary Mitchell's killer and that I needed to collect everyone together one more time to gather the final clues. 'I hope you don't mind, but I've asked Montenari to join us after dinner.'

'Of course, Patrick, you must do what is necessary. I'm sure we can persuade Peggy to bring her party over here. May I tell her what's in store?'

'Absolutely. But I'd be grateful if she didn't tell anyone else.'

'Including Melissa?' Bernadetto tilted his head back slightly as he caught my eye, his face raised in a gesture of confidence... and also of challenge. I thought of one of those statues of a Roman orator, drawing himself up to his full height, his toga grasped in one hand, a scroll in the other. A proud man. A man in love.

'I think *I* should tell Melissa. Is she at the Palazzo Aschenheim?'

'No. She's resting upstairs, in my room. I'll ask her to come down and talk to you.'

Twenty minutes later, after a quick word with Melissa, I was able to telephone Montenari again to tell him all was ready. 'The trap is set, Signor Montenari. See you at nine o'clock.'

I spent the rest of the afternoon in our bedroom, at the desk, running various possibilities through, over and over again, in my imagination. And I knew that the time had come where the danger was not the imagination that came up with nothing, but the imagination that produced too much. I knew that I must not convince myself of any of the score or so scenarios I imagined, unless it was securely grounded in the evidence. Sometimes, in the past, when my imagination has run too freely, I have settled too quickly on one possibility and discarded others. This time, I had to be certain I did not fall victim to my own imagination.

Jinny had gone for a walk in the late afternoon, returning at about half-past five. As she entered the room, I rose and crossed to kiss her, and she presented me with a single red rose she had been hiding behind her back.

'A boutonnière for your dinner-jacket, darling.'

'Thank you, my sweet.' I kissed her again. 'And now we must dress for dinner.'

'Have you worked out a plan with Montenari?'

I was distracted for a moment by a slight pain in my neck, and reached up to message my nape with my right hand before answering. 'Sort of. I'm afraid we're going to have to leave a good deal to luck.'

'Are you all right, Paddy? What's wrong with your neck?'

'I've just been sitting here too long hunched over the desk.' I affected what I hoped was a reassuring smile. 'Nanny was right: posture matters. I shall have to have some more Alexander lessons when I get back home.'

'Are you really feeling up to this?'

'I'll be all right.'

'No booze this evening, Paddy. You'll need a clear head.' It was a resolution I had already made, but it was irritating to have Jinny insist on it. I restrained the urge to snap at her, and turned, instead, to the armoire to collect my evening dress. Jinny must have glanced at *Strangers on a Train* on the chest of drawers, because she went on: 'Isn't it lucky I happened to be reading Patricia Highsmith, darling? Otherwise we might never have worked it out. And she's a Texan, too, as it happens.'

I was not much looking forward to the evening. There is never much pleasure in unmasking a murderer. And I must confess that the afternoon's work had resurrected my appetite, so that the prospect of an evening of fine food without spirituous, or even vinous supplementation, added to my discomfort. I cheered myself up by promising myself a large brandy if everything went well.

The grandfather clock in the hall was striking six as Lady Scott and I descended the staircase and made our way out on to the terrace.

Only Jamie and Giorgio were out there already, and, as usual when we came upon them alone, they both assumed the guilty countenances of children caught in the pantry.

'Hallo,' Jamie said. 'Drink, anyone?'

'I think I'll have a little sherry,' Virginia said. 'And Patrick . . .'

'Will have a large tonic water with a dash of bitters and a slice of lemon.'

Jamie looked at me sceptically. 'I say, Patrick, are you all right?'

'I do wish everybody would stop asking me that. First it's Jinny and now you, Jamie. I am perfectly all right. A little bit tired, but otherwise in tip-top condition. And looking forward . . . thank you, Giorgio, that looks delicious, is there any ice? . . . looking forward to another excellent dinner at the Palazzo Longhi.'

In my experience, simply acting as if you are cheerful has a buoying effect on the mood. I set about acting cheerfully and my spirits lifted. For the next fifteen minutes I found myself regaling Jinny and Jamie with amusing tales from my years at the Bar. Jinny was kind enough, for once, to refrain from correcting my stories; normally, she is rather inclined to interrupt with, 'No, darling, I'm sure it was Suffolk not Sussex,' or 'Three, darling, definitely three. That was what you said last time.' But today she loyally supported every detail, laughing at lines she had heard a dozen times before. I was very grateful.

Bernadetto and Melissa arrived next, arm in arm, flirting happily with each other. They seemed finally to have accepted that Jinny and I were not going to disapprove of their relationship.

'So, Patrick, we are all in your hands.'

'What *do* you mean?' Jamie asked jovially. 'You realize he's on the wagon? Is it really such a good idea to leave the evening in the hands of a teetotaller?'

'He means', I said, 'that I am going to ask everyone to help me solve the murder of Gary Mitchell.'

Jamie's smile disappeared. 'Ah, so that's why everyone's coming from the *palazzo*. Don't you think it'll be rather painful for Jo-Ann Bouncer to have to discuss a murder with her own husband so recently defunct?'

'Well, Peggy can't really leave her on her own; and I think it may provide her with a distraction.' Jinny did not sound very convinced.

'Perhaps you could make it your business to keep her amused, Jamie?' Bernadetto turned to Jinny and went on: 'Jamie has such a way with the ladies.'

Jamie reddened slightly and mumbled that he was sure he would do what he could.

As the conversation trickled on lightly, I gazed across the canal at the façade of the *palazzo* opposite. A stone window hung precariously over the water from the first – or was it the second? – floor, elegantly carved in an elaborate tracery of vines and grapes, rising, like some product of the confectioner's art, to a single tiny spire, topped with a sphere. The irregular glass panes in a host of colours, many of them containing what looked like armorial bearings, glowed in the evening sunlight. From behind a curtain, loosely pulled back, the face of a little girl appeared, gazing out, as I was, over the water, her eyes shaded from the sun. What a city to grow up in, I thought. Everywhere I looked there were magical architectural details; and each of the rios that disappeared behind the great houses of the Grand Canal drew away into a different mystery. The *vaporetti* and the gondolas travelled by with their cargoes of tourists, none of them much surprised by the sight of three men in dinner-jackets with two ladies in evening frocks, being served cocktails by a liveried servant. In Venice, I imagined them thinking, this is how people live. We were, for a moment, part of the magic, extras on the Venetian stage.

At about a quarter past seven, Peggy Aschenheim's motorboat arrived. Peggy herself, and her daughter, were accompanied by Claudio Occampo. Melissa and Jo-Ann Bouncer, Peggy announced, would be along in a little while. Melissa had accompanied Jo-Ann to the Danieli to help her dress and to arrange to have the Bouncers' clothes packed and sent over to the Palazzo Aschenheim. 'That way I can make sure she's okay,' Peggy said.

It was a little after eight when we moved across to the dining-room. Melissa had arrived a quarter of an hour earlier, looking ravishing, as usual, accompanied by Jo-Ann, who was now dressed fairly simply. I thought this might be the influence of Melissa, but perhaps it was simply that the old Jo-Ann had dressed to please her husband. The effect, in any case, was not unpleasing, and I was delighted to find myself seated between her and Peggy Aschenheim, who had also recovered her boisterous gregariousness.

'I hope you don't mind,' Bernadetto announced to us as we were settling down at the table, 'but I've asked the cook to prepare a fairly simple meal.' Given the sumptuous way in which dinner parties in Venice – at least on the Longhi–Aschenheim axis – seemed to be conducted, I was prepared to wait and see whether this was truly disappointing news.

I am glad to say I need not have worried. Bernadetto's idea of a simple repast began with a vichyssoise, sprinkled surprisingly with fresh ginger, accompanied by a fino I was obliged to decline. Over this course, Peggy Aschenheim and I discussed how she had begun to collect art. 'It was Al's idea. I like ballet. And so, one day, he sees this ballet dancer in a window of a gallery on Madison Avenue. He thinks: Peggy will like that. Goes in. When he hears the price, he nearly has a heart-attack. It's a Degas.' She laughed her hearty laugh. 'So, he comes home and he says: "Honey, I was gonna surprise you, but I'm not gonna spend that kind of money for something you don't like. So come look." ' She sighed. 'Well, it was love at first sight. Of course, now I think our taste was kind of naïve, but it was a start.'

'Do you still have the sculpture?'

'Of course. It's a very sentimental thing for me. It's in my bedroom in New York. Once the guys we bought it from discover that Al has all this money, we get bombarded with invitations to openings. So I said to Al, "If we're gonna do this, I'm gonna find out about it." So I took art history classes at NYU, Columbia, anywhere I could find them.' Peggy bent forward and addressed Jo-Ann across me. 'You should do that, Jo-Ann, honey.

You should do some art classes.' Jo-Ann nodded meekly. 'Yeah, I'll do that when I get back to the States.'

'Have you enjoyed visiting the art of Venice, Mrs Bouncer?' She had said nothing much so far, and I was hoping to draw her into our conversation.

'It's Jo-Ann.' She grinned for the first time in a long while. 'I won't call you Sir Scott, if you don't call me Mrs Bouncer.'

'So, have you enjoyed all our museums, honey?' Mrs Aschenheim's tone was maternal.

'Oh, sure. You know something, Sir Patrick, I've been meaning to tell you something for quite a while. You remember you asked me the other day if I had been up to the ghetto?'

'Yes.'

'Well, I said no and I lied. I did go up there. You see, I didn't want Phil to know. He was kinda anti-Jewish – not, you know, a complete bigot, just a regular Texas anti-Semite, if you know what I mean – so I never actually told him I was, you know, Jewish myself. I felt bad about lyin' to you, though.' Jo-Ann glanced sheepishly in my direction, batting her eyelashes ferociously. She was speaking very quietly, whispering almost, so that I only just caught her words. 'I just wanted to put the record straight.'

'Thank you for taking me into your confidence,' I said. I had a sudden flashing image of Monsignor Galsworthy beaming delightedly at the repentance of a sinner.

The main course – after a few pieces of warm duck confit on a bed of crisp endives with a balsamic vinegar dressing – was a perfectly grilled salmon steak, which had been marinaded in something delicious but not quite identifiable, with tiny new potatoes, done in the English way with butter and mint. Giorgio kept me topped up with mineral water, but it was painful to watch the well-chilled Pinot Grigio, whose crisp grassy flavour would brilliantly have complemented the salmon, pouring freely into the glasses around me. I was just beginning to feel that I could really allow myself to summon Giorgio for a soupçon of *vino*, when I received a warning glance from Jinny. I resolved that the brandy I had promised myself would have to be a really substantial snifter.

'Zabaglione,' Mrs Aschenheim bellowed as the final course appeared. 'I just love it. Give me a simple meal at the Palazzo Longhi any time, Bernadetto darlin'.' She chuckled. 'I always have to diet for a month after Mr di Montebello leaves *la bella Venezia*.'

As the time came for us to move into the drawing-room, the

butterflies descended on my stomach. I was as nervous as I had always been before the opening of an important case. I knew that once the game was afoot, my nerves would settle, but, now, as I walked across the hall, sober and filled with good food, I felt like a condemned man, his last meal consumed, approaching the scaffold. It was ten to nine. In a few minutes Montenari would arrive, with Gerry Miller in tow, and the final act of the murder investigation would begin.

The two sofas in front of the fireplace had been moved back at my request, so that a *chaise-longue* from beside the window and three armchairs from the library could be added to form a circle. Virginia was seated to the right of the fireplace, on the end of the sofa closest to the wall, with Jamie next to her, and Georgie Bishop on his right. Opposite them were Melissa, Jo-Ann and Peggy Aschenheim on the other large sofa. Facing the fireplace, on the *chaise-longue*, were Bernadetto and Melissa. Claudio Occampo sat on one of the large wing chairs from the library. He was between Melissa and Georgie Bishop, closer to the latter.

I stood facing the company and the two empty wing chairs to Bernadetto's right, awaiting the arrival of Signor Valentino Montenari and Mr Gerald Miller, inwardly rehearsing my plans. As Giorgio finished serving the coffee, the room fell silent and everyone looked attentively towards me. I caught Jinny's eye.

'Have any of you read *Strangers on a Train*?' she asked brightly.

'I believe I have,' Peggy said. 'Or maybe I saw the movie. Wasn't there a Hitchcock movie?'

Jinny nodded.

'Two guys meet on a train and agree to swap murders, right?'

My wife nodded again.

'Now what made you think of that?' Bernadetto asked.

'I've just finished reading it.'

Another awkward silence. And into it the sound of the front door bell. 'Good,' I said, 'the last of the guests have arrived. Giorgio?' He was already on his way.

I made my way across to the door and greeted Signor Montenari and Mr Miller. And then I turned and presented them to the company. 'I believe you all know Mr Montenari. He is investigating the murders of Gary Mitchell and Philip Bouncer. And this is Gerald Miller. Mr Mitchell was his lawyer.'

'And my husband was his father,' Melissa said coolly. 'You do look rather like Milo in his middle years.'

'How do you do, Lady Hawksworth,' Mr Miller said. 'I've been looking forward to meeting you.'

I introduced the others. Montenari declined the offer of a drink, but Gerald Miller accepted the offer of a glass of brandy, and took a nervous swig as soon as it arrived.

'Georgie,' I said, 'would you mind translating the proceedings for Señor Occampo?'

Bernadetto said: 'We're all ears, Patrick.'

I had the floor.

25

'Forty-four years ago, Milo Hawksworth had an affair with an Australian woman named Linda Miller. It didn't last long. When they parted, they were not on very amicable terms, and Miss Miller neglected to tell Milo that she was pregnant. When her son was born, in October 1947, she named him Gerald Andrew Miller: and he is here with us today.

'And I think I can safely say that there would have been no murder here in Venice if Miss Miller had stuck to her resolve to tell her son nothing of his father. But early last year, on her deathbed, she repented and told Gerald that his father was Milo, sixteenth Baron Hawksworth of Hawksworth.

'Mr Miller spent the week after Miss Miller's death agonizing about whether to approach this stranger who had sired him. Then, in February, he wrote Milo a confidential letter. Naturally, Milo was surprised. Of course, he was suspicious: but he decided that if this young man was his son, he would do something for him.

'The matter was a delicate one, however. Milo was, after all, a very public man, a well-known and well-respected public figure. He didn't want anyone to suspect he had an illegitimate son until he was sure. He had also just discovered that he had a terminal cancer. He didn't have a great deal of time. And so he created an elaborate subterfuge. He pretended that he was worried about the security of Alexander's inheritance because of the fact that he and Melissa had married abroad. He asked me to contact lawyers in Australia and dig up records of the marriage, and he asked me to arrange for a private detective as well. All of which convinced me and all his friends that, while it was slightly dotty, he really was worried about Alexander's title.'

'Convinced me, too,' Melissa said. 'He made me sign affidavits about Alexander being our son and our marriage having been voluntary and all sorts of nonsense.'

'But while I was making these investigations, Milo was writing letters to the boy, asking him questions about his mother and his early life; and using the same detective to see if he could confirm the boy's story. Finally, convinced that Mr Miller was sincere, he asked him to send him a blood sample. The analysis made it certain beyond any reasonable doubt that Gerald Miller was his son.

'By now it was October of last year. Milo knew he did not have long to live. He decided that it would be too painful for him to meet his son, and so he wrote him a letter . . .' I reached out my hand and Gerald Miller rose and gave me the photocopy from his breast pocket. I read out loud parts of the letter we had seen that afternoon.

'I . . . am dying, now, and I do not think it would do much good for us to meet. I have enough else to do in the time I have left. You have a brother, Alexander, who will inherit my house and my title, because your mother and I were not married. You have two sisters, in Bolivia, for whom I have also made generous provision.'

I waited for a moment as Georgie Aschenheim Bishop finished translating. Claudio Occampo seemed interested at the mention of his own continent. *'Ah, en Bolivie . . .'* I heard him say to his interpreter.

'There are more of them?' Melissa said.

'Two. In Bolivia. Shall I read on?'

Melissa nodded. 'Sorry.'

'After I die, you should find Melissa, my wife. Take her this letter, and she will introduce you to my friend Sir Patrick Scott. If you persuade him you are my son, as you have persuaded me, he will tell you what I have done for you. He will be able to lead you to your brother and sisters. . . .

Your father,
Milo Hawksworth'

'Amazing chap, Milo,' Jamie said. I looked at him disapprovingly. 'Sorry, old chap, do go on.'

'At some point, Mr Miller asked his friend and lawyer, Mr Mitchell, to make enquiries as to what his rights were in relation to his father's estate.'

'I waited until I read that he'd died. Of course, I'd told Gary all along about everything. He was my best friend.' There was a slight catch in his voice. I could see that all the ladies were moved. If I don't get a move on, I thought, they'll all be weeping.

'It took no time at all to discover that, since his father knew of his existence, it would be hard to claim anything that Milo had not chosen to give him. When Gary suggested that they at least ask for a copy of the will from the solicitors, Gerry said no. His father had told him to approach his widow and, through her, me. So that was what he was going to do.

'And so he wrote to Melissa in . . .?'

'In March.' Gerald Miller spoke out firmly.

'. . . asking if she would meet him. Melissa got her lawyers to write back and tell him that she did not wish to hear from him again.'

'Well, of course I did. I thought it was some dreadful con-man trying to take advantage of a rich man's widow. And anyway, Milo had never told me he had sired various bastards around the globe.' Melissa shrugged and then snuggled up to Bernadetto on the *chaise-longue*.

'I can see that we're going to get along just fine,' Gerry Miller said sarcastically. 'But, speaking as one of the bastards, I see you didn't have to wait long to find someone else to warm your bed.'

'Mr Miller, you are my guest, here,' Bernadetto said, rising angrily. 'And you will not remain my guest if you abuse the woman I love.'

'Come on, you guys,' Peggy Aschenheim said. 'It's natural he's upset, Bernadetto.' She turned to Gerry. 'But you have to understand that your father wasn't living with Melissa when he died. They hadn't been living together for nearly twenty years.'

Gerry raised his hands to his face and exhaled noisily. 'God, did I get the wrong end of that stick.' He uncovered his face. 'I'm sorry, Lady H. My apologies.' You can't help but admire the uncomplicated way Australians go about things. I half expected him to stand up and offer to make up by shaking hands.

'Do go on, Patrick,' Melissa said. 'This is riveting.'

'Finally, as you know, Melissa, he sent you a copy of this letter. And you agreed to meet him here in Venice last week. Which is why Gerald Miller and Gary Mitchell were travelling down to Venice on the Orient Express with us.'

Montenari raised a finger to catch my attention. '*Scusi*, Sir Patrick. One question for Lady Hawksworth. May I ask why you did not tell anyone you knew why Mr Mitchell was here?'

'She was sure it would lead you to suspect her. I advised her against it.' Bernadetto spoke firmly. 'If it was anyone's fault, it was mine.' Melissa looked down demurely, like an obedient wife. The effect was not altogether convincing.

'I have now to imagine what Melissa was thinking as the date approached for the arrival of her son's half-brother. You had seen the will. You knew that, since Gerald was Milo's eldest son, the vast bulk of his wealth would go to Gerald. I imagine you thought, too, that if Gerald appeared, Alexander would lose a great deal. You could have asked me, but you knew from the letter that Milo had asked the boy to contact you first. And you knew that I would have told you if I had heard of a son with a claim to some of the estate. So, if you could stop the boy from getting to me, he might never know what he had missed.'

'My dear Patrick, this is all wild speculation,' Melissa said.

'Well, why didn't you ask me about it?'

'I wanted to see what he was like first. I thought it would be fun to present you with a little surprise while you were here.' Melissa was coy, almost simpering. 'I didn't see why I should have all the unpleasant surprises.'

'No indeed. And you arranged another unpleasant surprise for me, didn't you?'

'What do you mean?'

'I'd mentioned in passing to Bernadetto that I was going to have to bring down a lot of papers to do with Milo's estate. About a month ago, Jamie told you about a young Englishman he'd met. A petty crook named James Pritchard. You had the bright idea of using him to see how much I knew. So you left him a note, some money and a return railway ticket to London, at the Pensione Scarpia, and told him that he'd get a thousand pounds more if he managed to steal my briefcase on the way down. You also made sure that the Australian party travelled down with us, because you knew that once I met them here in Venice, suspicion for the theft of the briefcase would fall on them.'

'Really, Patrick, you've been reading too many Bella Sharpe novels.'

I shook my head firmly and pressed on. 'When you got the briefcase, you found that Mr Pritchard had made a mistake. Gary Mitchell and I had exchanged cabins: Pritchard got Mitchell's briefcase. But when you opened it, you discovered you had hit, by chance, upon a real treasure trove. The briefcase had all the papers to do with Gerry Miller's search for his legacy. The briefcase was monogrammed G.M. You made the obvious conclusion. And when you saw the pictures that Gary had taken of himself in the booth at Victoria Station, you assumed that they were pictures of your husband's son.'

'If I took the briefcase, where is it?'

'Actually, you don't know, do you? One of Peggy's servants saw it in Mr Occampo's room on Sunday. The police now have it in their custody. Mrs Bishop, would you ask Mr Occampo how he came upon the briefcase?'

'*Vous parlez d'une serviette en cuir?*' Occampo said. I nodded. '*Oui, j'ai trouvé une serviette avec le monogramme G. M.*' Claudio explained that he had seen the briefcase in the bathroom at the Palazzo Aschenheim, near Melissa's room. He had opened it, he said, to see who it belonged to. And then, when he saw the papers were in English so he couldn't actually read them, he put the briefcase in his room, meaning to ask around later. He was sorry to say it had slipped his mind; he had thought nothing more of it until just now.

'Artists are so absent-minded ... Al was just the same,' Peggy Aschenheim clucked.

Now I knew how the briefcase had travelled from the cabin, where Pritchard stole it, at Melissa's instigation, to the room of Claudio Occampo at the Palazzo Aschenheim. The evidence of Melissa's involvement in the theft of the briefcase was now irrefutable.

This fact was not lost on Melissa. 'Look, Patrick, even if I thought Mitchell was Milo's son, I couldn't have killed him, could I?'

'Indeed you could not. You were safely ensconced in bed with a sprained ankle, an Italian doctor and Peggy Aschenheim all ready to affirm an alibi. But you could have arranged for someone else to do it.'

'Don't be ridiculous.' This was Bernadetto. 'The briefcase arrived in Venice only twenty-four hours before Mitchell was stabbed. You can't find a hired killer in that sort of time.'

'No, you can't. Not even someone with Mafia connections could do that, probably. And so there I was stuck until Philip Bouncer died and Jinny read *Strangers on a Train*.'

There was a long silence as everyone looked about in puzzlement. 'In *Strangers on a Train*,' Jinny explained, 'the idea is that if two people swap murders, then they can make sure that each of them has no motive for the murder they do commit and the perfect alibi for the one for which they do have the motive. If I do your murder, why should anyone suspect me? Especially if we're practically strangers?'

'Who had the motive to kill Philip Bouncer?' I didn't wait for an answer. 'A woman he beat regularly, who had to wear sunglasses to conceal the black eyes he gave her. A woman who will inherit all his riches. A Jewish woman who couldn't tell him she was Jewish because he was just "a regular Texas anti-Semite".'

Jo-Ann sat still, next to Melissa, shaking her head. 'I can't believe I'm hearing this. You think *I* killed this Australian guy? How the hell would I do that? And how could Melissa here have poisoned Phil? This is f — ing crazy.'

'You just told me, over dinner, that you were in the ghetto on the afternoon Gary Mitchell was killed. When I first brought it up you denied it. Then you must have realized that other people might have seen you and so you invented the story about not wanting your husband to know you were visiting a Jewish museum.'

She shook her head and murmured: 'I don't f — ing believe it.'

'You two were together in London a few weeks ago.' I spoke to Melissa and Jo-Ann. 'Each of you discovered the other had someone you wanted out of the way: I imagine that's when the planning began.'

'Imagine away, Patrick, my dear. This is all a complete fantasy. Signor Montenari, I hope you aren't taking any of this seriously.' Melissa was remarkably self-assured.

Bernadetto was seething with rage. The muscles in his jaw were working away mightily. Finally he spoke. His voice was taut with restrained anger: 'Patrick, I won't have you making these outrageous allegations against Melissa.'

'No, I can see that you wouldn't like it. After all, you were in on the plot, too.'

As he leaped towards me, Montenari stood up and placed himself between us. 'If you assault Sir Patrick, you will be arrested by the policemen who are waiting outside the *palazzo*. And I can assure you that this is a crime for which the evidence will be sufficient for a conviction.'

I continued. 'I can understand why Melissa stayed with Peggy when she visited Venice in the past. Melissa was Milo's wife and he was a powerful man. It wouldn't have done to flaunt your affair with Lord Hawksworth's wife. But I couldn't understand why this time, now Milo is dead, she didn't come straight here. You told us a cock-and-bull story about respecting our Catholic sentiments: but you'd allowed us to think that you were engaged in an affair with Jamie. No doubt, in part, this was a ruse you'd developed to keep Milo off your tracks; but it would have offended a Catholic with those sensitivities rather more. It was only when I discovered that Melissa had invited the Australians to Venice that I realized why you had agreed that she should stay with Peggy once more: it was because she had to be able to contact the Australians without any risk of being seen by me. When Melissa told you they were coming – this was only arranged a few weeks ago – you had already invited us. You could have withdrawn our invitation, but you didn't want to do anything to rouse my suspicions.'

'You haven't any evidence for any of this,' Bernadetto shouted. 'It's all the most monstrous bluster.'

'I don't think so. Mr Montenari?'

'My men have searched the Palazzo Aschenheim. We found Sir Patrick's papers in Lady Hawksworth's room. Even without Mr Occampo's recent testimony, we had evidence to support Sir Patrick's story.' Montenari looked around. 'Do you have any more for us, Sir Patrick?'

'We have Mr Mitchell's briefcase and we have Mr Occampo's testimony that it was in Melissa's bathroom. We have Mr Pritchard. We have motives. We have opportunity. I think we all know now what really happened. I was hoping that somebody here could help me corroborate a little more.' I looked around expectantly. Nobody spoke. 'Very well, let's see what progress we can make with the events at last night's dinner. I wonder if you could just help me with a few more details, Mr Occampo. You left the dining-room at least a minute before Melissa ... Lady Hawksworth.' Georgie began to translate. Occampo was attentive; he looked like a man ready to be as helpful as he could. He nodded as she finished and then looked expectantly at me. 'When you walked along the corridor to your bedroom, you could have seen the ledge under the window of the lavatory through the windows. Did you happen to look out?'

Claudio Occampo listened. Then he shook his head.

'It's very important, Claudio, to recall everything you can.'

After a brisk exchange, Mrs Bishop said: 'He says that he was hurrying to get his glasses from the bedroom. He didn't look out of the window. He's sorry.'

'One of the maids' – I paused to look at the notes of my phone conversation with Montenari – 'was busy turning down the beds at that time. She was still there when Melissa screamed; she said she'd been tidying up your room for at least ten minutes. She doesn't recall seeing you up there. Are you sure your glasses were in your bedroom?'

Claudio looked uncertain, now. He spoke to Georgie Bishop. 'He says the maid must be mistaken.'

'Are you sure you went up to your bedroom?' I asked again. Mrs Bishop began to translate. 'I don't think that's actually necessary, Mrs Bishop. You see, he understands English very well. Let me ask you this: if your glasses were in your bedroom, why did you join us from the drawing-room when we all rushed out after Melissa screamed?'

Señor Occampo seemed uncertain what to do. He tried asking Georgie to translate, but she pulled back from him in revulsion. 'Was it perhaps because you had travelled along the ledge while Melissa ran screaming towards us and entered the drawing-room from the terrace?' Still he looked at me as if he did not understand. 'You used a blow-pipe, probably a Bolivian Indian blow-pipe, to deliver the poison, through the window of the lavatory. You were able to recover the dart in the minute while Melissa was running back to fetch us.' Still he said nothing. 'Would it help,' I said, 'if I told you we know your real name? Mr Montenari?'

Montenari opened his briefcase and took out what looked like a photocopy. 'His name is Alberto Salinas. He is not a Chilean painter but a Bolivian art dealer. And he is married to Lord Hawksworth's daughter, Consuela.' This revelation produced a rewarding range of shocked responses from the assembled company. I had asked Melissa and Jo-Ann to play along with my charade: I had not revealed this element of the denouement.

'And since you worked on Lord Hawksworth's Bolivian estate as a farm manager for many years, you speak good English, as indeed does Consuela herself.' I was watching Alberto Salinas, alias Claudio Occampo, as I spoke. I wondered when he would break. 'I spoke to your wife this afternoon. It was early morning in La Paz. She told me you were often away now pursuing your career as an art dealer. But you've been due back for some time now; she's been wondering where you are. So naturally she was willing to fax me a photograph.' Montenari held it up.

'When Milo died, a letter was sent by Ellis to the girls in La Paz. I haven't seen it, but I assume that Milo told them that they had another brother. When you read the will, you saw that if that brother died, Alexander and your wife and her sister would be able to share all of Milo's vast wealth. You came here to stay with Peggy Aschenheim, because you had found out that Melissa would be here. You assumed, rightly, that the son would come first to Melissa.

'When you found the briefcase last Saturday, you thought that you had found the man you needed to kill. You found the photographs in the briefcase and you thought they were of your wife's half-brother. The correspondence told you that Mr Miller was here to meet Melissa. So, all you had to do was to go to the hotel, follow him, and tell him to come with you to meet Melissa. You took him to the ghetto and stabbed him.'

'It's a lie.' Alberto Salinas's English had only the trace of an accent.

'Ah, so you *do* speak English.'

'You cannot prove I was in the ghetto.'

'We've had a forensic team in your room all evening. If there's one drop of Mr Mitchell's blood, or one hair of his head on your clothes, your shoes, your carpet, they'll find it.' The phone rang.

'I think that will be for me,' the magistrate said. 'I'll take it in the library.'

'No – I'm afraid, Mr Salinas, you are a double murderer.' Georgie Aschenheim Bishop shrank further away from him and Jamie put a protective arm round her. My words had a similarly chilling effect on the three women on the sofa facing her. Melissa and Peggy each took one of Jo-Ann's hands and stared at Alberto Salinas. 'Yes,' I went on. 'You see, once Phil Bouncer got an idea, he followed it up. He met Occampo. Peggy said he was a fine painter. So he called his people in New York and asked for some slides. They came. He liked them. He decided to buy. He did all this without telling Claudio here, Mr Salinas. It was only before dinner last night that he finally mentioned that he'd bought one of the super-realist sheep.'

'Hyper-realist, dear,' Jinny said.

'Something he said must have led Mr Salinas to think that Bouncer would soon be on to him.'

'He was right,' Melissa said. 'There was a package waiting for him at the hotel this afternoon. A catalogue of one of Claudio Occampo's shows. His picture's in it.' She glared at him. 'And he doesn't look at all like you.'

'Oh my God,' Peggy said, covering her mouth with a bejewelled hand. 'I should have checked. It never occurred to me that someone would fake being Occampo. I was so thrilled when I got a call from a New York dealer saying that Occampo wanted to meet some of the people who collected his work seriously. I mean he's such a recluse. I couldn't resist.' She sighed. 'It's all my fault.'

There was an electric silence. Salinas looked about him, as if for a moment contemplating escape. Then Montenari spoke from the doorway. 'That was my forensic people. The blow-pipe we found in Mr Salinas's room has traces of the poison that killed Mr Bouncer. The pathologist says it kills in a couple of minutes, just the way Mr Bouncer died. And you should have thrown away the shoes you were wearing in the ghetto along with the clothes. We've got traces of blood of Gary Mitchell's type. Alberto Salinas, I arrest you for the murders of Gary Mitchell and Philip Bouncer.'

As we were debriefing that night, Jinny said: 'There's one thing I don't understand, Paddy. Why did you try out my *Strangers on a Train* theory? I mean, you never actually believed it, did you?'

'Remember: when we gathered in the drawing-room, we still had no physical evidence to connect Salinas with Bouncer's death. I was sure he had killed Gary Mitchell, but I wasn't certain he had killed Philip Bouncer. All I had was a possible motive and a hunch based on the fact that there are lots of exotic poisons in South America. To convince myself, I had to be confident he was lying about the business with his glasses: that there wasn't an innocent explanation of why the maid didn't see him upstairs.

'You see: if he'd been innocent, he would just have said he remembered the glasses were in the drawing-room. And if he was guilty and he thought I suspected him, he would have said the same thing, trying to explain away his lie as a misunderstanding, perhaps. It was only if he thought I *didn't* suspect him that he had a reason to stick to the lie: changing the story now would only draw attention to himself. Better to brazen it out. And so I had to ask him about it when he was sure I didn't suspect him. The rest was easy. I asked Melissa and Jo-Ann to help me convince Salinas that I suspected them so as to catch him off his guard. Maybe I should have told Bernadetto, too, but then he wouldn't have put on such a convincing performance.'

'I think you just wanted to see how long you could have us all spell-bound with your fancy intrigue.' Jinny smiled.

'Really, Jinny, that's very ungenerous of you.' I don't think my good wife found my stern tone altogether convincing. Her smile remained. 'But I must admit there was one other reason: I wanted Jo-Ann Bouncer to feel she'd played a part in catching her husband's killer. He may have treated her appallingly, but she loved him.'

Jinny shook her head and giggled. 'What a sweet man you are, Paddy. And I just thought you knew we all enjoyed charades.' And then she kissed me good-night.

26

Two days later, we finally reached the Hotel Serbelloni in Bellagio. Peggy had insisted that we take her car – the Silver Cloud – and chauffeur – Bruno Marcello – and so we appeared in the grandest style. (Bruno's cousins in Como didn't see very much of him, since he immediately made friends with a young woman of the place, who offered to put him up.)

On Friday, 1st June, we breakfasted together on the balcony of our room, on croissants and hot chocolate, scrambled eggs and sausages, and fresh figs which tasted as if they had come from one of the trees in the Garden of Eden. Across the lake, its waters blue as the robes of an angel by Titian (or is it Tintoretto?), a perfect village of red-tiled houses lay in the sunlight under the steep cliffs that rise to the Alps. Occasionally we would hear a voice in the village, as the day began, echoing across the sound of the lapping waters. Ducks and sea-gulls bobbed in the bay, awaiting the crumbs of the tourists in the restaurant of the Hotel Florence. Jinny had found a copy of Tuesday's *Financial Times* in the village and was busy solving the crossword. I gazed out meditatively at this sublime scene.

'He seems a nice enough chap, Gerald Miller,' Jinny said, suddenly. 'But I wonder if he can really step into Milo's shoes.'

'We shall have to help him. I think the first thing is to make sure he gets on with Alexander. Then they can spend time together at Hawksworth. I'm sure that's what Milo would have wanted.'

'Milo should have made it plainer what he wanted. If he hadn't created all these complications . . . Funny, isn't it? Because Gerald's such a decent chap, those Bolivian girls Salinas was trying to help will actually get some of the money.'

'I feel rather sorry for the one he married, though. I mean, it's turned out her husband was only after her money.' I closed my eyes and breathed in deep of the warm and fragrant air. Perhaps we might visit Bolivia and meet the two of them, I thought, not knowing much about the place or what there was to visit. 'That man Salinas was devilishly clever. He found out that Melissa would be staying with Peggy. Anybody who sells art knows about the Aschenheim collection: all he had to do was to find a reclusive Spanish-speaking painter that Peggy was known to be interested in.' Thinking over the whole business was most satisfying. I had made a couple of wrong steps, it was true, but in the end I had hit the jackpot. 'Funny chap, Milo. Melissa was convinced that if she tried to divorce Milo, he'd have them both bumped off. Milo had so many sides we never saw.'

'Do you think that he would have done it?' Jinny sounded genuinely puzzled.

'I don't know. But there was a sort of gratuitous unpleasantness in making Gerry Miller come to me through Melissa; it's as if he wanted to rub her face in the fact that he'd had a son before Alexander. Makes you wonder. And he did have his tentacles everywhere. He'd have been hard to escape if he wanted to make their lives miserable. You remember how he chased off all those girls who were after Alex's money. Besides, I'm not sure Bernadetto hasn't rather enjoyed the excuse to keep some of his bachelor ways. Some men' – I made sure I went carefully here – '. . . I mean, not a chap like me, of course, but some men find marriage . . . constraining. With Melissa able to come and holiday with him whenever he wanted, he could have the best of both worlds.'

Jinny hurrumphed. 'It's a jolly good thing they're getting married at last, if you want my opinion.'

'Absolutely. It'll be a splendid wedding.'

'I still can't quite forgive Melissa for trying to steal those papers. And making sure that the Australians were on the train so there'd be someone to blame. I mean, if Pritchard had actually got your briefcase, then the police would naturally have suspected them: since your papers had to do with Gerry Miller.' She sighed. 'And then all that subterfuge. Staying with Peggy, so that we wouldn't meet Gerry Miller when he turned up. And then actually stealing the papers.'

'We always knew she was resourceful . . . remember . . .'

'If you bring up that business of that scavenger hunt thirty years ago one more time, Paddy . . .'

I beamed at Jinny. 'I wouldn't think of it.' There was a knock at the door. I got up and went over to open it: there was a waiter with a rather grand envelope on a silver platter. I opened it. It was a letter from Bernadetto and Melissa. 'They've invited us to Seville this autumn.'

Jinny looked up in surprise. 'Really?'

'The invitation just came.'

'In the *Italian* post?'

'Actually, Bernadetto sent it with the chauffeur.'

'What a ridiculous extravagance. What does he say?'

' "My dear Scotti," ' I read, ' "I trust the Hotel Serbelloni is living up to its reputation. Melissa and I are looking forward to seeing you again soon at the wedding. We have so much to thank you for. This is just a note to say that we are expecting you in Seville in the autumn. We shall gather our party once more ... though Jamie, alas, will not be able to be with us, as you know ..." '

Jinny interrupted. 'What does he mean? "As you know".'

'Oh, I say, I *am* sorry. I forgot to pass this on. I asked Bernadetto why we'd never seen Jamie in Spain. Apparently, he can't go there because ... well, apparently he misbehaved under a campanile, so to speak, in Seville and Bernadetto arranged for him to be let off if he promised not to come back.' I rushed through the explanation in the hope, of course, that my good wife would forgive this failure of communication.

On Lake Como, apparently, forgiveness comes easily. 'Go on with the letter.'

'That's it, really.' I scanned the rest of the page. 'Suggested dates, that sort of thing. Then they both send their love.' I handed her the letter and settled back down in my chair. I took a sip of chocolate and nibbled my fig. 'Seville in the autumn.' I sighed with pleasurable anticipation. 'It's Bernadetto's and Melissa's way of making up. We shall have a lovely time. And the Muse always smiles on you there, my love. Bella Sharpe's latest adventures will no doubt profit from the visit.'

Those of you who have read *Last Train to Venice* will agree, I am sure, that I was right.